St. Nic, Inc.

By

SR Staley

Published by:
Southern Yellow Pine (SYP) Publishing
4351 Natural Bridge Rd.
Tallahassee, FL 32305

www.syppublishing.com

This is a work of fiction. Names, characters, places, and events that occur either are the products of the author's imagination or are used fictitiously. Any resemblance to actual persons, places, or events is purely coincidental.

The contents and opinions expressed in this book do not necessarily reflect the views and opinions of Southern Yellow Pine Publishing, nor does the mention of brands or trade names constitute endorsement.

ISBN-10: 194086920X
ISBN-13: 978-1-940869-20-9

Front Cover Design: Jim Hamer

Printed in the United States of America
First Edition
August 2014

Dedication

To Claire, who asked the question, and
Evan, who needed an answer.

Also by SR Staley

The Pirate of Panther Bay
A Warrior's Soul
Renegade

Coming in Spring 2015
Tortuga Bay

Find out more about SR Staley and his work at www.srstaley.com.

Acknowledgements

None of my books have been written or published in a silo, and that's as true for *St. Nic, Inc.* as the previous ones. Many people have graciously given their time and commitment to this project, spending hours going over manuscript drafts, providing edits, and candid feedback. All of this input has been considered, and the final story is much better as a result. First, I need to acknowledge my daughter Claire, who asked the question that prompted the backstory that eventually became *St. Nic, Inc.* I believe in Santa Claus. But the story would likely never have made it onto paper without my son Evan, who needed an answer. Unfortunately, the answer came too late to keep the idea alive, but I hope he can forgive me by knowing I at least have tried to rectify past injustices!

I also need to acknowledge those who took the time to read parts or all of the manuscript. I can honestly say that this manuscript would not have moved forward without the candid and honest feedback of Chris and David Nadler. Michael Whitehead, Terry Lewis, Liz Jameson, Emily Timm, and Diane Henderson also provided what seemed like harsh, but always helpful, comments as part of my Tallahassee-based critique group. Thanks also go to Amy Chavez and Bill Staley for reading early versions of the manuscript and helping shape the story and setting. Doug Dandridge provided immensely valuable input that helped frame the setting of the North Pole. My publisher, Terri Gerrell, also deserves more than a little credit for believing in and staking part of her business on the success of the story and characters. I am looking forward to a long collaboration with Southern Yellow Pine Publishing and their great stable of editors and graphics artists. Finally, I want to thank all my fellow authors in the Tallahassee Writers Association—published and aspiring—for their inspiration, commitment, and support for our craft. They are a unique community that helps make stories like *St. Nic, Inc.* become reality more often than they probably realize.

SR Staley

Praise For the Author

When the talented Sam Staley tosses DEA agents, moles, computer whizzes, and a multi-national CEO into one action-filled plot, you get *St. Nic, Inc.* a story that sparkles like the North Pole on a sunny day. *St. Nic, Inc.* offers a fresh vision of what modern tools like the Internet and high-speed delivery services could accomplish in the hands of the right Little People. This heart-warming reimagining gives us reason to believe—and fall in love all over again with our most cherished time of year.

Donna Meredith, author of *The Glass Madonna* and *Wet Work*

St. Nic, Inc. is a magical, innovative, and fresh continuation of the beloved Santa Claus myth. Staley has honored the past while ushering one of the world's most cherished and inspirational stories into the 21st century. *St. Nic, Inc.* artfully combines the action of a Tom Clancy novel with the insightful social commentary and multiple levels of experience of George Orwell's *Animal Farm. St. Nic, Inc.* is a great novel that would make a great movie.

Mark McNees (DMIN) Author of Immersion: *Live the Life God Envisioned for You* and *The Six Symbols of the Gospel*

St. Nic, Inc. is a thrilling and imaginative tale of the delusions, intrigues, folly and dangers of government bureaucracies running amuck to stop the secret goings-on at the North Pole. Can Christmas cheer survive the CIA, IRS, DEA, FBI, et al.? Find out in this intriguing and joyous, must-read book by Sam Staley."

—David J. Theroux, President, The Independent Institute; President, C.S. Lewis Society of California

SR Staley

1

Joy Gault may have closed her eyes, but she couldn't be sure. All she knew was that when she focused her eyes back on the monitor, the blinking light was gone. And a 100 million-dollar undercover operation may have just collapsed.

"Jesus Christ," she muttered, refreshing her screen over and over again as she pecked at function and control buttons on her computer keyboard. "Where the hell did you go? Getko's going to flip out."

She looked up, a silent plea for help lost in a now cavernous empty space that contained the energy of dozens of analysts during regular hours. She didn't have to look at her watch to know the hour had ticked well beyond 9 p.m. She was alone. God knows she wanted to be with Rocky right now downing a cold lager at the University Pub four metro stops away from her basement hovel.

Joy leaned back in her chair, lifted her hand to her eyes, and brought them down on her cheeks, praying that somehow the blinking light would reappear. The map on the monitor gaped at her, all the lines, dashes, and dots solid and calm.

"Shit."

2

"Any change?" a hollow voice asked from the darkness.

"Not much," a deeper voice responded, its tone distant and cavernous.

Keep your eyes closed, Peter told himself between waves of pounding, throbbing aches that surged from one side of his head to the other. The pain told him he was alive, but his eyes seemed to be glued shut, and something told him to keep them closed.

"Brain activity ticked up about ten minutes ago," said the huskier voice.

The fog that seized his thoughts kept Peter from knowing whether the voice was a man's or a woman's.

A shiver shimmied through Peter's body. He grasped at anything that seemed like a familiar thought. But the blackness held him and the pain drowned his thoughts. *Keep your eyes closed.* He was enclosed in a room somewhere, he decided. He could feel its stillness in those seconds between swells of agony. Barely a breath passed over his naked arms, but every hair seemed to stick up to grab at the periodic ice-cold wisps of air. His covered legs began to shake. The shivers moved up his body until his teeth chattered. He couldn't control them.

Keep your eyes closed!

"Shivering," the huskier voice said.

Is that an older female voice? Peter wondered through the clacking of his teeth.

"Circulation's starting on its own," the women continued.

"Good," said the hollow voice. "That's progress. Let me know if his status changes."

The throbbing now seemed to pitch boulders from one side of his skull to the other, crushing any hope that Peter could concentrate on the voices or what they said. He was so cold. Why couldn't he just die? Get it over with.

"Wells will want to talk to him as soon as he is strong enough," the hollow voice said again. Peter sensed it was a woman's voice, but he couldn't be sure.

A sudden sense of abandonment swept through Peter. These voices were not friends. He was alone. He felt the insides of his head become thick and stuffy, just like when he would cry as a little kid. Now he didn't want to cry. He wanted his head to stop thumping. And he wanted to move. His body lay silent, his hands, feet, legs, arms, useless even as they seemed to bounce up and down with the cold.

"What about the other one?" That was the hollow voice again. Or perhaps a new voice. The words seemed crisper, more defined.

What other one? thought Peter.

"She's in a lot worse shape," the husky woman's voice said. "We're keeping her alive on a wing and a prayer."

A girl?

"What about the dogs?"

Dogs?

"Yeah, they took the worst of it." A wave of pain released Peter's senses, but he couldn't track who owned these words. "Only two survived. We thought we could save four, but one passed last night and another passed this morning. We're not sure if the last two will make it either. Dr. Labonte's keeping an eye on them."

Peter was adrift. Nothing seemed familiar or attached. He was floating, and the air was strange. And this strange carried an aura of weird, and that weirdness began to twist Peter's brain into spirals. A girl. Dogs. Doctors. At least two doctors. Was he in a hospital? Dogs....

"Any clues in the gear?" Hollow voice again. This was also a woman, he mused.

Peter noticed an uncomfortable pause between thumps of pain before the second woman's voice responded, "I'll give a full briefing later." She paused. "Apparently, they were trying to reach the North Pole."

Abrupt laughter speared the silence in the room as their cackles seemed to shake his bed. Pain seared through Peter's body, unleashing

3

an uncontrollable moan that immediately extinguished the laughs and all other sounds around him.

Feet shuffled.

"Keep me posted," the hollow-sounding woman snapped.

A door opened and closed with a crack.

The closing door dispersed some of the fog that clouded Peter's brain. Dogs, woman, cold… the North Pole?

Peter felt the gentle hands of someone caressing and kneading his arms.

"Okay, okay," said a man's voice. A different voice. A third owner. Where was he?

"Your fever broke three days ago," the man continued in a soothing tone, as if in response to a question. "I know you can hear me; the monitors show conscious brain activity now. Don't worry. We're taking care of you. No one's going to hurt you in here."

Peter opened his eyes. Blink. Blink.

3

White.

Everything was white. Every thing was white.

Was this Heaven?

Or Hell?

Peter stared at the ceiling, a pure white ceiling that was completely flat. He didn't even see a light over his head. Floor lamps, he reasoned, holding his breath as if preparing for another surge in pain. Nothing.

His eyes roamed from one side of his head to the other. He tilted his head to the left, then to the right, knowing that a sudden movement would bring back the pain he knew was lurking inside his skull. Nothing... but white.

Peter dipped his chin to look down his body toward his feet. His toes pushed up from a grey, wool blanket, the only non-white object he could see. At least his feet were still there. He turned his eyes up, barely catching the top of a wall of cabinets just above his head. Someone had just talked to him. A man. But he couldn't see anyone. How big was this room?

What appeared to be a stainless steel door was on the wall beyond his feet. Something else that was not white. He could now see more cabinets and a counter with a stainless steel washbasin to his right. On the left were a few chairs and a small, portable writing table. It reminded him of an eerie 1940s style hospital room. *Well if these are the Pearly Gates, I'm not impressed; I'll go back to* terra firma. Peter let his head dip back into the comfortable pocket of a lush pillow, ready to close his eyes.

As his eyelids slid to a slit, the man thrust his face into his vision, forcing Peter to blink and open his eyes wide. "What the…?"

"Howdy!" the voice cackled as the face peered clinically into his eyes. "We were worried about you. You were touch and go for about a week." The man fiddled with some wires, and Peter soon traced their quivering movements to an IV connected to his arms, chest, and head. "We're still running tests and monitoring your brain. So please be patient. We want to make sure everything's under control before you start moving around."

The face disappeared.

The man's appearance was so fleeting Peter barely had time to catch his breath.

The man's face continued to dart in and out with a nervous quickness. *ADD*, Peter thought, *or more likely ADHD*.

The face disappeared and Peter felt hands work his arms, rubbing and rolling the muscles. The hands left his body, and he heard the scrawl of a pen on a clipboard.

"Yes sir, we've been working overtime on you," the voice said, as if suspended in an aura around Peter's head. "We haven't seen anything close to this in twenty years, mostly deal with colds and fevers. We had an outbreak of meningitis five years ago; whew, that was a close call. We had a vaccine available soon enough. Boy, airlifting in something like that is tough."

Airlifting?

"Ooops, I shouldn't be talking to you like that. Just don't mind anything I say. Doctors around here think we nurses babble too much, and they're probably right. They would fa-reak!"

The face appeared again, this time from the right side.

"So, how you doin'? Do you think you can talk? Ahh, don't worry. You're awake. That's the important thing. The talking will come soon enough. I can't wait to tell Dr. Patten."

Peter tried to study the face this time: clean shaven, fine lines, wavy brown hair, gentle brown eyes. The face seemed slightly out of proportion, but he wasn't sure in relation to what; Peter couldn't put his finger on it. The face disappeared again. "Got to go. Dr. Patten will want to hear the news. Don't try to get up. I'll be back in a few."

Peter heard the door snap open. Just as his eyes caught sight of the door it closed, and the nurse was gone.

Peter's head spun: dogs, cold, airlift, weeks, another man, another woman? He tried to sort through the images, but the throbs of pain interfered, sending him into occasional recesses of darkness. What did he remember? He remembered being very cold. He remembered the dogs and a sled, instruments, and food. He remembered an ice desert so familiar he considered it a common occupational hazard. Then, he saw the youthful face of a blonde-haired woman. Who was she?

The blackness seemed to recede for a moment as a sharpness returned to the images in his thoughts. He opened his eyes, looked at the walls and his feet, and tried to lift himself up.

"Owww," he screamed, clutching his head. He rocked back into the bed. Where was the girl with the blonde hair? He knew the face… he knew that woman.

A wave of energy surged into Peter's arms and hands. He grabbed the rails on his bed and winched himself into an upright position. The blanket slid down his torso and stomach, exposing a hospital gown that lightly covered his body. He looked around and noticed a closet next to the cabinets on his right. He swung his legs over the side of the bed and started to reach for the floor.

"Whoa there, Mr. Peary!"

Peter froze. "Huh? What?"

Peter looked around the room until he saw a man leaning against the wall behind the head of his bed. His brain still felt heavy and thick, but the images formed in his brain seemed familiar even if the person creating them was not. The man appeared to be average height, an African American in his late thirties, with short cropped hair, wearing a stylish sweater and well-worn cargo pants. No white smock, notepad, or pen.

Peter lifted his hand to his head, as if to keep it from rolling off his shoulders. "How'd you…?"

"Don't worry about it," the man said, barely moving from his position against the wall. He leaned into Peter in an exaggerated way, as if about to tell a child a secret. "I came in the door," he whispered. He winked and pointed his thumb at himself. He pushed off the wall, stepped toward Peter, and extended his hand. "Name's Jeff."

Peter took it, surprised by the firmness of the stranger's grip. Jeff moved like a businessman, he thought. Not the pin-striped organization man, but someone closer to an executive at one of those tech companies that rose out of nothing to make a gazillion dollars. His beard was a little rugged, too, close cropped with just enough length to prove he could grow one.

Jeff relaxed but continued to hold Peter's hand. "You've been through quite a lot. I don't think I would be trying to move too quickly. Let the doctors take a closer look before you start moving about."

"Thanks for the concern."

Jeff paused. "No problem." He let go of Peter's hand and picked up the clipboard on the counter. He scribbled something with a pen that materialized from inside his pants' pocket. "So what brings you to these parts?"

"What do you mean?"

"What brings you to this area? We don't get many visitors."

Peter turned his head toward Jeff as he sat on the bed. He looked around, trying to catalogue unfamiliar items.

Jeff glanced over to the bed. "You're in a hospital."

Peter shook his head. "Which hospital?"

A slight smile crossed Jeff's face. "Oh, I'm not sure you're ready for that yet."

Peter felt blood well up his veins.

"I mean," Jeff said, turning his eyes back to the clipboard as if rotating a dial to lower Peter's blood temperature, "you should concentrate on getting stronger."

"What happened to me?"

"You had an accident."

Peter closed his eyes and waited for another throb of pain.

Jeff opened a folder attached to the clipboard and flipped through a couple of pages. "From your records, it looks like there are a number of reasons you could be here, and not all of them were accidents."

Peter's face reddened. He couldn't remember. Jeff knew more about him than he did at this point. Pain pulsed through his head and out his temples.

"Precisely," Jeff said as if reading the blank look on Peter's face. "Why don't you lie down and get some rest. I'll be back in an hour or two. Let the doctors and nurses do their job."

Peter cursed as he flopped back on the hospital bed, lifting his hands to his head as pain throbbed through his brain. He struggled to think. "You aren't a doctor. Who are you?"

"I'm Jeff. Jeff Wells. That's all you need to know."

Peter sucked in a deep breath. "What happened to my dogs?"

Jeff sighed. "Two survived. They won't be able to pull a sled again though. We'll take care of them."

"What are you going to do with them?"

Jeff walked to the foot of the bed and smiled. "Don't worry. I'm not going to have them put down. We have a nice place for them to retire here."

"I don't care about that," said Peter, a memory materializing from nowhere. "I bought them in Nome. If they're still alive and healthy, I want to sell them, recoup some of my investment." Peter tried to conceal his own shock at what he had just said. It didn't seem right. How could he say that about his dogs? He was sure what he said was true, but he couldn't picture it in his mind.

Jeff shook his head. "Tell you what, you tell me how much you want for them, and I'll buy them. We can use them around here. They're good companion dogs and they like the climate. I'm partial to the older one, the one with the dark line down his back."

They like the climate? Huskies? What about the dog with the dark line?

9

4

The door to Peter's hospital room opened again, and the now familiar face of Peter's nurse entered the room. The nurse immediately recognized Jeff Wells standing at the bed and seemed alarmed. "Oh no, sorry, Mr. Wells! I didn't realize Mr. Peter R.B. Peary was up and around."

"Well, Fred, I did." Wells pulled his shoulders up and straightened his back.

"I guess it's your job."

Wells looked at Fred like a cat refusing to acknowledge the annoying presence of its owners.

Peter sat stunned. His nurse looked like every other man he knew, just smaller. Much smaller, perhaps four feet tall at the most. His brown hair was a little long, almost shoulder length, and he clearly worked out. As a nurse in a hospital, poking people the size of Jeff Wells, he couldn't be a shrinking violet. And Wells' reaction to his presence when he entered the room said as much.

"What's wrong?" the nurse asked in a casual tone, noticing Peter's dumbfounded look before turning to his work.

"Nothing."

"What do you mean, nothing? You look like you've just seen an alien, a close encounter of the third kind." The nurse's attention snapped toward Peter. "Or perhaps this is a close encounter of the short kind? Ever see a little person before?"

"Well... no. No. I haven't. I mean, I don't have any friends that are...."

"Little people." Fred's tone reflected annoyance, as if something unwanted from his past had just been unearthed. "We're called little people. We're not Munchkins."

"Of course, I know that," Peter shot back.

Fred returned to his work. "You'll get used to us around here."

The surreal aura of the room returned as the visual clarity of Fred, the little person, sent Peter's brain into a cloud of unfamiliarity. "Get used to who?"

"It's okay," Fred said, lifting his palm like a stop sign. "I may be a bit sensitive. I'm sorry. No one's reacted that way to me since I left Los Angeles more than ten years ago."

"Fred!"

Fred sent his hand toward Wells, as if to swat him out the door. "Chill out, Mr. Wells."

Peter looked at his nurse. "Your name is Fred?"

Fred pointed to the embroidered name tag on his uniform. "That's what it says." He looked at Peter and smiled. "Maybe in another minute your head will have cleared enough to read."

"Um, yeah," Peter sputtered, lifting his hand to his head. "I guess my brain's a little scrambled still."

Fred looked at Wells. "What are you going to do with him? Beam him back to the Lower Forty-Eight?"

Peter's head felt like it was spinning again. Dogs and sleds were fuzzy memories, but they were sharpening. And didn't someone say his gear indicated he was heading toward the North Pole? He remembered mushing a dog team on the ice. He must be somewhere in the Arctic. But where? The polar ice cap was a shifting mass of ice; nothing permanent this big could last long before falling into the Arctic Ocean. Maybe he was somewhere just south of the ice cap, perhaps the northern reaches of Alaska or the Northwest Territories. Was this a military base? Jeff Wells projected military formality and distance, always ready to cast someone aside to save the mission. Fred was certainly not military. But, still, Peter's recovering instincts said he knew military jocks pretty well, and Wells didn't fit that mold, either.

Wells pounded a file folder on the cabinet shelf with his forefinger, as he stared at Fred. "You know we're on alert. We don't know where Mr. Peary came from, or what he's doing." Wells turned to look straight into Peter's eyes. "And he's not going to tell us anytime soon."

11

Fred rolled his eyes. "He's got a severe concussion. He's lucky he can remember his name."

Peter looked around the room, and shook his head. "Where am I?"

"I'm afraid Mr. Wells is right about one thing," Fred responded, looking at Wells, then Peary. "I can't tell you that. We're under alert—Level Three to be exact—and that means I can't give you much specific information. Rest assured, though, we'll take good care of you."

"Am I under arrest?" Peter blurted. "What have I done? You can't keep me here, not against my will."

Wells laughed. "Unfortunately for you, Mr. Peary, we can. We're not under U.S. jurisdiction. In fact, you're not under anyone's jurisdiction except ours."

Peter's headache thumped through his forehead again. "What do you mean?"

Wells started for the door, then turned. "Mr. Peary, we'll talk soon. Right now, concentrate on getting better. I don't know how we will resolve this, but we'll find some way out of it."

"Peach of a guy," said Peter as the door closed behind the back of Jeff Wells.

"Ahh, don't worry about it," Fred said, as he prepared another dose of pain medication. "I've worked here a long time—longer than Wells. One thing about Wells is he's a straight shooter. Eight years in the Navy, six as a SEAL, seven as head of security around here. Did some other private security stuff for several years before coming up here. Florida, I think. He's tough, but fair. If he says he'll find a way out, he will."

"What do we have to find a way out of?"

Fred plunged a syringe into Peter's IV, and the cold flow of a chemical began to work its way through Peter's veins.

"Jeff isn't such a bad guy," Fred continued, ignoring Peter's question. "He's got a tough job. And right now, tensions are high, very high. Someone's about to upset more than eighty-five years of hard work. Lots of people—high-level people—are very interested in you, your dogs, and your friend Sheila. Oh, I just checked on her. She's still unconscious… in a coma, but stable. Dr. Patten thinks her prospects are good."

Sheila… Sheila; he knew Sheila. They were together with the team of dogs. They were headed north on the ice. Did she have blonde hair? "How did I end up here?"

The thumping in his head began to lessen.

"You fell through the ice, of course."

Peter didn't remember falling through the ice. If the ice broke underneath them, he would be dead. His instincts told him that, even if his brain couldn't. The ice was thirteen to fifteen feet thick this time of year, sixty in some places at the top of ridges created by colliding ice sheets. That was like falling off the roof of a two or three story building into freezing water. His clothes would have been soaked, pulling him under. He suddenly felt cold again, as he thought about the frigid water closing in around him, soaking through his clothes, drowning him within minutes. That is… if the ice didn't close in on him and crush him first.

Peter R. B. Peary closed his eyes, confused but calm, and let the drugs seduce him into a deep sleep.

5

A thick folder dropped onto the desk of Special Agent Miles "Gek" Getko on the fourth floor of the eleven story modern building at 700 Army Navy Drive in Arlington, Virginia. Gek smiled as he thought about how he was about to show the agency he was "back." All he needed was the final piece of the puzzle, and everyone would know he was Number One, the best of 681 agents in the narco-terrorism division of the U.S. Drug Enforcement Administration.

"This is the latest from the Caribbean," Joy reported as the folder hit the desk. "But I think we have a problem."

The dark circles under Joy's eyes told of long, boring days viewing aerial photographs, bank records, telephone logs, and that blinking dot on the computer screen. She stood quietly, waiting in her well-worn jeans and rumpled, un-ironed, white blouse. Her glasses projected a studious look, befitting the image of a Georgetown University graduate from the Walsh School of Foreign Service. Her well-toned body suggested someone religious about a daily workout and a little too adventurous to be stuck in an office nine hours a day.

Getko looked up. "You know, Joy, I don't like surprises." He lifted his eyebrows, as if expecting her to continue.

Joy fought back the depressing thought that she may now be doomed to the bowels of the DEA's surveillance unit. She wanted nothing more than to be four metro stops away with Rocky, his black and blue rugby-abused fingers clamped around the handle of a mug of cold beer, his eyes longing for her company after a long day of work on K Street in downtown Washington, D.C.

She pulled back strands of her long, brown hair as she placed her finger on the folder. "The North Pole expedition is no longer tracking."

"What?"

"The signal just disappeared."

"Damn. That complicates things. The last thing I want to do is bring another department into this mess. This program can't afford to lose another agent."

"Another agent? Just one?" Joy puzzled. "I thought we had two on that mission."

"Damn," Getko repeated, rolling his eyes toward the wall. He turned them back to Joy as if he were about to add something but thought better of it. His eyes coasted back to the folder she just dropped on his desk. "Okay, where are we with the project?"

Joy hesitated, surprised by Getko's focus and subdued reaction. Getko was usually giddy about spilling information and insight into intelligence operations as if she were his protégé. It was uncomfortable—he was in his mid-fifties, after all—but she wanted to get out of that abyss of a command center, stop looking at those blinking dots on her computer monitor tracking agents and get into the field. Now, his silence made her feel uneasy and awkward.

Joy picked up the folder and flipped through several pages. "George found a string of $10,000 cash withdrawals from four banks: the Primero Banco Nacionale in St. Thomas, the Virgin Community Bank in Jamaica, the Atlantic Coast States Bank in Miami, and the Third National Regions Bank in Tallahassee, Florida. The problem is, he couldn't trace the accounts very easily. I spent three weeks trying to track them! George spent another week after I couldn't find much. Apparently, these guys are transferring money from lots of different banks in the U.S. We think there are at least 300 people involved. These people have quite a network."

Getko looked impressed. "Joy, sometimes it's hard to think of you as junior analyst." Joy shifted her weight uneasily. "You've been here just six months, and you can practically run the money laundering section!"

"George is a good supervisor."

"Yes, George is very good. But so are you."

"Well, I was in the white collar division of the Department of Justice before moving over here."

Getko raised his eyebrows as if to say "enough!" and Joy acknowledged his order with a nod. Joy's heart skipped; perhaps her promotion to the field was closer than she thought!

Getko looked at the files again. "The accounts. They must have a common link."

"Many of them, about 14.2 percent, are under the name of Nikolai Barsukov, or some derivative of that name."

Getko's eyebrows turned up. "Fourteen percent? Is that enough to make a match?"

"Statistically, no," Joy said, but then paused, embarrassed by her brashness. She had to be careful. She loved statistics, and this project excited her. Still, she didn't want to torpedo a promotion by making it seem she was running it, even though Getko reminded her of a squirrel, willing and happy to hoard the spoils of his success. "Well, George doesn't think it is. But we've been able to cross-match movements of individuals in each of the locations, and trace some of their trips from city to city. We're about 65 percent sure we've got a 100 percent map for the people in the 14.2 percent."

"What about the other 85 percent?"

"We're still working on them. Statistically, we can probably match another 20 to 25 percent."

"That would bring the percentages up to about 40 percent or more."

"Yes, sir, statistically speaking." Joy tried to keep a smile from beaming across her face. She had to stay under control. Stay focused, just like what they'll want to see in the field.

"That's enough to draw up a plan and begin the operation." Getko picked up the folder and let its spine fall on the table, forcing the papers inside into a neat stack with edges aligned.

Joy looked at Getko.

"Is there a problem, Agent Gault?"

Joy hesitated but didn't divert her eyes from Getko. "Statistically speaking?"

"Statistically speaking."

"I didn't think we had enough to get final authorization from the agency administrator for the funds and equipment."

Getko looked at her, surprised. "When do you have time to read procedural manuals?"

Joy paused, again, shifting her weight. "Lunch?"

16

"Hah! Ambitious, too. Joy Gault, you have a future at the DEA!"

Getko leaned back in his large office chair and clasped his hands behind his head, looking up at the ceiling. "Where's Barsukov from, Russia?"

"Hard telling. I talked to Cheryl at the Department of State's Russia desk. She thinks he's Russian. The Caribbean Task Force believes Barsukov is a Russian Mafioso, laundering money through family and friends in New York City, Philadelphia, and Miami."

"That would fit. Moscow's pissed off about Britain and Germany. They can't shake them loose from us. When France signed on to the international drug law enforcement compact, they went ballistic. They've got enough savvy from the old days to work an undercover, narco-terrorism op to get at us."

Joy shifted her weight steadily from one side to the next. "Sir, do you want me to get George? As head of the Caribbean Task Force, he'll have a lot more say on this project than I will."

"You're right," Getko nodded. He lifted the telephone on his desk and pushed a button. After a moment, he grimaced as the call turned over to voice mail. "George? Miles. When you get back in the office, give me a call. I've got Joy up here, and she's pointed a few things out in the report I think we should discuss."

Getko thumbed through more pages of Joy's report. "What's with this series of money exchanges in Los Angeles?"

"We... George... doesn't know. George had me run a few cross checks with South Florida banks."

"Keep me posted on where that goes."

"Yes, sir. I'm sure George will explain more of this in his next briefing."

Joy opened her mouth to say something, felt better about it, and waited. Getko paused as he flipped through the pages and looked up. "What else? You were going to add something."

"Sir, it's really George's position to say anything more."

"Cut it Joy. George isn't here. He's probably getting a beer at the Pentagon as far as we know. I don't have time to let this stuff stew."

"This may be a wild goose chase," Joy said, "but we're spending a lot of time tracking down bank accounts."

Getko rolled his eyes and let the folder drop to the desk. "Trust me; we're on to something." He glanced back up at her, realizing something else was weighing on her mind. "Why? What's wrong? What are you thinking?"

"George and I found that once we get two levels down in the account names, the number of people with links to the bank account expands by two or three times the original number. We have to be careful. We don't want to make a mistake and go after someone who's innocent. It's sort of like the Six Degrees of Kevin Bacon."

"The what?"

"You know, the Bacon Game," Joy snipped, thrown a little by Getko's obvious ignorance. "Kevin Bacon? The movie actor."

Getko lifted his hands as if to say, yeah, so?

"Well, take an actor, actress, or director in Hollywood. Pick any movie they worked in or on. You can connect them with Kevin Bacon within six steps through other actors or directors they've worked with. Usually, it only takes two or three steps."

"So, what's the point?"

"It's based on probabilities and frequencies. Just because you have connected, say Cate Blanchett to Kevin Bacon, because Jim Cameron directed both of them in different movies, doesn't mean that Cate Blanchett and Kevin Bacon know each other. It's sort of like guilt by association, three times removed. We're running the same risk here. We can connect people, even build a case against them, even though they don't know each other or haven't committed a crime."

Getko smiled as if to say how quaintly analytical. He would need someone like Joy when he finally broke out of the Caribbean money-laundering vortex. One more big score and he would be able to do that. Then, he would be able to go after the Russians.

"Joy, I don't think we have to worry about that," said Getko, putting her folder aside and picking up accounting ledgers. "No one takes out cash these days unless they are running drugs, buying illegal guns, or laundering money. If they aren't, they should know that it raises suspicions; they should expect to be questioned. All they have to do is show us they're upstanding, law-abiding citizens in our interview, and they're off the hook." Getko pointed to two tables on the ledgers. "Besides, the patterns are consistent. Look at all the money changing hands in South Florida and the Caribbean, prime drug trafficking areas. The link to Latin America—Colombia, Peru, Ecuador, Venezuela—it's obvious. We're definitely onto something big... very big."

"Bimini Triangle?"

A toothy grin cracked the intensity of Getko's face. "Could be, could be. That would be big, wouldn't it?"

"Yes sir, it would."

"It would also save this task force." Getko's billion dollar sting in Bimini netted more than three dozen arrests of high-level drug dealers throughout the Caribbean, Central America, and the Southwestern U.S. That's when the DEA created the Caribbean Task Force, usually just called the CTF, and put Getko in charge. The sting was a cash cow: luxury cars, ocean-going cigarette speed boats, a corporate jet, and other confiscated loot generated tens of millions of dollars, financing years of undercover ops for the CTF. Then, South America was added to the mix—more countries, more drug operations, more targets.

That was before 9/11, and the feds started directing funds to Afghanistan and Iraq. Now, the money had slowed to a trickle. His success was bleeding his operations dry. Getko needed another big score. This was going to be it—Bimini Triangle II—with a twist: gun running.

"What's the code name for the operation?"

Getko lifted his fingers into a prayerful position in front of his nose, deep in thought. "Given the season, we'll call it *Jamaican Snow.* Can you let George know? Tell him the project and code name have the highest security priority. No one but us can know about it—not even the administrator's office."

Joy's body stiffened. "Um, don't you need budgetary clearance?" she asked, knowing full well Getko was breaking protocol.

"Let me handle that," Getko said, once he saw Joy's apprehension. "I'm well within my authority as division head."

"Of course. I just thought that Congress was trying to crack down on independent operations."

"Of course," Getko snorted, shaking his head. He looked out his window over South Fern Street across the 14th Street Bridge and toward the Capitol. The bronze Statue of Freedom's sword and laurel wreath of victory were invisible at this distance despite its place 300 feet above the Mall.

"Did the same article that talked about how Congress had to clamp down on law enforcement operations also discuss how discretionary accounts were essential in filling mission critical operations?"

"Well, no, sir."

"Did your seminar readings at Georgetown discuss how Congress knows about these accounts, but funds them every year after subjecting division heads and the administrator to extensive questioning in public hearings?"

"No, sir."

"We need these accounts. Otherwise, we'd never make any headway against drug lords and terrorists."

Joy waited. "Sorry, sir. I know you wouldn't work outside your authority. I just—"

"Thank you, Agent Gault."

The formality of Getko's words told Joy to shut up and leave the room. But she didn't, and what he said next worried her even more.

"I want arrests by Christmas. There'll be a big bonus in it for the whole team if we wrap it up."

Joy stepped back, as she checked her jaw from dropping open at the order.

Getko glanced at Joy. "It's a tight time frame, but we can do it. That's another reason I want you on the team. You have a lot of knowledge about the project that we couldn't hope to bring another staff member up to speed on quickly enough. Bimini Triangle closed down in three months. Our task force has already been working on Jamaican Snow in one form or another for about a year. We should be able to wrap it up by the end of the year."

"But the North Pole mission—"

"That's the key. We've got to find out what happened to our agent up there."

The dots weren't connecting. If the North Pole mission was critical, and their agent had dropped into nowhere, how could they finish the operation so fast? They had to track down the agent, conduct an investigation, recalibrate the operation, bring a new agent on board—Joy's head began to spin with details.

George would have to figure it out. Most of the task force was downright giddy about the prospects of another big score. They would keep their jobs and get a big bonus. But it all seemed so sloppy. That's why Joy liked statistics—clean and direct.

Joy cringed as she thought about her division's sloppy, investigative work. Mistakes would be made to wrap up Jamaican Snow by Christmas. She could see them emerging in the dollars, flowing through layer after layer of transactions among the four banks she was tracking. And those mistakes would become statistics. The question was whether the mistakes would help them, or destroy them.

A hollow rasp crackled over the intercom on Getko's desk. "Deputy Administrator Colson on line two."

Getko looked up at Joy, dismissing her with his eyes as he reached for the phone.

"Hey, Chuck," Getko said cheerfully before the receiver plugged into his ear. "What's up?"

6

"I've been going over some of these requests, and I have a question about the CTF investigation."

"Sure, Chuck, fire away," Getko said into the telephone receiver. "If I don't have the answer, one of our team leaders will write up a quick memo."

Getko swiveled his chair away from the door. The room was small. Looking out the windows gave him a sense of openness unavailable in the cramped walls filled in by files, desks, and chairs. He heard the door click as Joy left the room and the digital lock kicked in. Getko relaxed. "What's going on?"

"Well," Colson said, "you've got this request for snow gear. Now, the last time I checked the weather report, it wasn't snowing in the U.S. Virgin Islands."

Getko chuckled. "No, you got me there Chuck! But it's winter in South America, and we're in the steeps of the Andes."

Colson's doubt was evident in the silence on the other end of the phone.

Getko's heart quickened. He let a quick breath escape from his lungs, letting his shoulders fall. *Relax, he's fishing. These political appointees are clueless.* "Chuck, I'm not sure what else I can tell you that's not already in the files."

"Come on, Miles." the deputy administrator snapped. "Don't jerk me around. These are serious dollars and resources you're asking for here."

Getko played the scenarios in his mind: being fired, reassigned, or, if successful, promoted. The CTF couldn't be disbanded quickly.

Bimini Triangle created a cushion in Congress for him, even though its feathers seemed to have had their luster patted down with each passing session. In national politics, ten years was a career, fifteen a lifetime— six administrators, four deputy administrators. Colson was number five. But public hearings would muck up narco-terrorism initiatives everywhere. Not just in the DEA. Everywhere. Colson didn't want the spotlight on DEA special ops. Why was he fishing? Getko and the CTF could be a prime target for getting sacked now that the fiscal hawks in Congress were putting the budget deficit on the front burner again. Jamaican Snow would keep his cushion fully fluffed.

"Chuck, this is all legit. It's the Andes. We've got a huge lead on a massive money laundering scheme that spans our southern border and both seaboards, from Los Angeles to Miami. We need interagency cooperation and the resources to do a winter operation."

"I need more than that, Miles."

"Okay," Miles lied. "We've got a string of fourteen wholesale cocaine and heroin processing labs identified in the Andes, running from Peru down to Chile. Our intelligence shows that these labs are a new breed. The producers have found a way to break the coke down to reduce its weight and bulk. Mules can pack as much high-charged powder in a belt's inseam as they carried in a pouch strapped to their stomach five years ago. They transport it into the Caribbean, then it's distributed in the U.S. The revenues from the national drug gangs in the U.S. are massive. We need helicopters to airlift about fifty agents and soldiers into the territory. If we shut these labs down at their source, we shut down a multibillion-dollar network overnight."

"That's dollars. We know dollars don't mean anything. What's the bulk? How much of the supply would be disrupted?"

"About 80 percent of this new type of coke; 10 percent of the total supply coming into the United States."

"Crap, Miles, that's a big score."

"Yes, sir. We could make a big dent in the market with just a couple of million dollars and some winter gear."

Getko's throat tightened as the silence on the other end of the phone stretched from half-seconds, to seconds, to a half-minute. Was his lie too big? He mentally checked the story. He had added enough truth to make the lie believable. He hoped. He drew in a silent breath, letting the oxygen rejuvenate his lungs.

"Who do you want to work with?"

23

Getko relaxed. "We have to keep this completely under wraps for obvious reasons. I want to work with agencies capable of keeping complete secrecy."

"Hmm. That means you can't go with conventional law enforcement."

"No," confirmed Getko. "I want to work with the CIA or Special Forces."

"Well...."

"Look, Chuck," Getko said, invoking his smoothest, most consoling tone. "This is an international conspiracy. The CIA's Crime and Narcotics Center has lots of data not available to the general public that we can use. More importantly, the Office of Transnational Issues can help coordinate these interagency efforts because of the national security implications."

"But those are intelligence gathering agencies. You're proposing field operations."

"Chuck, do you really think the CIA is only involved in collecting data?"

The deputy administrator's end of the line fell silent... again.

"Look, Chuck, these foreign countries will be happy we're going after these guys and busting up their cartels and production. Besides, we have intelligence that suggests they have ties to Afghanistan and Syria. It's a global, money laundering scheme that's feeding drugs to our kids and funding terrorism in the Middle East.

"The political situation on drugs is like terrorism in Pakistan. The governments don't want to be involved if they can help it; it just creates a domestic, political problem. If we go in, they pound their fists over sovereignty and independence, but they'll be happy it's us, not them, going after the drug lords and terrorists. We create a political IOU we can cash in later. Either way, we win by going in on our own, without local law enforcement or their government's help. They won't have any qualms about us sending in whatever troops we want to stop this. With the CIA on board, and units from the 3rd Battalion of the 20th Special Forces Group, or the 7th Special Forces Group out of Eglin Air Force Base, I think we can take these drug operations down. After all, their specialty is in-country operations."

"Pakistan was pretty pissed off when we went in after Osama."

"Exactly. And our relations with the Pakis are better than ever as long as we stay out of the headlines."

Colson paused again, but Getko felt the momentum shift. Getko let the fingertips of his free hand drop lightly to the table top, his middle finger beginning a silent drum beat, as if sending warning signals to his boss three floors up on the phone.

Getko held his breathe. He told a lie like this to set up Operation Bimini Triangle. That was a huge risk, too. But it worked. But this lie was different. Getko's middle finger started tapping more quickly. Canada wasn't a banana republic. He nodded to himself. This was the right thing to do. Success would vindicate him. The Special Forces would ensure his success. He just needed airborne troops for insurance. It worked in Bimini. Why not with Operation Jamaican Snow?

"Okay, I'm signing off on this request."

Getko let out a long sigh of relief.

"But listen up, Miles. I'm not going to tolerate rogue agents under my watch. This operation better come off without a hitch. You're walking a fine line from here on out."

"Yes, sir."

"Keep me posted regularly and often. I want to know who you're working with and what they're doing."

"Of course, Chuck. Just keep in mind most of the agents and troops won't know anything about the mission until twelve hours before the operation starts. The only people knowing the details will be me, you, and the commanders of any Special Forces or CIA detachments. As you know, we're also concerned about a possible mole inside the agency. We can't afford to let any hint of this operation leak out, so we're going to keep it buttoned up from head to foot."

"Good idea. I see this other update on the mole investigation. I'll get Internal Affairs to step up their efforts."

"And one more thing," Colson said, his tone stiffening the hair on Getko's neck. "Anyone with a Special Forces background is there purely for backup and advising. This is not a military operation. It's a narc operation through and through."

As the phones hung up, Getko spun himself around in his chair, feeling like a little kid who had just pulled a fast-one on his parents. Yep, he would keep the deputy administrator completely informed— once he could file a report, detailing the breakup of the world's most extensive and corrupt drug ring. *Imagine*, he thought to himself in amazement, *a network so complex it extended from the tips of South America to the North Pole. Sheer brilliance!*

25

SR Staley

7

"You've got to do better than that."

Nicole began to pace, hoping the steps and her breathing would rein in her testiness. Sure, two intruders falling through an ice crevice was distracting. But she needed to know what the intruders were up to, and whether they knew anything about her operation. This was not the time for Wells to mess up.

"I know," Jeff Wells said, his voice rising in protest. "We just don't know what to make of it."

Quicker, shorter steps did little to calm her. She lifted her hand to her chin as she turned. Nicole's personality was much bigger than her small body would suggest even under normal circumstances. She wasn't a dwarf, but she was somewhat shorter than average for an American woman. But even a five-foot-five woman was diminutive next to the large, fit body of her chief of security. Waves of light brown hair tossed over her shoulders with each step, stirring the air and the mood in the small office. She stopped. "Jamaican Snow could shut us down."

"It's certainly got the potential." Wells lifted a folder and let it slap down on his thigh as he sat watching Nicole, as she stood next to her desk. "It depends on where the DEA takes it. They're staying south for now."

"But we can't count on that. Our mole says Getko is thinking north. His team's traced dozens of links to bank accounts, and he's close to connecting them to our North Pole operation."

Even after six years, Wells had trouble adjusting to Nicole's machine-like efficiency when it came to The Business. His instincts, combined with relentless training, kept him calm and alive in Afghanistan and the first Iraq War. But the feeling that Nicole's green eyes could penetrate deep into his soul made him shift his weight in the chair.

Once Nicole entered a room, no one, not even Jeff Wells, could mistake her beauty as a crutch. Like her father, and his father before him, Nicole embraced her Dutch heritage and drive to keep a laser-like focus on the business of running The Business.

"True," Wells said at last, "but we don't have any real evidence Getko's actually moved on that idea. Besides, he would need authorization from the deputy administrator, and no paperwork has been approved for a North Pole operation."

Nicole chafed at Wells' bureaucratic approach. She wanted to yell: *Trust your gut!* "We can't wait for proof. I think we have to explore all the options. We can't afford a break in security. Not now. Not as we're gearing up."

Wells gave her a sideways look. "Okay, I'll put two more guys on it, and put a few more in our posts in L.A., D.C., and Miami. We'll elevate the threat level."

Nicole hated prodding him this way. He knew his job, she tried to remind herself. Like her, he had to report to the directors.

Wells scrawled notes onto the screen of a small tablet—a modified version someone had smuggled out from under the nose of Apple's head of R&D, right after Steve Jobs passed away. Rolf's shop at NP Software had tweaked the technology, taking it to another level. The third-generation technology did little to improve Wells' scrawl or slow his frantic writing every time Nicole pushed him like this. When Nicole pushed him, he reacted with uncharacteristic impatience, a weakness that would have killed him when he was out in the field in the Navy's Special Forces. Wells' stylus seemed like it was about to push through the screen and into the circuits and chips below.

Nicole concealed a sigh as she thought of her father and the wistful longing to leave The Business she felt each time NP Software made another technological breakthrough. Nicholas III had seen a global vision for The Business. She hated spending so much of her life in these cavernous ice dwellings, especially as a child. But his smile was infectious, and his laugh could lift her spirits more than anything. His smile was widest and biggest, and his laugh fullest, when he was talking about The Business. She needed that, especially after the death of her mother when she was in grade school. She missed it now.

"What's wrong?"

Nicole looked up to find Wells staring at her. "Come on, Nic. I know something is troubling you. What is it?"

"Nothing." What was the point trying to talk to him? His parents were still alive and he was forty-three years old. She had lost both her parents by the time she was twenty-one. "What about Peter Peary?"

Wells touched the screen on his notebook. "Basically, he's a washed-up explorer even though he's just twenty-six."

Nicole cast a surprised look at Wells.

"Yeah, your age." Wells looked at Nicole, about ready to say something, then turned his eyes back to the notebook. "Peary was a child prodigy of sorts. We ran an Internet, FBI, and INTERPOL search. I called in a few chits here and there. We rebuilt his career on paper."

Wells touched the "enter" button on the tablet, and papers began shooting out of a high-speed laser printer a few feet away. "He lost five people on an expedition on Mount Everest when he was twenty-two years old. One of the guys was a good friend and mentor, Richard Van Dorn. He'd been climbing for thirty years and this was his tenth Everest attempt. Peary couldn't take the pressure after his death. Of course, he was barely out of college. Who would have expected him to?"

Wells stopped. He looked up at Nicole. "Sorry Nic. I didn't mean...."

"Don't worry, Jeff. It's no big deal. Go on."

Wells paused.

"Seriously," Nicole implored. "I know I'm forty!"

He laughed. "Well, you certainly act forty!"

Nicole smirked. "Yeah?"

Wells waited again, surprised by her lightheartedness.

Nicole's smile disappeared. "Okay, okay, so I'm a prude. I can still take a joke... most of the time."

This time, they laughed together.

"Now go on before I'm forced to get serious again!"

Wells' laugh faded into a smile, and he looked down at his tablet's monitor again. "The pressure was too much. He had graduated from Georgetown with a second degree in geology. His first degree was awarded to him by Florida State University at age nineteen, after he graduated from high school at fifteen... go figure. He was an Air Force brat and spent his high school years in Pensacola, Florida. He was enrolled in graduate school at George Washington University. He dropped out after the Mt. Everest accident, just a semester shy of graduating. Or, at least he didn't take classes. He basically disappeared after that for about two years. About eighteen months ago, he resurfaced, trying to rebuild his life and, apparently, his reputation as a winter explorer and guide."

"So, he's an unfocused, washed-out explorer."

"Nicole, he lost his best friend and mentor in a bonafide climbing disaster. The accident got a lot of press at the time. We scanned about 500 articles during the crisis and a few post-accident wrap-ups; more than 400 were from a single Reuters wire story that got picked up throughout North America, Argentina, Chile, Japan, and Kenya. It was just one climbing accident. It happens when you're in the Death Zone on a mountain that kills 25 percent of the people who attempt to reach its summit."

Nicole's nose twisted as if doubt were morphing her face. She stood up and seemed to absorb her office, pausing at two widescreen television monitors that blanketed one wall. One sparkled with blue, green, white, and red blinking lights that appeared to be linking cities and states, and traveled across oceans. Just last night, she had tracked the movements of their freight on this world map, using their satellites to scan street grids and neighborhoods where cargo seemed to have slowed to a crawl. Every movement of every truck and courier was plotted with a blinking light indicating its location and status.

She studied the lights before saying, "He's weak. He doesn't have the discipline or focus to turn his passions into success."

Wells' cheeks hardened as the muscles tensed. "He's brilliant, Nic. Until Mount Everest, he showed more drive and ambition than anyone his age. He was ranked first in his age group and *Exploration Magazine* named him one of the top twenty world climbers to watch. Don't dismiss him. He could be the guy."

"Okay, okay," Nicole relented. "Maybe I'm judging him too harshly."

Wells turned his eyes to the wall and away from Nicole, hoping to break the invisible beam that seemed to drive his frustration toward her. "There is a pretty big, glaring question mark in his record, though. Somehow, he scraped up enough money for this expedition. He was facing some pretty hard times, so he would have been a good civilian candidate for the DEA's undercover operations. They pay pretty well, now that they can seize assets and sell them off at auction. He had no money or assets. He was trying to rebuild his life. We don't have much evidence, but he's our #1 prospect for DEA stooge."

Nicole nodded. "What about the girl?"

Wells fell into a chair at the desk and clicked through more files. "Sheila Livingston. From what we can tell, she's also an explorer and another of Peary's friends; at least for now. She may even be his girlfriend. We suspect she got the financing for the expedition, but again, the trail is far from clear. Nothing too spectacular in her career, though. She had a savings account that could have bankrolled it. Most of her explorer work was done under Peary before he went off the deep end. She seemed to drop out of his life before the Everest incident. Apparently, she started graduate school at American University in Washington, D.C., and busied herself with academics and writing a few technical papers. Nothing connects her to law enforcement. But we're still running checks. No husband or boyfriend that we can find right now."

Nicole stopped pacing and was now sitting behind her contemporary-style desk. On top of the desk, directly in front of her, was a laptop computer. No drawers or cabinets were nearby, but three widescreen monitors hung behind her, consuming the wall like an inverted, tech version of wainscoting. The screens were blank, but she could easily swivel her comfortable office chair, computer on her lap, to see them all at one time.

"Well," Nicole said, twisting in her chair, arms behind her head, "she's not going anywhere soon. Julie... Dr. Patten says she's got a pretty severe head injury; the surgical staff is worried about brain damage and clotting. It's touch and go."

"Man, that's a tough break." Wells twisted his chair to face Nicole and the rest of the room. Nicole's office was stripped down. A few photos adorned bare walls—a picture of her father, grandfather, great-grandfather, and others deeply involved in The Business—but little else other than the massive video screens. A second contemporary desk hugged the back wall with yet another laptop, although it showed little life, or interest in engaging the world, at the moment.

"What?" Nicole asked.

Wells blinked and diverted his eyes back to the folder in his lap. "What do you mean 'what'?"

"You were staring at me."

Wells scrambled to come up with something. He had been distracted when she threw her head, tossing her hair away from her eyes. The move was functional—she had hair obscuring her reading—but he wasn't prepared for it. Now she had caught him in a momentary gaze. "Were you like this at MIT?"

"What? Where did that come from?"

"You're so intense. Your profs must have loved you. You probably worked on your computer programs all night to debug them and get them right."

Nicole flushed with embarrassment. She loved working on those programs. A grin cracked her face as she remembered coming up with the idea that made all Windows-based operating systems obsolete. She had started working on the underlying programming language after enrolling in an on-line university course in computer programming at fifteen. They never knew she was just a high schooler! MIT let her take it to the final steps with the help of a brilliant family friend, Rolf Hackett. She installed the program on all NP networks, and they were able to process more information, more accurately, and at greater speeds than any system in the world. It was her pride and joy. It doubled their revenues in the first year! Then, Father died. The fun seemed to stop right then and there.

"I can have fun," Nicole said. "I'm twenty-six for God's sake! In the Lower Forty-Eight, having fun is legal once you turn twenty-one."

Wells' smile, like Nicole's, was a little more forced this time.

Nicole tapped a stylus on her desk next to her laptop. "It's just we're moving into the busy season. I need all my energy focused on making sure things don't screw up. About 650 million people are depending on our networks working this year; that's 50 percent growth over last year, and it puts quite a strain on our systems."

And you, Wells thought. "Well, your father wasn't nearly as intense, and he seemed to keep things on track well enough."

Nicole's beauty disappeared into a deep frown. "You didn't know my father!" She caught her breath. "He's gone. I'm a different person. I run things my way." Wells should have known to avoid the reference to Nicholas Klaas, III. Nicole almost always shut down at the mere hint of a reference to him or his name, almost like she felt his shadow, stalking her in the command center of The Business.

"Okay, okay," Wells apologized. "Sorry, Nic. I just meant it might do you some good to chill out a little. Remember, I know what pressure is; I was a Navy SEAL. And I saw real action, with people shooting at me and trying to blow me up."

"Well, hooray for the armed forces!" Nicole regretted the outburst as soon as she said it. She needed to chill out. She knew her attitude had changed when she became president of NP Enterprises and left NP Software to Rolf. She just didn't like to admit she didn't enjoy the job as much. She looked at the pictures of her father, grandfather, and great-grandfather. They would be so proud! She huffed. The responsibility for carrying out their legacy rested squarely on her shoulders, no one else's.

Each day as her feet hit the cold floor of her bedroom thirty feet below the Arctic Circle (thanks to the creativity of her town's engineers), she prayed she had a knack for more than developing cutting-edge software. She wanted to be as good at running NP Enterprises as her father was. Where did he find the time? She always seemed to be scurrying about. She just didn't have time to do it all, and running the business was critical right now. *I can relax once the family legacy is intact*, she kept telling herself. *Just stop comparing yourself to Father! Or, Grandfather. Or, Great-grandfather.* She was different. Better!

Any romantic thoughts, no matter how fleeting, flittered out the room and to the surface of the ice as soon as Wells saw Nicole's souring expression. "Sorry, Nic. You're doing a great job. It's just some of us are worried that you're burning the candle at both ends. We don't want you to burn out."

"Yeah, right," she said, her voice too light to be taken seriously. "Thanks for the concern. I don't see anyone else jumping up to do this job. Besides, my candle's in the World Book of Records for the longest burn. Don't you have a plane to catch?"

Wells looked at his watch and then looked at Nicole with a torn expression. His plane was scheduled to leave in just three hours. It would take him nearly an hour to get to the landing strip. This wasn't the time to leave, especially with Peter Peary and his ex-girlfriend bunkered down in the hospital. Too much was riding on Nicole keeping her head in the game. If she slipped, the entire operation could be jeopardized.

Wells made a mental note to monitor Nicole's behavior, though he was no longer clear in his own mind if it was for personal or professional reasons. Everyone needed to focus on his or her job to keep the DEA from destroying everything. This wasn't the time for indecisiveness. But even Jeff Wells, the internationally recognized security expert, didn't know how important that decisiveness would become within the next 100 hours.

8

The video monitor in Nicole's office crackled as the image of a man with wavy blond hair and strong features morphed onto the screen. Thick eyebrows, deep dimples, and a piercing look seemed to hide his age as short, thick fingers from his right hand stroked his chin. A painting hanging on the wall seemed oddly large as a silhouette for the man's face, a visual confirmation that the man was a dwarf. Nicole and Jeff didn't notice.

His face lit up as soon as he realized Wells and Nicole were watching. "Hey Chief!" the image said lightheartedly.

"Hey, there," Nicole responded. "Whassup?"

"Yo, yo, man. Jes chill while I give you the low-down on the dude in the hospital."

Jeff Wells rolled his eyes.

The dwarf chuckled… and then became serious.

"I've got some information for Wells. We've been tracking down the cash withdrawals. A couple of big payments were made in LA's Toytown, but that shouldn't have raised any red flags for the government. Cash transfers are common these days, and we ghost them through Japanese, Chinese, and European retailers."

Wells tapped the conference table. "I think you're right on that one. I think we're looking for some vacationing workers."

"Right," confirmed the dwarf. "Some of the crew went to South Florida and the Caribbean for vacation this summer. Turns out, we had three sets of six go down within a twelve-week interval. Each used cash transfers to pay for hotels, lodging, and even a cruise. We think the feds picked up on those transfers and that's what got them interested."

"Hmm." Wells' voice seemed to growl with irritation. All vacations were supposed to be cleared to avoid these kinds of problems.

Wells' eyebrows curled in thought. "Where was the security breach?"

"We think they're just new to the process," said the dwarf. A beep inside the control room interrupted the dwarf's report.

"Here," Nicole said, passing a headset with a microphone to Wells. She tapped a button on her laptop and the second screen lit up.

"Just a minute," Wells said to no one in particular. "I've got to get these things on. I hate it when we have to split signals."

The face of a distinguished looking woman with a sharply defined jaw took over the second screen. A tinge of grey in her well-groomed, brown hair betrayed middle age despite youthful cheeks and lips.

"Hello, Dr. Patten," Nicole said.

"Hello, Ms. Klaas," Patten said with the Boston drawl, lengthening the vowel sound of two a's in her last name with a high nasal tone. Nicole found the distinctive accent a comforting reminder of her time studying at MIT. "Aw... you alone?"

"If you toggle to the right of your screen, you can get a widescreen, continuous feed video of the entire room. There. As you can see, Jeff Wells is the only one in the room with me and he's on another secure line, so we can talk freely. What can you tell us about our visitors?"

"Not much change, except for Peawee," she continued with her accent dropping the "r" in Peary. "Weaa still watching Sheila Livingston closely. I don't recommend moving her. Peawee, on the other hand, is fit to be tied. He wants to leave his room. We need to make a decision about him."

Nicole tapped Wells on the shoulder, signaling him to end his conversation. The security investigator disappeared from the first screen, leaving Patten's image alone on the wall. She looked young for someone in her late-fifties, hardly showing any wear from her med school days at Johns Hopkins University and ten-year stint at Boston's Mass General.

"We can't let him walk freely," said Wells. "We don't know enough about him or what he's doing up here."

"He's arrogant," Patten interjected, shaking her head.

"That's saying something, coming from the chief surgeon at NP Medical Center!" said Nicole.

Nicole felt a particularly strong bond with the older East Coast doctor, despite the formality of always using "Dr." She wanted Patten to like her. After all, they were both women with executive responsibilities. Shouldn't they have a bond of some sort?

"Yeah, well I broke out of that when I came up heeaa," said Patten, failing to pick up on the joke. "Peawee's pushing hard to get out, asking all the right questions. He's had enough *incidents* in international territowee to know the ropes. We need to evacuate him soon."

Nicole looked at Wells. He paused before nodding. "Ready the helicopter. I'll go down and talk to him. We'll ship him back to Nome. We can make it look like he got lost and *miraculously* found his way back."

"That's fine, Mistaa Wells," said Patten, her tone unconvinced, "but we have to deal with Livingston, too."

"Just let him think she died," said Nicole.

Wells looked at Nicole. "That's a bit cold, don't you think?"

Nicole let out a puff of air. "This is business."

An awkward pause overcame the trio. "Nicole, theeaa best friends," Patten reminded her. "He'll look for her."

"Wells, you've met this guy," Nicole said. "Put 25K in his pocket, and he'll be off on his next expedition. Right? His friends are expendable."

Wells caught his breathe. "How do you know all this?"

"I read your file on him."

"I'm not going to send Livingston to Anchorage until I know she's stable and in full recovery," Patten said, her voice becoming more insistent.

Nicole looked at the image in the video monitor. "You realize we think he might be a DEA agent, right?"

"It doesn't mattaa," Patten said. "We have to do the right thing for them both."

"I understand," Nicole said, "but we have other information that makes us think we have to monitor these two closely."

"What?" Patten's eyes seemed to expand to the size of saucers. "Don't you think I should be briefed? I am a community directoah."

Wells shook his head. "Not yet, Dr. Patten. We'll bring you and the other directors into the discussion as soon as we have information that warrants it."

"I think we should be informed soon, Mistaa Wells."

"I understand your concern." Wells looked at Nicole before turning back to Patten. "But paper only tells you so much. Peary's got passion, that's for sure. And he's impulsive. But he rises to challenges. He won't let anyone put one over on him. I'm telling you, we've got to tie up all the loose ends, or he will be back. Even if he's not DEA, he can be dangerous."

Patten was shaking her head. "I'm not comfoatable with this."

Wells looked at Nicole as if they had just been caught in a bedroom by their parents. "Uhhh, it's just a theory, Doc. We had a couple of minor breaches and the feds are curious, nothing we can't handle. My guys are on it."

Patten remained expressionless as her mind seemed to tick through different implications. "If Peawee is DEA, then this is more than a minor issue."

Wells cursed to himself. Nicole drew in a breath and closed her eyes. They both seemed to envision the incessant haggling that would subsume the village's fifteen directors with Dr. Julie Patten at the helm. They couldn't afford the hours sequestered in a board room.

"Julie, we are still assessing the situation," Nicole said, her voice steady. Nicole didn't seem to detect Dr. Patten setting her jaw at the informal reference to her name.

Nicole tried to hide her concern behind the mask of a CEO running a billion-dollar enterprise. Peary and Livingston were security matters, not community mascots. The community directors had to let her and Wells work it out.

"We don't have anything to report yet," Nicole continued. "Rest assured, once we know something concrete, we'll brief you and the full board."

Patten nodded her head. "We may need to move quickly. Perhaps I should infoamally brief some of the other directoahs."

"That's not necessary," Wells said, hoping his quick reply would hide his near panic. "Bringing them together now would signal a much greater level of concern than is necessary. Our current problem is to dispatch Peary at the earliest possible time. Once Livingston can be

37

transported, we can move her to Anchorage. She probably won't remember a thing."

Patten's eyes seemed to lose focus, as if she were distracted by something else. "Well, okay. Let's see what happens in the next couple of days. If this looks like it's going to take longer, I'll go to the directoahs. It's my responsibility."

"Agreed," Wells said. He needed to move. Fast.

Nicole's eyes glanced to Patten, and then fixed on Wells. "That still doesn't solve our problem with Peary."

"I know," he said. "Look, give me a few hours to work on this. Right now, we need to get Peary out of here before he sees too much."

"Agreed," said Patten, a hint of suspicion lingering over her word.

A black line appeared over the top of the video screen, and a stock-market ticker began running across Dr. Patten's forehead.

Nicole's face lifted to the scrolling numbers. "Hey, guys, I've got to go. The distribution numbers are coming in with new orders. I need to make sure the network is secure and functioning."

Patten's face clicked off the screen, and Wells rose from his chair. He unplugged his laptop and secured it in his briefcase. As he turned to say good-bye, Nicole was already clicking away on her keyboard, focused on the numbers passing across the screen.

"See ya," he said, not waiting for a response. "Got a plane to catch." The door closed and the digital lock engaged automatically behind him.

***

Nicole scanned the steady stream of coordinates, numbers, and letters flowing through her computer and into the network, any thought of Peter Peary was tucked away into the confined memory of his hospital room. Expanding into Africa was harder than she had expected. Most of the routes to Europe, Japan, Hong Kong, Philippines, and Thailand were intact. Accounts receivable were flowing in. They were gearing up for the big fall push.

That reminded her—she needed to check with Rowdy on the new distribution software and encryption codes. Keeping the flow running smoothly and efficiently was her job, and if she didn't do it, the entire world known as "NP"—the business and the community—would grind to a halt. Four generations of Klaas work would be lost, locked into the secrets of the arctic ice.

She looked at the clock, ticking off seconds in the corner of her monitor. Walking to Rowdy's office would take ten minutes. Perhaps they could grab a beer at the pub across the street and discuss the next phase of this expansion.

Nicole still had no inkling that the challenges emerging from the daily ticker would soon be the least of her worries.

9

Peter Robert B. Peary, one of the world's best cold weather explorers, was ready to move. His skin crawled each time he thought that he might have to spend another minute in the tiny hospital room. It was small, sterile and, worst of all, boring. He didn't know why he was there, or how he got there, but he had had enough. He had to get out, even if his memory had more holes than Swiss cheese.

Peter swung his legs over the hospital bed. No dizziness and weakness. Whoever these people were, they were keeping his body nourished. This was a very strange place. Strange people coming in and out of his room. A strange ninja security guard ready to pounce at any slight. And, Fred, the nicest of them all, was his nurse and a dwarf!

It was time to learn more about this bizarre prison and his compassionate keepers.

Peter R.B. Peary didn't have time to mull over the "whys" now, or even the "hows" about his escape. His brain was clearing, and he could chart a course through the squall.

Peter shifted his weight to the pads under the ball of his foot to minimize any thump that might come from plopping down on the floor. He stepped toward the closet and opened its door. Just as he thought—clothes were hanging and neatly stacked, as if his shirt, shoes, socks, and pants were begging him to put them on. They had had enough of being locked up in that closet too. They were ready for fresh air and a new adventure, perhaps, even a quest.

Peter stared at the clothes. At least, they seemed like his clothes. He couldn't remember specifically how he got them. They just looked comfortable, like he had spent a lot of time in them already. He put each garment on, piece by piece, trying to remember each article as they covered another part of his body. They felt intimately familiar, natural, and comfortable. For a moment, Peter just stood there, drawing strength from the cotton and wool. The boots slipped over his socked feet easily. *Hmm.* His clothes were clean, too.

Peter shut the door and found himself staring into a mirror. He looked like an explorer—the spitting image of his great-great-grandfather, Robert Peary.

"Of course," he nodded with unassuming recognition, one more hole in the cheese filled in. "I was on expedition." He looked at the clothes again. They were winter clothes. "I was on a winter expedition… to the arctic… to the North Pole. Just like Grandpa Bob."

Peter's grin widened as he recognized the figure in the looking glass. He pulled his shoulders up and peered into his face, clean shaven and a little more familiar. Boy, he looked young. For some reason, he seemed to remember twenty-six looking older.

He patted his shirt and pants, feeling the pockets, inspecting the seams. Everything seemed to be in place, except—no winter coat. He searched the further reaches of the cabinet, but his hands clasped at nothing but air. If he were in the arctic, wouldn't he have had a coat? Even if he had been airlifted, they would have taken him to Fairbanks or Anchorage, still too far north to be without a coat this time of year. He shook his head. He couldn't let that detail bother him. He was going to get to the bottom of this weirdness, coat or not, or die escaping from it.

Peter pushed his hands across the smooth skin of his chin and cheeks. The hospital's good hygiene didn't shave away his thirst for adventure. Like his ancestors, plowing the ice before him, a successful expedition could absolve past sin. He had known for years that those sins were the ones that drove him. But why? They weren't his to own, let alone embrace. But something dark was there, in the deepest reaches of his mind, even though he couldn't see it. He just felt it, something in one of the black holes of his memory.

Peter looked around the room again. He was, for sure, in a hospital. Something must have gone terribly wrong. But what? Not a brawl. He was now sure of that. He still couldn't remember the details, but he had a vague recollection of a conversation in his hospital room about dogs and a friend—a colleague?—near death. He must not have reached his original objective.

He closed his eyes and let his explorer's instincts embrace the images, sounds, and feelings flowing back into body and brain, bit-by-bit.

Peter's eyes shot open. The answers were outside the hospital room door. He turned from the mirror to face the door and listened. He was alone. Now was the time to move.

As good as his instincts were, however, they were still too ragged to pick up on a small camera lens, carefully tucked into the track lighting above.

***

Peter stepped to the door and tested the doorknob—unlocked. For the first time, he had to force his body forward, to overcome the natural caution that kept most people from venturing beyond the familiar. He let out a full breath and reminded himself that all adventure worth pursuing required overcoming some mental resistance. Well-oiled hinges seemed to hide his impending escape, as the heavy metal door opened a crack. He peered into a white-walled hallway.

"This is the most boring hospital I've been in for a long time," he mumbled. Peter struggled to dampen an ever so slight notion that he was drawn to this place. Jeff Wells was a piece of work… and that strange woman who left his room so quickly when he was barely conscious. Some weren't so bad: Fred, for example. Peter grimaced as he recognized the draw this strange, new experience seemed to hold for him. At least his headache was no longer surging.

Peter stepped into the hallway. At the end was a standard neon exit sign, pointing toward two doors that looked like a stairwell. *Two hundred feet, and I'm free*, he thought. It seemed so simple!

For all the hand wringing Wells made over leaking information, getting out of the building seemed easy enough. A flight of stairs led to the main floor where a window revealed a much busier hospital with people moving in and out of rooms. The hospital was small—just two stories high. *This must be a small town.* Peter could see the main exit another 100 feet away, but he would have to go into the main hallway where everyone would see him. He felt naked.

"Be bold," he whispered to himself.

He opened the door and strode into the hallway as if he did this every day. No one seemed to notice. He spotted the exit and focused on the doors, avoiding eye contact.

Seconds later, Peter was beyond the hospital walls and… outside? An eerily cool calm slapped him in the face, as soon as the doors closed behind him. The air was crisp, about thirty degrees Fahrenheit, but unnaturally still. His cold-weather experience reminded him of the calm before a major storm, and he became uneasy. He clutched for his coat, forgetting he couldn't find it in the hospital room. The dangers of exposure rushed his thoughts, freezing his boots in place for a moment. A few degrees colder and he would be forced back into the building to avoid hypothermia. The thought of being put back into his hospital room pushed his feet forward.

The memory of a snow storm, a blinding snow storm, made him pause as his feet touched a carpet of crystallized water. The streets were well lit, but he had the feeling of being closed in. Usually when outside a building, he felt free. Now, he felt trapped, almost as if he were in a cave.

Peter stepped outward, and his foot fell on the ice with a crunch. That was odd—his boot didn't slide. He looked down and saw dark streaks along well-worn paths. Of course: it's sand. Sand created a grip on the ice.

Peter walked. Once he rounded the corner of the hospital, and was safe on the street and among people again, he thought he could figure out where he was. People were moving up ahead, and he thought he saw a snowmobile cross the street up a block. This town must be very far north if snowmobiles were allowed on the main streets, he reasoned. A dusting of crystallized snow left footprints, and without the slightest trace of a wind, Peter realized he could be tracked. *All the more reason to pick up the pace.*

Peter reached the road and gazed, puzzled, up and down the street. The street was, like everything else he had experienced since waking up, very odd. He couldn't place it with any of the North American towns he had experienced, or anything close to Katmandu, or even a Masai village near Mount Kilimanjaro. The American architecture was obvious, but the street lacked the bustle of automobiles, buses, and trucks. Each of the buildings was no more than two floors high, and a raised sidewalk connected the store entrances, like an old Western town. And there were people, lots of people, coming into and out of stores. All the stores had unique names: Charlene's Hardware, NP Retail, Stan's Clothier, Winter Pharmacies. He couldn't see a chain store or franchise; no department stores, either.

NP. He saw and heard those letters a lot. Peter chuckled as he thought of the North Pole. Impossible! The North Pole was a point below a moving ice sheet. He was in a real town—with a hospital!

Peter turned the images of the town and the barren snow fields of the North Pole over and over in his mind, trying to make sense of it, oblivious to the puzzled looks of passersby as he meandered forward. His head spun with spontaneous clues and dead ends. The wood-frame store facades were reminiscent of an old mining town, but he knew they were too far north for serious mineral deposits. Oil exploration? That would explain the secrecy that laced Wells' evasive tone. No, Peter would see some sign of drilling equipment and companies, and nothing was nearby.

Then, Peter stopped dead in his tracks.

10

Dusk held the street while a frozen mist sparkled in the low light of street lamps. Peter struggled to make sense of the scene before him. The road dead-ended into a roundabout in what appeared to be the town's center. A two-story building loomed in the center of the circle, the name NP Software barely visible over a set of double doors. People scurried across the street and into the building in a scene more like a movie set in the Old West than on New York City's Wall Street, or, for that matter, Wisconsin Avenue in Georgetown. Snowmobiles plowed their way around the building along the circle, patiently yielding at the intersection, and a crosswalk shepherded a group of people across the street. Except for the absence of cars, this was the normal stuff of any town.

The biggest oddity was something Peter never could have expected, and it hit him like an avalanche. Fred was everywhere. All kinds of Freds. Old Freds. Female Freds. Professional Freds. At first, Peter thought they were children, passing him on the wooden sidewalks, but they were adults, just like his nurse. Peter guessed every third or fourth person he passed was a dwarf. Why hadn't he noticed this as soon as he started walking up the street?

He clenched his fists as he tried to check the frustration, tightening his throat. A well-seasoned explorer's senses would have alerted him immediately to something so obvious.

He focused again on the street. Many of the dwarves were dressed in everyday clothes. Others were wearing business suits or casual business dress, despite the obvious late evening hour—or was it that obvious? He was now doubting his own senses—the streets seemed to be as busy as a regular business day in Anywhere, USA.

Peter's stunned gaze shifted again, this time to the architecture. The buildings puzzled him. They weren't the normal wooden structures that pieced together small towns and outposts in the tundra. And the design was Western, not Inuit or some other Eskimo, Native American, or Canadian tribe. The air was cold, and the darkness was reminiscent of Alaskan winters when night would spread through the day for twenty hours at a time. The scene was so strange, so surreal; Peter was sure his brain was retreating back into its Swiss cheese form.

Peter felt the presence of people walking past him. Some were staring.

"Are you okay?" came a voice next to him. The dwarf's overcoat barely hid a smart two-piece suit with an engaging, colorful tie. Rubber galoshes protected his shoes, although his hands were bare.

"Yes, yes," Peter said, dismissing the query in a faux businesslike fashion. He needed to at least project normalcy. The man turned, prompting Peter to change his mind. "Well, wait a minute," he called.

The man stopped, rotating his body so he could look at Peter.

Peter stumbled, trying to grapple with the sudden feeling he had just made a terrible mistake. He pushed on. "What town is this?"

The man's eyes darted away from him, and his mouth opened as if he was about to say something, but he paused. He cocked his head. "What do you mean?"

"I'm sorry," said Peter, even as he realized he should shut up. "I must have taken a wrong turn and ended up in this town. I couldn't find it on the map, and the store signs aren't very helpful. Can you just point me to City Hall or to a convenience store? I'll just get a map."

"Excuse me?" the man asked. "We don't have a city hall."

"What?" Peter pushed his puzzled look aside to adopt a mask of confidence. "Oh, yes, of course. Small towns often don't have a city hall." He lifted his eyes to the top floors of the buildings, jumping from window to window, even as he knew avoiding eye contact would only deepen his Samaritan's suspicions. "Well, do you know where I can find a convenience store? Then I can get back on track and be on my way."

The stranger's face relaxed, and a small smile drew his lips wide, though his eyes maintained an awkward focus. "Let me introduce myself. I must apologize for being so rude. My name's Rolf Hackett.

My friends just call me Rowdy. College nickname—I'd just as soon forget how I earned it, but it's kind of stuck."

"Sure," said Peter, adopting his new found friend's earlier bewilderment. "My name's Peter Peary."

Rowdy let out a boisterous laugh. "Your parents certainly had a sense of humor!" Peter scowled. "Oh, sorry. Bad joke. You know… Peter Peary… PP… name alliteration. Yes, well, why don't we go into the pub down on the corner? You look like you could use a cup of Joe, or cappuccino, or latte. Whatever. No Starbucks here, but it's good stuff, imported from Brazil. I can get a map from the bar keep, and we can see how we can get you back on the road."

"Great," said Peter, relieved he might now get answers to his questions.

They turned right at the roundabout and walked another 200 feet when Rowdy turned to open the door to a tavern with a hanging sign that read "Nick R Baaker." Rowdy pulled his jacket off, dusting flecks of pinpoint size water droplets off his sleeves. He waved Peter to a booth two spots down from the front door.

"Sit down and kick up your feet. Rest a little bit. I'll grab us a couple of drinks. Hmmm. You look a little worse for the wear. Perhaps a coffee rather than alcohol to start out?"

"Yeah, that would be great. Black." Peter had better keep his wits about him, and coffee might just keep him amped long enough to figure some of this out. He looked back to Rowdy. "Actually, do they have a vanilla latte?" Rowdy smiled and turned toward the bar against the back wall.

Peter huffed with irritation; all his money was stashed in his gear and dog sled. Dog sled? The dogs! Another hole filled in. He knew what happened to the dogs, but what about the sled and his gear? He checked his pants and shirt with both hands, and tracked down Rowdy with his eyes. "Rowdy, wait! I'm sorry, but I left my money in the car."

Peter caught his breath—he hadn't seen one car in this town. Where were the cars?

"No problem," Rowdy reassured him without skipping a beat. "This one's on me. You can pick up the next one. Prices of Joe aren't that bad here. We have a special import deal that keeps the price down; much lower than Fairbanks or Anchorage."

Finally! Peter had a clue. He must be somewhere in Alaska. No, that couldn't be. Wells told him he was outside the U.S. Was Wells lying? British Columbia? The Northwest Territories? Another dead-end.

Peter was so busy putting pieces of the puzzle together he lost track of Rowdy approaching the barkeep to place the orders. Peter took off the fleece shirt he was using as a makeshift jacket, stretched his arms, and rubbed his eyes. He was weaker than he expected. How long had he been in that hospital bed?

He tried to gather his thoughts, grateful for the respite from the odd goings-on in the street. His sudden fatigue distracted him from noticing that Rowdy was spending a long time ordering two coffees, or that if he had watched Rowdy's conversation with the barkeep, he was mouthing more words than "one coffee, one vanilla latte."

Rowdy picked up their two coffees—one vanilla latte and one cappuccino—and brought them over to the booth where Peter was looking much warmer and more comfortable. "Hope you have a few minutes. I don't mind talking to strangers in town."

Peter tipped his cup toward Rowdy and smiled.

Rowdy returned the gesture. "Cool. I'm meeting someone else here in a bit to discuss business, and I can use the company." He sipped from his mug and then raised his eyebrow at Peter. "So, where you from?"

"The South mainly."

Rowdy gave Peter a knowing tilt of his head. "Well, that's a big expanse of land."

Peter smiled and nodded as he searched for details of his life. "Born in Dayton, Ohio. The family moved to Florida when my father was transferred in the military, but I eventually went to Washington, D.C. to finish college."

"Finish college?"

"Yeah." Peter hesitated, hoping another memory would make its appearance. "Took some classes at Florida State University." He thought some more.

Rowdy's eyes widened a bit. "That's quite a bit of moving around. Going from the south to the north… that doesn't happen very often."

A weary smile fastened itself to Peter's expression. "Need to follow opportunity, I guess."

"And get away from the folks, I'm sure."

Another memory washed in front of his eyes. "Well, Mom and Dad really liked the Redneck Riviera. They still live there."

"I had an engineering intern from Florida State a while ago, when I was working in the Lower Forty-Eight. He said good things about Tallahassee, although I suspect he had a busy social life."

Peter sipped his coffee. "I don't know much about that. My college was mainly on-line. My mom would drive me into Tallahassee every two weeks so I could meet with a professor. Actually, I usually ended up meeting with a graduate student."

"Couldn't afford living in Tallahassee?"

Peter looked at his coffee. "I was fifteen."

Rowdy's eyebrows popped up on his forehead. "In college at fifteen?"

"Yeah. I guess I was a bit of a nerd."

Rowdy smiled. "You certainly don't look like a nerd now! I never would have guessed."

Peter smiled back. "Thanks... I guess."

"Pleasure's all mine!"

Peter looked up from his coffee. "And, you?"

"Grew up in Southern California—SoCal."

Peter glanced around, remembering the winter-like coolness in the street. "Seems like quite a change of climate for an Angelino."

"Been here fifteen years now."

"Really? This place must suit you. What made you move?"

"Opportunity. There aren't many professional opportunities for those of the dwarfish persuasion on the Silicon Coast of Malibu and Santa Monica. Little people are considered one step away from Munchkins. It's hard to get away from some legacies."

Peter had never thought about that, but from what little exposure he had had to Southern California, the culture didn't suit those outside the mainstream—physically that is. "I can understand that."

"How so?" asked Rowdy with what appeared like genuine interest. "You look trim, fit—the embodiment of the ideal male specimen."

Peter chuckled. "That may be true, but there's more to a man than his body."

Rowdy lifted his cappuccino. "*Touché, mon ami!*"

They clicked coffee cups in midair.

Peter gave a wistful sigh. "I suppose I have a tendency to follow my passion, not my brain."

Rowdy cocked his head in curious approval. "And what is that passion?"

49

"Snow, ice, living on the edge. I'm an explorer." At least, that's what he thought. The Swiss holes hadn't filled in to become cheddar yet.

"How old are you? You can't be that experienced. What's your most challenging expedition?"

Peter's head snapped up a few inches, surprised at how crisp the mountain memories had become. "My most successful expedition was climbing to the summit of Mount Washington. I was with a dozen novice climbers, and we got up in record time." *Wow*, Peter thought. *That memory was vivid. I was the youngest, too.* Peter's eyes sparkled with satisfaction.

Rowdy seemed to be reading his thoughts.

"Awfully young to be taking risks like that. I'm not sure I would have approved, if you were my son."

Peter frowned. "That's what my parents said." He looked at Rowdy. "They were wrong. I led the others to the summit. They followed me! I even beat the guide."

"Okay, okay! I didn't mean to doubt your abilities. No, no, you seem quite capable if you ask me." Rowdy looked down at his cappuccino, lifted it to his lips, and took a loud slurp.

Peter sent Rowdy a challenging look. "I bet you had parents who supported you. You didn't have people telling you 'don't do this,' 'you've got to do this'—people that didn't care about what you wanted."

Rowdy's eyebrows came together as anger flushed through his cheeks. "Everyone doubts us. We're too small to do this, or that. They think because our bodies are small our brains are small, too. And the bullying. How can we defend ourselves? We have to outthink, outsmart, out work everyone!"

Peter sat, looking into his coffee, and then gave his mug a slight tip, letting the brown liquid swirl. "I guess we're more alike than we think."

Rowdy looked up at Peter, letting the anger recede into the pub's vacuous space. He tipped his mug at him. "Perhaps we are, young Peter."

The odd pair sat for a few more awkward moments. Peter glanced around the pub, noting in the back of his mind that the only patrons left in the bar were an average-sized couple on the other side of the room and a dwarf on a stool at the bar. That was curious, Peter thought. More people seemed to be in the pub when they entered.

"So, Mr. Rowdy, what do you do?"

"Eh? Oh. Software development."

"Software? Geez, that's pretty intense."

Rowdy's head swayed in momentary thought. "It's not much different than being an explorer. The difficulty is just of a different sort. Can you imagine me pulling a 200 pound man up a crevice on an ice-covered slope? I could handle myself, but it would be much more difficult leading a team. I'll stick to computer programming."

"Sounds like you have a passion," Wells said, his hands cradling the warm mug.

"I picked it up as a hobby in high school. Then I took a few classes in college. I majored in business administration and built up my programming business on the side."

Peter nodded. He dabbled in programming, even got straight As, but it didn't excite him. "What's your claim to fame?"

"I was one of the principal architects of the NP 2000 operating system."

"The what?"

"Oh, you're probably a Mac man," Rowdy chuckled. "It's an operating system like Windows, except it jumps light years ahead. We work mainly with networks and large corporations. It's a hybrid of company-owned software—proprietary software—and open source. We can parallel process information about twice as fast as Microsoft, Oracle, and IBM-type systems, and do it more cleanly at about one-third the cost."

"You travel a lot?"

"We've doubled revenues each year for the past five. My business employs about 200 people right now, half of them programmers. The Internet means I hardly have to travel at all anymore. We have sales offices in LA, Chicago, New York, and Boston, and I go to the Lower Forty-Eight a couple times a year. But, for the most part, I'm content to stay up here with my family."

Peter sent a puzzled look Rowdy's way. "You don't sound like you miss being down there."

Rowdy dipped his head and extended it over the table top toward Peter. "Look... I've got a BA in engineering from Purdue, and a master's degree in computer science from Stanford." Rowdy paused.

"You know what? With all the hullabaloo about productivity in the Silicon Valley, I couldn't land a job anywhere. I'd walk into the interview, sometimes even make it to the third interview, and, for some reason, I would be told 'I just wasn't the right fit for the job.' Bunk. They couldn't get past my height. I did pretty well on consulting jobs, mainly contracts over the Internet and remote jobs."

Rowdy lifted his finger and pointed it directly at Peter. "The Internet's a great thing. No one has to see you. You're judged on your performance. That's it.

"But I wanted more. And I needed a business with real employees and staff to make my dream come true. I partnered up with a brilliant woman who no longer had the time for software development. I met with some venture capitalists up here. They gave me seed money—with a 40 percent ownership stake in the business, mind you—and we're a raging success. Easy as pie!"

Peter looked at Rowdy, his eyes intent. "You don't sound bitter. I would be angry about being shut out."

"Well, as an employer, I see things a little differently now," Rowdy said with a distant, philosophical detachment. "I admit, I give preference to people of smaller than average stature. But I make sure they're good, the best. Bill Gates was right: the computer industry is changing so fast, you can't afford to have mere competents working for you. If we dally for six months, we're dead in the water in the seventh."

Peter leaned back in his chair, letting his fingers drop to the table as he closed his eyes. Maybe this guy was as nice as he seemed.

He opened his eyes and looked at the dwarf, fixing his attention on his eyes. "So, Rowdy, how do I get out of here? The coffee and company's great, but I need to get going."

Rowdy's eyes darted down at his near empty coffee cup, and he began to fidget.

"Rowdy, what's wrong?" It was a challenge more than a question.

Peter felt the blood begin to rush into his arms and face. He thrust his body across the booth seat, lifting himself to his feet just as a ringing signaled the opening of the pub's front door.

11

Jeff Wells could see Peter's body bulge with rage as he lunged across the table at the dwarf. Rowdy ducked and scrambled toward the back of the booth, dodging Peter's hands.

"Stop!" Rowdy yelled. "Peter, stop! Before it's too late!"

Peter clutched at Rowdy, sending their coffee mugs crashing to the floor, shards of porcelain scattering under tables and chairs. Rowdy jumped on the table, lunged across the back of the booth for the door, but Peter nabbed the back edge of his coat. He spun him around, a fist raised, cocked, and ready.

Before his knuckles plowed into Rowdy's face, the human talons of Jeff Wells encircled Peter's wrist and wrenched his arm behind his back, as the security officer's palm sent him face down onto the table. "Dear, dear, Mr. Peary. You didn't think you could get away that easily did you?"

"Damn you, Rowdy!" Peter rasped.

Handcuffs etched into his wrists. Wells lifted Peter's head and spun him around, holding him nose-to-nose. "I don't think your discharge papers from the hospital are in order."

Rowdy stepped over to Wells. "Jeff, don't be too hard on him. I honestly don't think he knows where he is."

"Well thank God for small favors! We'll take it from here. What did you tell him?"

"Nothing really, we talked about my business mostly." Rowdy stepped closer to Wells so that he couldn't avoid looking at him. "Jeff, remember: we aren't in the U.S. We have The Code."

"Don't worry Mr. Hackett. I'm not doing anything contrary to The Code."

Rowdy crossed his arms, sending a stern look toward Wells.

Wells lifted his hand as if waving off Rowdy. "Don't worry. We aren't going to hurt him!"

Rowdy shook his head.

Wells stopped to face Rowdy directly. "Don't worry, Mr. Hackett. Nic's even involved. We've got the right people on this case."

Peter pursed his lips, his eyes hard. He looked down at Rowdy, his anger turning to contempt. "Why did you do this to me?"

Rowdy began a short, nervous pace. "I'm sorry Peter. I'm sorry. You'll understand soon enough. Just do what Wells tells you to do, and everything will work out. Trust me, Peter. It will work out!"

Two other men, both wearing grey flannel shirts with NP Security patches over their front pockets and on the shoulders of their shirts, appeared out of the background and began to pull Peter out the back door of the bar.

"Look, Peter," Rowdy said, his voice high-pitched and loud. "Play it cool. I'll get representation for you. Just ride this out; don't rock the boat. I'll be in touch."

***

Peter heard the back door to the tavern close as his feet slid over a dusting of snow and ice. The two security guards held his arms, pulling and steadying him as they moved through what appeared to be an alley.

He heard a metal latch turn, and a door swung open as an invisible force pushed him into a grey void. He landed on the vinyl of what must have been the back seat of some sort of a van, squeezed between two men. He could tell by the way they pulled him that no dwarves were in this security detail.

The van was small, reminding Peter of the European vehicles that seemed to fit in every nook and cranny of towns and villages sculpted out of prairies and hillsides in the European Middle Ages. No windows, either. The van's wheels crunched against the wintery road outside as it picked up speed in silence. An electric motor?

Wells sat in the front seat as another guard pulled the vehicle out onto the streets. Peter closed his eyes and rested his head. He prayed

Rowdy was true to his word even though Peter knew he had no reason to expect he would be.

12

"What do you mean you can't find her?" Getko blurted.

"She seems to have disappeared," Joy Gault repeated, still standing in front of the thick wooden desk that separated her from her boss. The room seemed tiny, now that the door was locked and secured.

Getko rose from his desk and began to pace, running his hand over the middle of his scalp through threads of near non-existent hair. Joy looked out the window at another overcast fall day in Washington, D.C. It was a nice change from the oppressive humidity of the dog days of summer, but she missed Vero Beach, where the Atlantic Ocean winds seemed to guarantee sunshine and swept the humidity off the coast.

A loud thump startled her as Getko's hand fell onto a stack of papers on his desk. "Is she dead?"

"We don't know, sir. It's a real possibility. We haven't had any signal for ten days. The tech guys have tried to restart the device, but they haven't had any luck. We're trying to track down her last moments by going over old satellite photos and infrared readings. It's as if they just vanished off the ice pack."

"Vanished?"

Joy couldn't tell from his tone if Getko was puzzled or annoyed.

"Yes."

"Did they fall through the ice?"

"That's a possibility," Joy said, "but that would not have disabled her homing device. We had several devices that should have allowed us to track them. Even the lead dog had a GPS chip placed under his skin, so it wouldn't be dislodged by the sled's harnesses. We should have been able to find them in the belly of a polar bear."

Joy pulled out two photos from a manila folder and hesitated for a moment, as if trying to determine which place on the desk would cause the least disturbance. Getko snatched them from her hand.

Joy craned her neck over the middle of the desk to point to two white dots on the black and white photograph. "It's clear on the first photo, dated September 23rd, that their position is here. You can even see the tracks of the sled. The infrared readings show the warmth of the sled runners. It doesn't take much heat to show up in that climate."

Getko looked at Joy with deadened eyes. "Obviously."

"Yes... well... look at the photo dated September 24th. It's only a six-hour time difference, but our satellites weren't in place to take consistent pictures any earlier. Peary and Livingston are gone. We can't find any sign of life within a fifty-mile radius. It's as if they—"

"Vanished." Getko looked at the photographs for a few minutes. "If they were dead, would the satellite pictures show their bodies?"

"In theory, yes," Joy said. "But at the temperatures they were experiencing, the infrared readings wouldn't be very helpful. Virtually any heat would have been long gone by the time these later shots were taken. We're checking with NASA, the National Weather Service, and several private satellite companies to find readings or photos more recent than ours."

"What about the dogs?" Getko asked. "I don't see any sign of them on the photos either."

Joy nodded. "That's what makes the whole situation even stranger. We would expect to see some form of life. Even if they all died, they would have died at different times and some trace of body heat from a dog or person would be clear from the picture. The dogs are hardier than humans, so they would have died later."

Joy pulled out photos of Peter Peary dressed in his heavy mountain climbing coat and gear. The other picture included Sheila Livingston in a puffy down parka clearly dressed for an ascent. Livingston's expression was serious, but void of anxiety or worry. Peary's eyes danced with expectation. "Both Peary and Livingston were skilled survivalists." Joy continued. "They would have sent out an emergency signal of some sort. Even if they were attacked by a pack of wolves or polar bears, we should have seen some sign of their expedition. There's nothing."

Getko stared at the documents. He couldn't ignore the creepy feeling of satisfaction he felt from the news. They must have been surprised and taken below the surface by something. If his theory was right, Livingston must be underground. The drug money must be going north, not south. Nothing else could explain her disappearance. Or Peary's. Or the dogs for that matter. It was time to mobilize.

"When did you lose official contact?"

Joy paused, recognizing that Getko had made an important decision about the investigation and perhaps, Operation Jamaican Snow. "She was supposed to report in two days ago."

"Two days ago? And no one bothered to tell me?"

Joy hesitated again. "We wanted to check the satellite photos to be sure. We finished our assessment ten minutes ago. I immediately came up here to inform you."

Getko's hands lifted to his face and then dropped down to the desk with a thud. "Let me get this straight. Ten days ago all the homing devices for a covert operation disappear. An agent misses her call-in seven days after their technology fails, and it still takes the home office forty-eight hours to figure out she's gone?"

The heat in the small, box-like office seemed to increase dramatically. Getko turned toward the window, whirled back to face Joy, and then turned again to pace. The image of Rocky, holding a frozen mug of beer, loomed large again in her mind.

"Gek," Joy said. Getko threw a piercing lance of a stare toward her. "Agent Getko," she corrected. "Livingston missed a call-in by twenty-four hours eight weeks ago when she and Peary were provisioning in Nome. We tried to contact her directly, even dispatched an undercover agent to find her. She was very insistent that we avoid any direct contact, particularly once she and Peary were on the ice. Any hint of surveillance and she was sure her cover and the mission would be blown. We couldn't be sure this was a real problem, not just a technology malfunction caused by cold weather, until we reviewed the satellite photos."

"What do you mean you couldn't be sure? When an agent fails to call-in at the appointed time, it's a problem. I don't care what the agent says; there can be no excuse for not checking in." He shook his head, looked at the photos again, shoved them back in the folder, and threw them into Joy's arms. "Joy, I'm very disappointed. I thought you had better judgment."

Joy clenched her teeth as she fought to contain her instinct to lash out. This was her boss, she kept telling herself. She was playing too valuable a role right now, and she couldn't blow it. She couldn't let herself be fired, when her role was so critical to so many people.

Getko was mad for a reason, she told herself. The DEA administrator would terminate the Caribbean Task Force if he found out about this. Getko couldn't afford to have an agent's death on his record, let alone a blown operation of this scale. Operation Jamaican Snow would have to be scrapped if this became public too soon. He might as well dig up the early retirement papers now and start filling them out.

Getko paced as Joy turned to leave.

"I haven't dismissed you yet," he snapped.

Joy stopped and executed a crisp turn, only to see her boss ignore her and continue his calculated pace.

"Agent Getko," Joy said, after a few more maddening paces. "Are we going to delay Operation Jamaican Snow until we can be certain of the North Pole expedition's fate?"

"No!" Getko slowed his steps, deep in thought. "How long has it been since you lost contact with Livingston's radio transponder?"

"That's just it," Joy said, "we haven't. We're still receiving signals. We lost their GPS and satellite tracking, not their radio signals. But their radio's been silent for ten days. We were supposed to receive a Morse code check-in two days ago. It didn't come. We weren't too worried because the same thing happened earlier in the trip. We assumed they were holed-up in bad weather."

Getko stopped in mid pace. "How do you know she's missing?"

"We don't," said Joy. "We've just lost contact. We can't be 100 percent sure she's injured, dead, or even missing. All we really know is that we can no longer track them with our technology."

Getko looked up, a sparkle in his eye. "All right, so why do you think we have a problem?"

Joy straightened her shoulders, sending a curious look toward Getko. "She hasn't checked in. If she had reached the objective, she would have checked in to relay the coordinates and give us instructions to move forward. We haven't heard anything from her."

Getko nodded. "She could be in the hands of the cartel."

"Yes sir, but we don't think that's what happened. They would have killed her."

"Maybe that's why the transponder has been silent."

"Possibly, but the cartels know our equipment and MO. They would have searched her body for anything electronic and disposed of it fast, probably before they killed her. They couldn't risk discovery of any sort. They would have tortured her first, of course."

Getko's cheeks flushed as emotions welled up. Livingston's DEA file flashed through his memory. He fought to contain the tears he could feel forming under his eyes. While Peary was drowning himself in self-pity in the bars on Wisconsin Avenue and around Dupont Circle, Livingston's father was being laid to rest six feet under. Getko could see the crime scene photo of her father's lifeless body in a pool of his own blood, all because he stumbled into the wrong neighborhood as a drug deal went sour. The coroner said he didn't even know what hit him before his body hit the pavement.

Sheila Livingston would have blown a hole through the polar ice cap to get rid of a drug-running operation. And that's why they recruited her. That was part of what bugged Getko. The cartels have been silent on anything north of Belize for the last week. There was virtually no violent, drug-related, clandestine activity on the internal wire service. Getko stroked his chin, as if it might stimulate some brain activity.

"Okay," he said after several moments. "Where do you think we should go? What's the consensus of the task force?"

"We still think the evidence is pretty thin," said Joy, trying to use her tone to warn Getko not to move forward.

"Nonsense. We've got the paper trail from L.A. to Miami to the Virgin Islands, and then back north… somewhere."

"But the line is a faded, gray one, not a clear, black one." Joy stared at Getko.

Getko didn't seem to notice her warning. "What's the cover for this operation?"

Joy half shook her head but answered her boss: "Toys."

"Toys?"

"Yes, toys. We've traced three successive links of money in downtown L.A. from a place called Toytown. It's not an official neighborhood. It's a cluster of renovated buildings in the old warehouse district east of downtown Los Angeles. A law firm is somehow tied to all the transactions."

"What law firm?"

"Ebson and Associates."

"That doesn't ring any bells. Tell me more about them."

"They have about a dozen partners, another dozen associates, and a few clerks." Joy looked into her file again, checking figures in a thin, typed report. "Most come with pretty slick credentials: degrees from Harvard or Yale, University of Chicago. Here's an odd one: University of San Diego. He does a lot of property development and land-use law. Another has a law degree and economics degree from UCLA. His work focuses mostly on estimating damages for civil liability cases and contract disputes. In addition to toys, they do the usual entertainment, patent, and trademark work. Most of the attorneys stay out of the courtroom—corporate law most of the time." Joy decided to leave out the only quirk in the firm's profile: more than half of the attorneys and staff were little people. "We haven't found any record of illegal activity."

"Until now." Getko's tone was ominous.

"Ever," Joy reiterated. "They haven't done anything illegal. They're clean. Even our legal division can't find anything."

"It's the pattern, Joy, the pattern." Getko lifted his arms, and the arc seemed to quicken his pace. "What else do you know about this law firm?"

"They have only a few big clients. They aren't very broad based, concentrating mainly in the toy industry. They manage the corporate transactions of a cluster of twelve businesses in Toytown that make up, as well as we can estimate, about 25 percent of the total revenues earned by the businesses located in the district."

"Wow," said Getko, his pace pausing. "Those must be big numbers."

"They are," confirmed Joy. "Toytown's practically a city in itself; it has more than 500 businesses and generates a billion dollars in sales each year."

"So this law firm manages the corporate affairs for businesses that have combined revenues of $250 million per year?" asked Getko in disbelief.

"Yes, sir."

"How much are they worth? What is their market capitalization?"

"Each business is private. Our analysts estimate their market value at about a billion each."

"A billion dollars each? They must be profitable."

"They appear to be."

"Unless," Getko said, "they are laundering money."

"That would fit your theory. Privately owned businesses of this size could easily launder millions of dollars each week. Without an independent audit by a firm experienced with laundering accounting techniques, we can't verify where the money is coming from. They have private auditors, but we can't be certain they're straight arrows."

"What else?"

"Just that the last estimate from L.A. County and the Census Bureau was that Toytown employs about 5,000 people, mostly Asian and Latino immigrants."

"What? Hello?" Getko said, pounding his head with his finger. "A large immigrant labor force in an industry with a substantial export-import business would be the ideal setting for money laundering!"

"Yes," Joy said. "But agency investigators have not been able to detect anything illegal or even remotely shady about their business."

"They must not be looking in the right place." Getko's gut told him something was going on here, and that something was very big. The scheme was all falling into place. The drug money was laundered through the toy companies in Los Angeles, with the aid of a local law firm. Money transactions were laundered through bank accounts in Miami and the Caribbean, to put the money on the streets so it would be harder to trace. The Latino and Hispanic communities would be an ideal cover for networking and transactions to South America and the Caribbean. The Asian connection seemed a bit odd—were they missing something in the investigation? Was heroin also part of the scheme?

"How does the North Pole fit in?" Getko asked.

"The paper trail is hard to follow," said Joy, now weary with the briefing. "But we were able to commandeer the manifests of some of the shipments into the toy distribution companies and hack into their computers for distribution records."

"How careful were you?"

Joy diverted her eyes to the folders in her hands. "Very careful."

Getko understood the stakes. Bypassing the legal system was a risky move, but he was sure they could build the case on harder evidence, without involving judges and government lawyers.

"Good. So we can make the connection through the computer records."

Joy hesitated. "Not quite."

"What do you mean?"

"The operating system is unique. It appears to be designed specifically for the toy industry with its own encryption codes and programming language. Our systems analysts haven't been able to break the codes yet and interpret the software."

"How long will it take?"

"They aren't estimating," said Joy. "They haven't seen anything like it before. To tell you the truth, I think they are baffled by it. I think it could take months."

"We don't have months," said Getko, frustration mounting again. "We don't even have weeks." He felt a wave of satisfaction warm his body. "It's a good thing we're not relying on this information to build our case in the courtroom."

Joy didn't look at Getko directly but checked the weather in the window—no sign of clearing.

"We have enough evidence without the distribution data to complete the mission and bust up this drug ring," he said.

Joy's shoulders slumped as she let her hands fall to her sides. The folder slapped against her thigh as she pondered the implications of what Getko was saying. "Gek," she said in a soft voice. "Gek, what are you saying?"

Getko looked up. "You know what I'm saying."

"Do you think this is wise?"

"Joy, I've been around the block more than once."

"Don't you think we should run this past legal first?"

Getko shook his head. "They'll just delay the operation. We don't have the time for them to review it."

Joy caught her breath. Getko was more concerned about a potential review from the administrator than the legal analysis.

Joy's boss rose from his desk and moved closer, gently laying his hand on the small of Joy's back, pulling his lips within an inch of her ear. "Joy," he whispered. "You aren't doubting me are you?"

Every muscle in her body tensed, to control the shudder that had started in her head and now raced to her toes.

"No, sir," she said, hoping the formality in her tone would buy her some time. Joy's heart ticked faster. *What did he know? What did he suspect?*

"Good," Getko said, slipping his hand along her waist to her wrist. He clasped his hand against hers, cupping it with his free hand. "Because, Joy, we're going on a ride. This will be the ride of your career, maybe even the ride of your life. If you ride this wave the right way, nothing can stop your ambition."

Joy's emotions told her to leave, to go meet with her team and prepare for the operation. Her brain told her to stay, to absorb everything Getko was going to tell her, to learn everything she could about what he was thinking, Operation Jamaican Snow, and his plans.

"Joy," Getko said, his voice raising to parlor volume, "we're about to go on an adventure the likes of which this agency has never seen. Operation Bimini was nothing compared to the complexity and challenges we face here in Operation Jamaican Snow. I need to know if you are with me on this. You are, or you aren't. If you can't handle it, I'll find someone who can."

He was bluffing, and Joy knew it, but should she take the chance he wasn't?

"If you decide not to come with me on this operation, it won't mean anything for your career in the agency."

Joy knew Getko was lying. If she didn't go along with his scheme, she was finished, whether the operation was successful or not.

Getko positioned himself in front of her, still cupping her hand. "Just let me know what you want to do."

Getko stepped back and leaned against his desk, holding both of Joy's hands and looking straight into her eyes. His were searching and confident. Joy hoped he saw the determination in hers.

"I'm with you, Miles. Of course, I'm with you."

Getko smiled.

13

"Stay put until the boss gets back."

Peter thought he was going to explode. He was back at square one, suffocating in another tiny, sterile hospital room. At least this time they stuffed him into a chair next to the bed rather than force him to lie in it.

Peter sized up his new surroundings: the now familiar featureless white plasterboard walls, stainless steel cabinets, a countertop with a washbasin and faucet—another jail cell as far as he was concerned. At least the room had a private bathroom. Still, he preferred the décor of the bar and even the company of Rowdy... until he stabbed him in the back.

Peter furrowed his eyebrows when he noticed a curtain, cutting off the front section of his room from the back. A double room? A glow flickered on the other side, as if there were a window to the outside. Peter patted his shoulders as if he could push the new found warmth inside the building through the veins and his body. He lifted himself from the chair, crossed over to the curtain, and swept it aside.

Peter's lungs stopped in mid-breath. This was a double room, not a single, and he immediately recognized the blonde hair framing Sheila Livingston's face. He leaned over the bedrail, and clasped his hands over hers. Images of a young girl and boy, playing on a beach, barreled through his brain as he bottled up gathering tears.

Sheila's body lay limp, only the warmth of her skin providing any hint of life. Bruises still pocked her face, and the swelling around her eyes after so many days of recovery made him wonder whether she would regain her eyesight. Her arms were still covered by the hospital blankets, and his fingers passed over hard plaster at her elbow. His heart sank with each inch of the cast as his hand moved from the wrist to her shoulder.

"Oh, Sheila," he whispered, cupping his hand to the side of her face.

"I'm disappointed." Peter didn't have to turn to know Fred was in the room with him. "I can't believe you tried to escape. The security company is very good, and this town is very tight knit. Strangers are easy to identify."

Peter continued to look at Sheila's battered face, glad it was Fred in the room. "Ya think?"

Fred moved around the room, checking a clipboard, inventorying cupboards.

"I don't understand," Peter said. "Why are so many people concerned about me?"

Fred didn't look at Peter as he checked Sheila's vital signs: heartbeat, blood pressure, IV, tubes. He recorded the readings on the clipboard, shaking his head. Finally, he looked up at Peter.

"You still don't get it, do you? You're an outsider. We can't let you go until we've checked you out. You seemed pretty reasonable earlier. I never would have guessed that you'd take off like that. Otherwise, I wouldn't have left you."

Fred checked Sheila's eyes with a tenderness no longer shown to Peter. "Good, we see instant dilation of the pupils. Very responsive. I'm not a doctor, but that bodes well for her eyesight when she regains consciousness."

"Where the hell am I?" Peter blurted. The echo in the room seemed to bring the walls alive.

Fred ignored him. He took out a key and opened a drawer underneath one of the cupboards. A shelf rolled out from the dark recess of the drawer, and a monitor sprang up. He pecked a series of strokes on a keyboard, and then banged the return key as if that alone were enough to communicate anger, disappointment, and betrayal.

"No need to yell," Fred said without looking at Peter as he entered information into the computer. Fred tapped a few more notes and then he closed the drawer.

Finally, his eyes darted back to Peter. He walked around the bed and patted Peter on the shoulder as he rounded the corner. "Don't worry, Peter, we're taking good care of her. We took care of you, didn't we? Just because we're detaining you doesn't mean we want you hurt."

Fred pushed a chair over next to Sheila's bed.

Peter accepted the gesture and let himself fall into the cushion, still holding the hand of the person his subconscious told him was his best friend. He didn't want to like Fred. He was his captor, after all, just like the guard outside the room and Jeff Wells. He sighed. Just like Rowdy. Here he was, held against his will, in some isolated urban wilderness, and he couldn't do anything but sit in a bland hospital room. He glanced back at Sheila and let another measured sigh escape.

"You two are close, huh?"

"She's my best friend." Yes, he remembered that now. And he knew he couldn't leave her, even if they left the door wide open. He wished he could remember more, a lot more, but his mind was blank.

"She'll get better, Peter. I promise you."

"What have I done?" asked Peter as he caressed Sheila's arm.

"That's a good question," came a gruff voice from behind him, sending Peter's blood into a hot boil.

14

Peter's entire body flushed with anger and resentment.

Fred felt the tension, and he stepped toward the front of the room.

"What have you done?" Jeff Wells asked. "Answer that question, and maybe we'll let you go."

Peter kept his gaze trained on Sheila. An image of a younger girl about seventeen years old at a picnic table on a warm, bright, sunny day, flashed before his eyes and stayed. He pretended to ignore Wells, although he caught Fred lingering by the counter as he wrote something on his clipboard.

"How is she doing?" Peter asked.

Wells stepped around the bed. "She'll live."

"What do you mean, 'She'll live'?"

"Look at her, Peary. She's lucky to be alive. If it weren't for the fact we have one of America's most skilled surgeons on staff here, she'd be dead."

"What's her status now?"

"Dr. Patten's upgraded her condition to serious. She's stabilized and out of any immediate danger. We need to keep her here for a while longer to make sure she recovers."

"I want to move her. I want to take her home."

Wells let out a huff. "Sorry, not going to happen."

Peter whirled. A guard stepped out from behind Wells. The guard was big: at least six feet tall and well over 200 pounds. Peter grabbed the bedrail with his hands, hoping to channel the energy into the metal frame and out from his fists.

"She's got her own doctors back home. She has a right to be treated by them."

Wells shook his head. Peter noticed an official-looking manila folder in Wells' hand for the first time. It was thick, full of papers. He began to shuffle through them.

"Yes, yes," he said turning through pages. "I see here that her doctors are some of the best in the District of Columbia. Pretty nice health plan, too, a virtue of the student health plan as a research assistant at American University."

Peter shot a sharp look at Wells. He didn't remember the specifics, but he knew it was true. How did he get that information?

"So, why can't you move her?"

"Because, Mr. Peary, I haven't approved the move."

Peter sensed Wells was stalling. "Why do you get to decide whether I come or go?"

"I am head of NP Security."

Peter turned his attention back to Sheila.

Wells thumped the file with his index finger. "You are stubborn. That's in here, too."

"Where did you get that?"

"We have our ways. Everything's computerized; we can hack into just about anything—a benefit of health-care reform."

"That's illegal."

"Not here. Not when it involves a Level Three Alert or higher. I'm authorized."

"By whom?"

"We've been over that before," Wells said.

Peter's teeth seemed glued together as he drew in a deep breath to calm himself, turning his gaze back to Sheila.

Wells slapped the folder closed, creating a loud smack that echoed across the walls, prying Peter's attention away from the bed.

The door opened and Peter heard the rubber-booted footsteps of another person, although its body was hidden behind Wells and the security guard.

"Okay, okay," said a new voice.

Wells' face seemed to freeze, only the slight pursing of his lips divulging a deep seeded irritation. "Hello, Ron."

A well-dressed dwarf walked around the two larger men and toward Peter, his presence keeping the security professionals rooted to the floor. Ron Cutler was barely four and half feet tall—big by dwarf standards—and he carried himself with the confidence and experience of a professional football player. Wells' worst nightmare, Peter mused: a dwarf with attitude.

"Let's see," Cutler said, launching his briefcase onto the empty bed. He looked at Peary. "You must be the new guy, Peter R.B. Peary."

"Stunning perceptiveness!" swooned Wells. "Your reputation as our cleverest legal mind is justly deserved!"

Cutler ignored Wells and looked at Peter, his deadened expression displaying the seriousness of his situation. "I've been retained to defend you."

Peter swayed as he began to think about the world around him. How many dwarves were running around this town? He had never met one before, and now he had run into three, up close and personal. No one would answer his questions. No one would tell him anything useful. Everything was so unfamiliar and strange.

A cold and windswept mountainside seemed warm and comforting for a fleeting moment. The image of a grey Husky with a dark line down its back popped before his eyes. Peter caught his breath. "I want my dog."

"What dog?" Cutler asked.

Peter looked past Cutler and over to Wells. "If I can't go home, I want my dog."

"I'm afraid that request may be too late." Wells nodded to Cutler. "You have an attorney. You'll have to work that through him now."

Wells' words seemed to shake Peter, but he continued to look at the head of NP Security. "Maybe I don't want him to defend me."

Wells raised his eyebrows and smirked, turning toward the wall as if trying to contain a laugh. Fred backed up against the cabinet, preparing for the show.

"What?" Cutler's question was so calm and deliberate his tone made the offense obvious.

Peter broke from his trance and turned his attention to Ron. "I don't think you should represent me. I want my own lawyer. Don't I get to choose who represents me?"

"That question proves that I'm more competent than you are." Cutler looked straight at Peter. "What makes you think I'm not competent?"

Peary shook his head.

"I'll repeat the question," Cutler said, eyes narrowed and focused. "What makes you think I'm not competent to defend you?"

And that's when Peter made a fateful mistake.

"Look," he said, "if I'm going to be defended in a court of law, I need someone with a presence in the courtroom. I just don't get the sense you can prepare and present my case effectively in front of a judge or jury. You don't know me."

Cutler brought a fist down hard on his brief case, creating a smack that forced Peary to blink. Fred pulled his clipboard up to his face to hide the smile he had given up hiding. Wells looked like he was about to keel over from the effort he needed to hold his tongue. Cutler directed a hardened gaze straight at Peter. "Why couldn't I present my case effectively in front of a jury?"

"People want a powerful presence in the courtroom," Peter said, a lightness in his breath that hinted at a trap Cutler had already laid for him. "I've read public opinion, studies, and psychological experiments that prove taller people have a more significant positive impact on people's perceptions than shorter people. Taller presidents have done better at the ballot box. Healthy presidents have done better than those with disabilities, whether they are suspected heart conditions or serious diseases such as polio. Why do you think Franklin Roosevelt never gave a speech in his wheelchair?" There, Peter thought, trying to keep from smiling at his brilliant, off-the-cuff rationalization. Those introductory history and political science classes at Florida State were paying off.

"Roosevelt misjudged the power of his own leadership potential," Cutler said. "He was trapped by his disability." Cutler stepped to within inches of Peter. "Do you think I have a disability?"

Peter hesitated, flustered, but didn't stop. "You're short. I don't think you can pull off defending me in court. It doesn't matter what I think. It matters what the jury thinks. And jurors don't respect short people as much as tall people. "

"So, my small stature is a disability," Cutler said, keeping his glare trained on Peter. "I can't defend you because... I can't reach the bench? I can't look at the judge straight in the eye, say you're innocent, give him compelling evidence, and have him rule in your favor? Is that it? Come on, boy, be more specific."

"Well, it's not a real disability." *Of course, often those with disabilities are the least able to understand their own limitations,* Peter told himself, particularly when it comes to other people's perceptions.

"Then what are you saying?"

"I'm saying that I don't want you to defend me because I want to put my strongest case forward. That case includes a commanding presence by my attorney, who can use his physical presence to make the case as well as the legal argument. This isn't a legal brief at stake here. This is my freedom. I'm not concerned about a judge. I'm concerned about the jury!"

Wells gave a sideways, baiting glance toward Cutler. "Ya know, Cutler," he said tapping his thick folder containing Peary's background, "he's got some experience with the law."

"First rule of cross examination," Cutler said, letting his eyes drop from Peter's gaze. He pulled out a velo-bound case book from his brief case with a clear plastic cover and held it up. "Never ask a question you don't know the answer to. I've been practicing law in the courtroom for twenty years. I have a 95 percent success rate, mostly with juries. The American Bar Association ranked me in their Power 100." Cutler thrust the book into Peary's hands.

Peter's cheeks flooded hot red. He thumbed through the pages, noting newspaper articles screaming Cutler's success in the courtroom and case after case of decisions stamped "Ruled in Favor, Cutler Associates, LLC." He failed to notice the other law firm also sharing credit for the cases won: Ebson & Associates, Los Angeles, California. Peter nodded sheepishly.

"I've been practicing law in this community for a decade, and I've never run into anyone with the brazen attitude you have displayed in the last few minutes. I'm defending you because a friend asked me to, not because I like you, or you like me."

Peter couldn't lift his eyes from the floor of the hospital room.

"Look at me, boy."

Peter tried not to obey, but Cutler's voice was overpowering.

"Look at me!"

Peter was surprised when he looked into Cutler's eyes again. They didn't carry condemnation or blame or disgust. He had every right to drop Peter's case. Yet, here he was, giving Peter the choice. Peary nodded. "I'm sorry Mr. Cutler. Of course, I would be honored to have you represent me."

"Well I'm still not done." Cutler crossed the room and leaned against the wall. "Guess what? The judge is a dwarf, too. The jury will also have dwarves on it. Even the prosecutor might be a dwarf. Do you know why? Because this town has more than 500 dwarves living in it, most of them professionals. That's 2.5 percent of the entire dwarf population in the Lower Forty-Eight."

Five hundred? That's an entire village. From the streets, dwarves weren't even the majority. The town must have 2,000 people. A town this size on the Arctic Circle? Paralysis seemed to take him as Peter tried to accept what Cutler had just told him.

"That said, I have a problem defending you." Cutler's comment brought Peter mentally back into the room. "I'm a civil attorney, not an immigration or criminal defense attorney. My record's not nearly as good on those cases. First rule of good decision making: Never make an uninformed decision."

Peter's blood started to bubble again. He couldn't help but feel the eyes of Jeff Wells and Fred bore into him.

Cutler let Peter brew for a few seconds. "But don't worry. I still bat over 500. My success rate is lower because I take the hard luck cases; the only attorney in town willing to do it, most of the time."

The room fell silent as four strangers—a nurse, a lawyer, a guard and a former SEAL—waited for Peter's next words. Peter sighed. "Well, what are you going to do?"

"Oh, so you've decided to stick with me?"

"Do I have much choice?"

"No." Cutler picked up his brief case.

Wells looked deflated. He turned a stern look to Peter. "Tread carefully, Mr. Peter R. B. Peary. The standard rules don't apply here."

Peter returned the look with equal sternness. "So you keep telling me. I think now, I should pay attention to my lawyer."

***

"Smart move, Peter," said Cutler in a much friendlier tone after Wells and the others had left the room. "Can I call you Peter? Now that we've got one of those attorney-client privilege things going on?"

"I don't know. I don't think I'm in Kansas anymore."

SR Staley

"You aren't. And neither am I as long as were getting our geography straight. But we have rules. And we expect everyone, including NP Security, to follow them."

Peter shook his head, weary from the verbal sparring. "Well, what are the rules?"

"Mostly the same as the Lower Forty-Eight," said Cutler, "with two big exceptions: immigration and residency. That's where your situation is a bit stickier than most. In this case, you're a security risk."

A security risk? How could Peter be a security risk to some po-dunk town in the outer reaches of the arctic?

Cutler hoisted himself onto the empty bed, bringing himself level to Peter's chest. He swung the briefcase over on the mattress and opened it. "Now, let's talk about your case—"

"Wait a minute. You need to answer a few questions first."

"I'll answer what I can," Cutler said, sifting through papers in the case. "But I'll warn you, until you're cleared of any security risk to this town... my town... I may not be able to answer everything."

"What's the deal with this 'security risk' stuff?"

"Peter, I can't tell you everything you want to know. Not now. I can tell you that the town is under a very serious threat right now. We have a mole, a spy, if you will, and we don't know who it is. So, security's pretty tight. That's why you're under suspicion. The only thing in your favor is the circumstance in which you arrived."

Peter's face went blank. "How did I get here?"

Cutler studied Peter's face for a few seconds. "You fell through the ice." Cutler's tone was matter-of-fact, as if falling into a town of dwarves through the arctic ice cap was normal. "It was hard for the investigative team to be certain. The shifting ice and currents are always tricky to judge. But we think you fell about twenty feet. You're alive because you landed on two of your dogs. They broke the fall." Ron let his eyes close, and a deep sigh filled his cheeks before he exhaled. "Unfortunately, the dogs didn't make it."

The image of a silver Siberian husky reappeared, bright green eyes full of anticipation looking up at him, a clear dark streak following her spine. *Penny*, Peter thought. *Not all of them are dead.*

Ron turned to the other bed and looked at Sheila lying on the bed. Peter stepped around the bed and put his hands on the rail. He picked up her hand, holding it between his palms. "They say she's going to live."

74

Ron nodded. "She fared much worse. As best the rescue team can determine, she bounced off the sides of the crevice enough to slow her fall, but the ride left her comatose. The doctors can't believe you both survived. Your recovery, in fact, is nothing short of a miracle. But that's a mixed blessing for most of us here."

Peter felt a tear crest his eyelid and start down his cheek. He lifted a finger to wipe it away. "You don't sound like a defense attorney."

"I'm not." Cutler seemed to adopt a new wariness of his client. "We don't have much reason to invoke the criminal code around here. I pinch hit. Our goal is to provide a peaceful and secure home and work environment. We still have an adversarial legal system, but we're moving to a less confrontational approach, based more on probing and investigation. We're really trying to get to the truth in these situations. It's not quite as cutthroat as down south, but these things evolve."

"So, are you going to defend me or let them do what they want?"

"I am your advocate, and Rowdy is paying me a lot of money to play that role."

Peter's head snapped up an inch at Rowdy's name. Cutler picked up on Peter's confusion. "He has a soft spot for average size people."

"Pffft."

Cutler let a small smile crack his lips. "Don't judge Rowdy too harshly. You were a stranger, and we keep very close tabs on who arrives in, and who leaves this town. Everyone leaving needs to register with NP Security and get approval. It's a formality really, but the precautions pay off. Rowdy didn't know who you were."

"So, why did he retain you?"

Cutler shook his head. "Something about Jeff Wells. Rowdy respects him, but he's a bit suspicious, SEAL training and all. It's been fifteen years since he left the service, but some people, like Rowdy, wonder whether he's tempered his tactics well enough for a place like ours."

"How does he know I will pay him back?"

Cutler looked at Peter, his eyes soft and the lines in his face receding as he became more relaxed. "He just wants to make sure you get a fair shake."

"Wells doesn't seem to be that concerned."

"His job is to keep this town safe. Wells is not an attorney, but he knows the rules. That keeps him from pushing as hard as he wants to. Right now, you're in the vice."

"Sounds like you're not so sure of me either."

"I'm not. The threat to this town is real, but this town exists and thrives as long as everyone plays by the rules—fairly. Wells knows that, too." Cutler looked straight at Peter, as if waiting for him to say something. "I'm here to make sure that justice is served in this case. If you are innocent, not knowing the rules around here can get you into real trouble. If you're a threat, you could still get into trouble. Either way, my job will be to make sure you get out of here, and in a way that doesn't threaten the existence of this town."

At that moment, Peter's brain cleared, pain-free for the first time since he woke up. "I'm at the North Pole."

Cutler smiled. "Well, I would use the word *at* rather loosely."

Peter nodded with new understanding. "I fell through the ice and landed on my dogs. I'm under the ice."

Ron raised his eyebrows, knowing that Peter needed nothing else to confirm his new-found revelation.

The full weight of his predicament began to sink in. This was not a normal town. This was a secret town—maybe even a secret society. Somehow, it was connected to the North Pole. Nobody knew about it, and they wanted to keep it that way. Any stranger was a threat, not just Peter R.B. Peary or Sheila Livingston.

"How can this place exist?" Peter stammered. Rowdy was running a global software company for God's sake! The hospital had some of the best trained doctors and nurses on staff. "What am I guilty of?"

"It's not about guilt or innocence," said Cutler.

"Then why am I being detained?"

Cutler laughed. "You know why."

"Then how do I get out of here?"

Cutler sized up Peter again. He looked down at his papers and shook his head. "I still don't know enough about you or your case to tell you. Let's just say we have ways, and they've been successful so far."

Peter looked at Cutler. "You mean I'm not the first to pay a surprise visit?"

Cutler ignored him. He pulled a pad of paper onto his lap and a very expensive ball point pen out of his jacket. "Okay, Mr. Peter R.B. Peary, how did you get here?"

Peter rolled his eyes. "Are you serious?"

Cutler lifted his hands. "I have to ask. Trust me. Just play along."

Peter shook his head. "I still don't know for sure. My memory's fuzzy. I'm an explorer. At least I think I'm an explorer."

Cutler looked at Peter, his pen unmoved over his pad of paper.

Peter shrugged his shoulders. "I'm pretty sure I'm an explorer. I have these memory snippets of the cold. Of expeditions. Of mountain climbing. This trip was to the North Pole, apparently by dog sled. Sheila was—"

"*Yes, y*es, yes," said Cutler, waving Peter off. "I know all that; it's in your file." He tapped the thick folder pulled out of his briefcase earlier.

"How does everyone know so much about me?"

"The Internet is a wonderful thing, but we only know the boring stuff. We don't know the interesting stuff. Like why you were really going to the North Pole. What were you trying to achieve? What was the purpose?"

Peter shook his head. "I don't know. I honestly can't remember. I was probably trying to set a record for the fastest trip from Nome to the North Pole by dead reckoning."

Cutler shook his head. "Yes, yes, that's in the file, too. We have a clipping from the Nome newspaper. There's even a mention in the *Washington Post*. The Associated Press sent out a clip, but most papers cut two-thirds of the filed article. We've got three dozen clippings talking about that. Why were you *really* going to the North Pole?"

"What do you mean? I had funding for this expedition, just like every other expedition."

"I don't believe you. Or, maybe you believe that, but it's not the truth," his new attorney said.

Cutler directed a desperate look into his pile of papers, and then lifted his head to look at him. "Peter, you dropped off the face of the exploring world for almost a year. It was after the Everest expedition. Who in their right mind is going to throw $3 million at a kid jinxed by a fatal climbing accident on Mt. Everest? You couldn't even get a cable TV channel to commit to underwriting your trip. Your video equipment isn't commercial grade. No, there's much more at stake here than reaching the North Pole—and you actually got to the North Pole."

Peter couldn't help but smile. At last, confirmation!

Cutler shook his head. "But you didn't reach your goal by the planned route. So I'm not sure it would qualify, although your backers would be happy to learn what you did discover, assuming your story checks out."

"Great!" shouted Peter, punching a victory fist into the air.

"Your backers aren't going to find out."

Peter's face fell into a grimace. "Why not? You can't keep me from telling them."

"We have ways." Cutler's tone was as ominous as it was serious. "But we're hoping the restraint will come from your heart. It's your choice which medicine to take."

Peter was confused—again. This entire experience was a nightmare with more twists and turns than a roller coaster with inverted loops and barrel rolls.

"I know," Cutler said, as if reading Peter's mind, empathy softening his expression. "Right now, I have to work on getting you some walking time. We'll eventually have to go before a judge, but we need some time to investigate and prepare our case. Our system here requires complete discovery on both sides; they know everything we come up with, and we know everything they come up with. Even though you're a potential threat, we still hold to the concept of innocent until proven guilty. The key word here is *potential*. If we find out you're a real threat, the ball game changes completely."

Cutler sifted through his files. "Besides," he said looking back up at Peter, "maybe we'll get a dwarf for a judge!"

Peter wasn't amused. "I'm no threat. I'm an explorer."

"I hope so," said Cutler with a wink. "But you know Peter, I already know you're much more than that. It's in your files."

15

Nicole Klaas immersed herself in the file—flipping pages, scanning, reading, memorizing—confident that Peter was back in his hospital room by now. She wondered if Cutler had arrived yet. Rowdy would surely send Cutler; he never spared a dime when someone needed a good legal defense. Right now, no one in town was in more desperate need of a good lawyer than Peter R.B. Peary.

The file was thick, and she wondered for a minute how she was going to make sense of the papers and photographs. Peter was young, but he seemed to live a life fuller than most people when they die! She had to admire that, even if he was here to bring her and the entire community surrounding NP Enterprises down.

Nic lifted a picture from the file and peered into the face of a boy with fierce, competitive eyes. He was fifteen when that photo was taken and had just descended from Mt. McKinley. What struck Nicole was his focus; it blazed a hole through the photo. The photographer had caught something in that picture about Peter's character that could only be felt, not described. He tamed the mountains. They didn't tame him. Even though he had reached the summit on his own and just completed his descent, his eyes glowed with the energy of a boy beyond his years, ready to turn around and do it all over again without a rest. If Peter Peary were working for DEA, he was dangerous. It wouldn't be their livelihoods at stake. It would be their lives and freedom.

"What's your story, Mr. Peary?" she wondered aloud. "You climbed Mt. McKinley without a problem. You knew the risks of Everest. So what happened to bring you down? And how did you end up here, in the backyard of my icy haven."

Nic shuffled through two profiles prepared by Wells and NP Security, oblivious to the blinking lights on the stock ticker screaming across the widescreen video monitors above her. Yep. Everything seemed to be there: the high-school transcript, the college application to Florida State while a high-school freshman, college application to Georgetown, the financial records for Top of the World Expeditions, the grant proposals for his trips that funded groups of rich amateurs whom had no business being on a mountain like Everest. Embarrassment forced her to skip over the dirt on his college girlfriend. It was all there. But where was the link? Where was the missing piece that put Peter below the surface of the polar ice cap? That link would either save or destroy her and NP Enterprises.

Nicole rapped the file with the tips of her fingers. She picked up the Reuters photo and caught her breath. August 25, 2009. She sifted through the file again, finding the electronic news clip she had seen with the banner screaming "Seven Climbers Lost in Freak Storm on Everest!" dated two days earlier.

"That's when you lost it," she mumbled. It wasn't just the failed expedition. That accident seared his soul. She let her finger pass over the youthful, adventurous Peter Peary. "You lost *him*." She looked at the expedition picture and the lean, grizzled white beard of a man whose confidence was built by experience, not the impulsive energy of youth. Nic nodded. "You built Peter, Mr. Richard Van Dorn." Peter lost much more than a friend during that storm on Everest.

Nic's heart felt hollow. "You lost it," she said, shaking her head. "You lost it. At twenty years old you lost it." At twenty, she was a junior at MIT, blazing new ground with a young Turk of an engineer by the name of Rolf Hackett. She smiled.

Then, her smile turned to a frown as sadness overwhelmed her. She clenched her fists and brought the knuckles up to her face and over her eyes, fighting back the tears she knew were about to come. She had to hold it together. She couldn't feel sorry for herself. She couldn't feel pity for Peter. She had to attend to The Business, and she couldn't let these creepy emotions cloud her judgment.

She let her hands fall to the desk, confident she had pushed the tears and memories deep inside. *There*, she said to herself, *you can't come out now.*

Nicole sighed and leaned back in her chair, staring at the silent monitors above her trusty laptop. She had built it from scratch as part of an independent lab at MIT, and then named it Silver. The professor almost didn't sign off on the project; he couldn't see how this freshman, with no formal education, could build a computer that powerful and fast, programming the mother board with the top-of-the-line chips, from scratch. Nic spent hours in his office, trying to convince him she could do it. He didn't believe her, but he signed off on the paper only after she showed him she would stay on track to graduate, even if the independent study blew up and produced nothing to grade.

She smiled at the machine. Those were the days. She didn't have to worry about employees. She didn't have to worry about the supply chain. She didn't have to worry about distribution. She didn't have to worry about government agencies or international treaties. All she had to do was build, and her father would take care of the rest through NP Enterprises.

Nicole leaned over and touched Silver's plastic casing. Of course, she had replaced virtually everything in it by now, but she couldn't bear the thought of giving up the casing. It sat there on her desk, like a warm, familiar friend.

Nicole spun herself around in her chair, throwing her head back to let waves of hair flit in the gentle breeze she created.

That first year at MIT! What a time. She had so much fun. She would work and work, find a wall, and shoot Rowdy Rolf an email. He was more than ten years her senior, but Rolf always turned her messages around in hours, generating pages of new ideas to try out. They texted and messaged, and even skyped when they ran into really hard problems. She would press the code she had been working on up to the camera so he could see every Greek letter, symbol, and doodle. Weeks went by before Rowdy had remembered she was on Eastern Time and was working well into the first morning hours! He was so angry.

Nicole laughed at the thought of Rowdy throwing a temper tantrum way up here under the ice cap as she blazed away, trying to fix the circuits and re-route the processors. Speed. She needed more speed. She wanted to make the most powerful computer ever! And they were close. Nothing was going to stop their revolution! She would work on the hardware. He would work on the software... and the marriage would revolutionize the world!

Nicole chuckled, remembering the first time she shut down her computer only to find the entire room pitch black. The light bulbs had burned out, and she hadn't even noticed, her work illuminated by the glow of her computer monitors and the enthusiasm of a revolutionary.

Five thousand miles away, Nicole knew Rowdy was just as caught up in the project. His software would make him rich, a giant in the computer industry, and a world leader. No one's research department was even close to coming up with something that could compete with their system. The program was so fast, so accurate, with room to grow. Microsoft would seem like a twentieth-century flash in the pan. Apple? A blip on the mid-century radar screen. Lynux? Please!

Nicole threw her head back again as she let those memories in the lab and dorm room take her. Their computers and program would transform her father's sleepy, third-generation business into a global powerhouse!

NP Enterprises would touch every customer, every supplier, every retail transaction in the world.

Best of all? No one would know it! It all depended on working out those two bugs and cleaning it up—twelve more months, tops. She didn't make any friends—at least not new ones—but she was going to change the world.

Nicole's smile began to shrink. She sighed as memories of those times testing software and developing code seemed to flood her heart in a torrent.

She was a junior and the spring leaves were full and bursting with color in Boston. She went strolling down the block, basking in sun released from clouds that had unleashed a drenching rain. That's when her phone lit up with Rowdy's name emblazoned onto the screen. She remembered the heaviness of her lungs when she answered, knowing he wouldn't be calling at this time of the day unless something was seriously wrong. No one had expected the heart attack that brought down Nicholas III. She had been so consumed by her ambitions that she hadn't spoken to him in weeks. She couldn't believe what Rowdy was saying, even though the words were clear. It wasn't news; it was a nightmare—a surreal horror show. She needed to get back to the North Pole. Fast.

The seconds on the phone to the airline reservation desk seemed abominable. Didn't they know her father was dying? She needed to get back. Charter a plane from Boston to Fairbanks, for God's sake!

Tears began to tickle her eyelids as she felt all over again the isolation of sitting in the airport, waiting, waiting, waiting. Each second seemed to distance her more and more from carefree men, women, and children, chatting just feet away, as they prepared to be whisked away to some enchanted destination.

He can't die, she chanted to herself, as if the mantra alone were powerful enough to change the inevitable. He couldn't die. Not before she could get home. Not before he knew of her project. Not before he knew what she had done for The Business—and for him.

But he did die, as she was flying somewhere over Saskatchewan. No one had told her, but she felt the grip and wrench in her stomach. Her sobs had almost driven the pilots to land the plane.

Nicole looked at the widescreen monitors that now surrounded her in the office under the icepack. Her body wasn't dying that day; it was her heart. And her passion was following her heart.

Nicole was five when her mother had died. She barely knew her. Her father was everything. He was the one who made sure she applied to MIT. He was the one who put up with her solitary nights, tinkering with computers and software. He was the one who encouraged her to try out her amateurish software ideas on NP Enterprises. He was the one who made sure the community directors would tap Nicole as the next president and chief executive officer of NP Enterprises. He wanted her to be the one who kept NP Enterprises going as a fourth-generation Klaas.

How could she say no when the directors made their inevitable offer? She owed it to her father. Dropping out of MIT was the only path. All her counselors and professors told her to stay in college, but they didn't know what was at stake, did they? They didn't know about NP Enterprises. They didn't know about the three generations of Klaases that preceded her. They didn't know that thousands of people depended on NP Enterprises staying healthy for their livelihoods. They didn't know how many children depended on NP Enterprises to be there every Christmas season, and the devastating effect it would have on them and their families, if the family enterprise disappeared.

Taking over the reins of the business was her duty. Her calling came by inheritance from her father, his father, and his father. It was the right thing to do. Wasn't it?

Rolf Hackett took over the controls of their project. Now, Rowdy is changing the world with his software, and her computer was keeping the dream alive.

Nicole swept away a small tear with her hands. She picked up Peter R.B. Peary's file and straightened the papers with neat efficient strokes of her hand. She looked at the picture of the expedition, excited explorers, ready to conquer the world. She looked into Peter's eyes on the photo. "Did you lose your father that night?"

Nicole put the picture in the file and reminded herself those days were gone. Now, she had a business to run, and it was a great business that employed thousands. It was an awesome business, an inspiring business. It kept her town alive. She wasn't going to let her father down. She wasn't going to let down the community and all those children, moms, and dads they supported every year. She would be damned if she would let some low-life DEA hack bring down four generations of Klaases!

Nicole's shoulders slumped. She and her father had the same goals, didn't they?

She looked at the clock on her computer screen. Wells must be interrogating Peter back in the hospital right now, she thought. She looked back at the file on Peter Peary, the washed-up explorer and desperate seeker of answers to questions that could not be answered. Was Peter a threat? Her eyes grew heavy and dull as she shuffled through a stack of papers, pulled from the file, this time putting them in a timeline.

The entire community was at Level Three Alert. She and Wells had to decide soon whether they needed to step up to Level Four. That would be serious. That would mean involving the community directors. That would be a nightmare.

Nine months of tracking the DEA threat still hadn't found all the pieces of the puzzle. Whatever the agency was doing, it was going for the heart of The Business. She needed to know where the shots were being fired. Was Peary one of those pieces? Was he the bullet? Or the gun? A trigger? Or the shooter?

"What are you looking at?" came a man's voice from behind her.

16

"Jesus, Jeff! I should never have given you that pass code!"

"Well, you did. You can change it if you want. But do you really think it would make a difference?"

"Well, uhh, no. You are the head of security. I guess nothing's really completely secret around here. Besides, someone needs to be able to get in here for security reasons."

"A bit ironic, isn't it? I'm the only one you trust up here with all these other people?"

"You know what I mean!"

Wells smiled and approached Nicole's desk. He knew every square inch of her desk and instantly recognized Peter Peary's file. He looked around, noted the monitors reporting the normal information and statistics, then pulled a chair a few more inches from Nicole's desk and sat down. He leaned over and tapped his thumb on Peary's file. "Are you angling for my job? I can offer you a position in my investigative unit if you're bored."

"Hah! As if that were on option."

"We've got to put that MIT education to work somehow."

"Three years doesn't count as an 'MIT education.'"

"Ahh, but that's where you're wrong Nic. Just getting into MIT means that you're qualified to run the world!"

Nicole scowled.

"Geez, lighten up. You know NP Enterprises is the heart and soul of this place. Without you, the entire town collapses. The spirit evaporates."

"I'm twenty-six years old. Don't you think I should be wasting my youth doing something else?"

"Like what? Developing a revolutionary computer program that will network more than 10,000 independent terminals at once with speeds so fast the human brain thinks it's instantaneous?"

Nicole didn't smile.

"Look Nic. You're the right person in the right place in the right job. Everyone knows that. Except you. Your great-grandfather started this business. Your grandfather practically killed it—second generation curse, you know—your father resurrected it, and you're making it into a global empire. Who could want anything more?"

"I don't know, Jeff." Nicole turned to the wall and lifted her hand to her head. "Ever since Rowdy's software business took off, I have to wonder about the changes around here. I sometimes think we're losing our soul."

Wells cocked his head. "I wouldn't worry about it. Everyone comes here because they want to be part of The Business...."

She turned back around to face Wells. "Unless you're a dwarf."

"Well, that's a special case. A little myth and legend helps, too. Combined with the job opportunities, it's a hard place to beat if you're under four feet ten inches tall."

"Yeah. And that worries me a little. Some of the people coming in are more interested in a good salary than the 'heart and soul'."

Wells raised his hands as if signaling Nicole to stop. "Nic, you know we've got a very thorough and secure review system. Everyone is interviewed three times, their résumés checked out, mined, and scoured for fairy dust. You've seen the process. We even track down their bosses from their first job as a teenager! They need more than a good résumé before we hire them and move them up to this wilderness. The apprentice program in LA and our people at Ebson and Associates do a good job of weeding out those who don't fit."

Nicole shook her head. "We have people up here who are not as committed to our dream."

"Your father was a wild man. I haven't known anyone with the drive and commitment he had to this place. Don't compare him to us mere mortals."

Wells looked at Nicole just as she looked at him. He pointed to the map of the world, with lights blinking on every continent, every country in Europe, North America, Australia, and South America, just about every country in Asia, and almost all the countries along the coasts of Africa. "Nicole, the growth of this business energized your father in ways I've never seen before. It was infectious. He knew you were the one driving it, and he was very proud of that. He wanted it to succeed for you."

"Well, his personality helped."

Wells leaned over the desk and looked directly into Nicole's eyes. "Nic, we're here because we believe in the soul. No one forced us to be here. Not even you. That's what counts."

"You underestimate the power of the grave."

Wells didn't respond, but his eyes hardened.

Nicole put her hand back down on the file. "Well anyway, what's the newest on Peary and Livingston?"

Wells straightened his shoulders and glanced down at the folder. "Not much new. Peary's terribly suspicious and antsy. If Rowdy hadn't reported him in the pub, we could have really been in trouble."

"I seriously doubt that," she said with the return of a whimsical smile. She knew NP Security's capabilities, and she had no doubt Peary was never very far from a guard or camera. Nicole picked up Peter's file. "I don't think he's our man."

"What do you mean?"

"My gut just says he's not our guy."

"I wouldn't put it past him. He fits our profile."

Nicole grimaced. "Yeah, Jeff, but you know what profiles are. They're somebody's guess at how we think people behave. They aren't reality." She leaned over the desk and thrust Peter's picture in front of him. "And this guy is real."

"This is an old picture, Nic."

"Hmm. It's not that old. Look at it more closely."

Wells picked up the photo and looked at Nicole, baffled. "So? He's got two eyes. And two eyebrows, a mouth, a nose—"

"Don't be funny."

"What? It's the same guy we have in custody three blocks down the street on the other side of the roundabout."

Nicole looked at him. "You don't get him, do you?"

"I've read his entire file! I know as much about him as you do. Actually, I know more about him. I've met him. You haven't."

Nic nodded. She plucked the picture from Wells' fingers and put it back in the folder. "No, it's not the same guy."

"Of course it's the same guy. He's just more of a kid. He's got the same unshaven face, same wavy hair. It's just now he's gotten out of college. He can drink a beer, but there's no way he will ever become a Navy SEAL."

Nicole let her frustration bubble over. "Jeff! Look at the eyes!"

Wells lifted a bland expression to Nicole. "Huh?"

"Look at his eyes! What do you see?" Peter's eyes were sharp, focused, and full of life and purpose. Couldn't Jeff see that? The boy in the photo had a real explorer's eyes. They weren't the same eyes she saw in the man in the hospital bed, pulled almost lifeless from the ice last week.

She knew. She understood. That was the same look in her dorm room and in the MIT lab during her first three years. Peter had also lost something. He no longer had that glimmer of purpose, that fire of life. Was it Everest?

"Nicole!" Wells said raising his voice. "This guy is not some lost child looking for a mother. He's a weather-hardened explorer. He fits the profile of someone the DEA would recruit. Don't get sentimental on me. I know you're young—"

Nicole burst out of her chair. "How dare you!" She lifted her hand, closed her fingers it into a fist, and brought it down hard onto the table top.

"Nicole—"

"How dare you even think that!"

Wells stood up from his chair and threw his hands up. "Nicole, I'm sorry! I didn't mean that. I just meant you haven't had as much experience at this as I have."

Nicole's eyes were on fire, but she stayed behind her desk.

Wells dropped his hands and his head lurched back as a bellowing laugh filled the room. "Now that's the spirit I was hoping to see in you!"

Nicole looked down at the desk, embarrassed. "I'm sorry, Jeff. I shouldn't have exploded like that."

He strode around the desk and took Nicole gently by the arms. "No, no, don't apologize. Nicole, that was beautiful!"

Wells' eyes were alight with pride and... joy! Nicole looked into them, as if seeing him for the first time. No, this wasn't a new person. It was a different side of him. His eyes were warm and inviting. His hands felt natural, holding onto her arms with confidence and gentleness. This wasn't the cold, calculating security guard who walked into the room with such stealth she didn't even know he was there until he spoke. This was a man full of life, who responded to a passion in her.

Nicole leaned closer to him. He didn't push her back or even slow her movement. He let her walk into his arms. His arms. They felt comforting and secure as they wrapped around her and pulled her close. She could smell the faint aroma of burning wood from a fireplace on his shirt, and knew he carried the scent at Nick R Bakker's pub. Nicole slipped a hand up to his face and put her palm against his cheek. She was surprised at how smooth his skin was. She had always thought of it as rough and coarse, like the ex-military man that ran a tough-as-nails security contracting company. But it wasn't. She let her head fall on his chest as his hands slipped under her arms. She felt his chest press up against her, as the smell of the campfire comforted her.

Nicole looked up at him. "Jeff...."

His expression was open, vulnerable.

Nicole lifted her lips to his, and they kissed. His lips were soft and welcoming. She held the kiss and pulled him closer. She felt safe, secure, like everything was going to be okay. And he was accepting her... without conditions.

She pulled her lips from his, and he let her, though she could tell he would take more if she wanted to give it to him. He was waiting for her. He wasn't judging. He wasn't asking. He was waiting for her. "Jeff—"

"Nicole," he said, his voice low and tender. "Let's just stay here for a while. Just like this."

Wells brought a hand up to her face and put his palm on her cheek, letting his thumb caress her nose gently as he pushed strands of hair away from her eyes. "You are beautiful."

They kissed again, holding each other, enjoying each touch, each caress, without prejudice, somehow also knowing this feeling might vanish with the tick of the next second.

17

Wells had left Nicole's office the previous night, cursing himself before he even hit the main door. How could he have kissed her like that? Good God, what would Nicholas III have thought? He would have killed him!

Wells shook his head as he made his way onto the street and started walking toward home. The crisp air under the ice cap was refreshing, and he needed a good cool down. He looked around, the stillness and quiet of the late hour providing a comforting isolation he couldn't savor during the constant motion of the work day. His thoughts welcomed the peace that came with the safe harbor of a village fast asleep.

Wells hesitated as he stepped down from the boardwalk onto the crystallized roadway. He drew in a slow, deep breath, careful not to let his exhale disturb the silence around him.

He stopped. There. A slight reverberation climbed up into his boots from under the ice. He resisted the tendency to look around, knowing that if the ice were breaking up, the clues would come from the splitting walls of the ice cavern, not any visual sign of a crack.

He tapped his phone and a gridded map of the town emerged with blue and purple splotches growing and shrinking. Nothing unusual, he noted to himself. No yellow lines emerging to trace cracks big enough to cause alarm.

After a few more moments, he continued his walk, satisfied that the tremor was just the normal grumblings of the ice pack, adjusting with the Beaufort Gyre, the ocean current that moves the polar ice. The village didn't shift that much given its closeness to the North Pole, but the four-year rotation of the ice pack challenged his security firm and the utility engineers every day to ensure their equipment stayed up and running. Wells looked at the screen on his phone, even though he knew any emergency would have set off lights and sounds that would have rattled him from his deepest sleep.

He started back toward home, and the mental wrestling match started to play out in his mind. Yes, Nicole was beautiful. Yes, she was smarter than everybody on the planet. Yes, she was somehow managing a billion-dollar global enterprise. But kiss her? He was practically old enough to be her father! Well, not quite, he reminded himself with a chuckle, unless he was a teenage father. He shook his head. Nicole was driving him crazy!

The fifteen-minute walk home did little to settle him down, even after doing a lap around the traffic circle and the NP Software Company. The fact that he didn't even think about Rowdy, Cutler, or Peter Peary disgusted him as he walked up the steps to the porch of his two-floor townhouse. He was off his game.

Wells stepped up to his door, pulled a brass key from his pocket, and inserted it into a hole in a box next to his door. A blue light began blinking over the box and he lifted its plastic cover. He then put his hand into a ceramic form that conformed to every detail. Wells continued to puzzle over his sudden attraction to Nicole, the momentary concern about the ice, both below and above, now only a distant data point, compartmentalized in a memory safe. He couldn't shake the kiss, its warmth, her accepting arms, her head on his chest. These memories warmed him in the night air, oblivious to the scanner doing its job, checking his palm and fingerprints against NP Security's database in less than five seconds. He heard the latch unlock automatically, and he walked into his home, so secure in his commercial grade system that the thought an intruder might have gotten past the technology did not even register a second thought.

***

Later, Wells lay awake, staring at the ceiling, still unable to banish the kiss from his lips. When was the last time he dated a girl, really? Definitely before he took on this exclusive deal with the North Pole. He couldn't risk dating someone not permanently attached to the village, or NP Enterprises. Besides, his breakup with Jennifer was awful. She liked the the fact he had earned an MBA from the University of Miami—financial stability, she thought—but her ashen face foretold their end the night he came home after diffusing a hostage situation at a shopping mall. The media had been beating the drum of a multi-store terrorist attack for twenty-four hours, reporting bombs discovered in trash cans and assault weapons behind every corner. The attack was sophisticated, but he could tell right away that the crime was really a robbery, not a terrorist assault. Wells knew for sure when he saw the robber's surprised expressions. They were using the fear of a terrorist attack, the mass hysteria it would inevitably create, as a way to induce panic and make the loot in the jewelry stores easy pickings. So they thought. Wells still could see the panic in their faces when they realized their bodies and souls were about to be riddled with bullets from real assault weapons, by trained professionals. The hostage was terrified and in tears, but never in real danger from the would-be burglars.

Jennifer couldn't deal with it even though he had told her everything. Perhaps he should have kept more of the details of his work secret. If she had stuck around just another month, she would have seen that the scenes plastered across the newspaper headlines, tabloids, and TV screens that had tortured her every sense were also the ones that sent Nicholas III looking for him. Nicholas impressed Wells with his vision for The Business and his need for a sophisticated but fearless approach to protecting the town as well as thousands of workers across the globe. For reasons still unclear to Wells, Nicholas had seen that sophistication in the way he diffused the hostage situation.

Six months later, four months post-Jennifer, Wells had an exclusive contract with NP Enterprises and a cushy job. His job was complicated by the tedium of overseeing tight security at a place no one knew about, or was even looking for, but he was out of harm's way— most of the time.

Wells drew in a deep breath as he thought for a moment of the life they could have had under the ice cap. Jennifer would have liked it. She would have adjusted… if she had just trusted him.

His mind drifted back to Nicole and the light brush of her hair on his chin. He smiled. Was what he did really that wrong? Twenty-six was young, but she was an adult. She could make her own decisions, right? It wasn't just him. How could he have let it happen? Where was his discipline? He needed to regain his focus. A billion-dollar enterprise depended on it. But he didn't have to worry about that until the morning.

***

Wells stood in front of Nicole's office, unsure of what to do. He couldn't remember ever feeling this way about a woman. It seemed so new. And fresh.

He took out his security ID and slipped it in an electronic reader about shoulder height. A small flap opened on the wall revealing a quarter-inch round camera lens, and he lifted his right eye for the scan. A few moments later, an indicator light flashed blue, then yellow, then green. The door opened automatically.

Nicole was at her desk—*did she ever sleep?*—and looked up as he passed through the door. She stood up. She smiled. "Hey."

"How did you sleep?"

Nicole let her eyes drift as her hands dropped to her desk, as if bracing her body to keep it from collapsing. "Okay. Last night was a bit... um... unusual."

He chortled. "That's an understatement!"

Nicole smiled as her cheeks turned pink.

"Umm, Nicole. I'm sorry about last night. I shouldn't have let that happen."

"Why?" Nicole seemed surprised, disappointed. "I didn't regret it. I was happy it happened."

"I don't regret it." Wells paused. "It's just... I can't let myself become emotionally involved with my clients."

"I'm a client?"

"Well, yes. You're my company's biggest contract."

"I thought you were hired by the community directors."

"Well, yes, but my highest priority is NP Enterprises. I need to keep a clear mind so we can keep you... the company and the village safe."

"A client, huh? Is that the way you thought of my father?"

Now Wells diverted his eyes. "Well, no. He was a great friend, even a mentor."

Nicole walked around the desk, "So, how am I different?"

Wells stood still. "For one, you're a girl."

93

Nicole grinned. "I'm glad the North Pole's chief of security could figure that out! Is that a problem? Kissing a girl?"

He laughed. "Not at all. Didn't you feel a bit awkward?"

"Actually, it felt completely natural."

Nicole was in front of the desk now and leaning on the table. She reached for Wells' hands. He resisted, but she used a gentle tug to bring him closer. "Jeff," she said, her voice soft. She ran her hand up his arm, to his neck, so her palm cupped his jaw, and her thumb just touched this side of his mouth. She gently pulled his other hand to her waist. "I know this is weird, but let's not try to figure it out just yet. Let's just try to go with it and take it day-by-day. I'm fine if it goes nowhere."

Wells relaxed and let her body fold into his. His hands completed a circle around her waist as he felt her against him. "I don't know, Nic."

"I'm an adult." She lifted her other hand to his face and pulled him close, bringing her lips almost to his as their noses touched. Her breath warmed his chin as she lifted her lips to his. "I'm not a child."

Wells sighed. His dipped his head so their foreheads touched. "This is going to get complicated."

"Going to get complicated?"

They smiled together as their lips touched for a second and fateful time.

18

"Be careful, Nic. Peary's our number-one suspect."

"Oh, don't worry about that, Jeff. I'm just trying to get inside his head. If he's the threat you think he is, we need to know how he thinks."

Nicole didn't believe that, although she was trying to convince herself that was the way to approach the problem.

She noticed the dim light that seemed to isolate them in her favorite booth in Nick R Baaker's, aware that most everyone had left for the night. The barkeep paused as he wiped the last of the glass mugs dry and sent a hopeful look toward the couple, sitting discretely in the back of the bar. She had purposely decided to sit across from him to make sure they would focus on the evening's agenda.

Wells stole a glance at Nicole as he began to pull Peary's file together from the assorted stacks, dispersed among empty mugs.

Nicole reached across the table to place her hand on his. "Uhh, those are mine."

Wells cast a startled look at her but didn't pull his hand out from under hers.

"I accessed the electronic files on Peary, too. These are my copies."

Wells looked over at his briefcase and saw it leaning against the leather-covered bench beside him, unopened. He opened his fingers to let hers fold into his. "Sorry. Just keeping them safe."

A twinkle flashed through her eyes, "Like you kept Peary safe?"

Wells opened his mouth to say something but shook his head and kept his lips closed. He lifted the index finger on his free hand and

SR Staley

motioned as if he were notching a "1" for Nicole on an invisible scoreboard.

"What about the girl?" Nicole asked, pleased with herself.

"Not much change. I can't find much about her, either. She and Peary were hooked up before the Everest accident. Then she went to college and graduate school. She's been a grad student ever since. American University. Working on a Ph.D. in counter terrorism. Nothing too far out of the ordinary, there."

"That's odd, don't you think?"

"Why? What's odd about being in grad school?"

"Not grad school *per se*." Nicole began to sort through her files. "I think it's odd you haven't found anything else on her. After all, she's in a Ph.D. program at American University in Washington, D.C., a powerhouse in government and international affairs. Power junkies go to grad school in D.C. She must have been busy somewhere around there on government time."

Wells acknowledged the point. "We're still searching. We just haven't turned anything up. She's been a good student, making mostly As, not surprising in grad school. We've been able to track down some of her term papers, and they're standard fare. They don't show an inordinate amount of brilliance. A lot of the material draws from her explorer days. It's almost nostalgic."

"That's an odd way to describe it." Nicole looked through another set of papers with the steadiness of checking computer code.

Wells let pages slap together as he turned them, as if searching for something specific. "We thought so, too. Through our interviews we found most of her friends think she idealized the past, but decided she had to get down to business. She submitted a couple of applications for jobs on the Hill, working as a legislative aide for congress, but she never received an interview. Nothing spectacular."

"Don't you think that's weird?" Nicole let a sideways glance slip toward the bartender, but he had disappeared from the behind the bar. "I think Paul's ready to close up for the night."

Wells glanced over toward the bar and chuckled. "He's probably afraid we're going to nab someone again and mess up his bar and the rest of his night."

Nicole smiled. "You do have a way of creating fun."

"That's what you call it?" Wells let out a light-hearted huff.

Nicole smiled and let her gaze fall back to the file of Sheila. "Her behavior seems like typical D.C. stuff, doesn't it? But her experience seems almost too routine, too mundane, too… normal. If she had that explorer's fire, why did she give it up? Peary's understandable—that mountain disaster was life-changing. And it was his fault, or at least he thought it was his fault."

"Yeah," said Wells, "but I think we would have turned up something by now."

"And the girl…?"

"You mean Sheila Livingston."

Nicole shot a hard glance toward her chief of security. "Yeah, Livingston. That girl didn't go through a life-changing event. She just gave up the life."

"That's not quite right," Wells said shaking his head. "She lost her father in a random murder a year after Peary went off the deep end. But she seemed to pull herself together—finished college, went on to graduate school." Wells turned a stack of papers, until he found the headshot of Sheila Livingston's father. "Funny. Not many pictures of them together. This photo is professionally done. I just haven't found anything in her or Peary's file that I find interesting. Besides, it doesn't have to be her father's death. It could also have been something as simple as disillusionment with the real world, or even finally realizing she and Peary would never be together as a couple."

"Oh, I get it," Nicole said, rolling her eyes. "Big, brave Peter Peary needs a near-death event that kills half his party for him to break down, ruin his life, and set out on a three-year drinking binge. Then, in a hangover induced conversion, he 'rediscovers' himself and sets out to redeem himself. Sheila Livingston, being the weaker sex, changes life's course because she breaks up with a boyfriend or loses her father in a random crime. She can't recover until said boyfriend gives her something to live for."

Wells glared at Nicole. "I didn't mean it that way," he said, his tone calling out her sarcasm. "In fact, I think Sheila was the more rational of the two. She had her head on straight and was going in the right direction. Peary's head was in the clouds—literally—and he didn't know when to stop."

A smile broke through Nicole's contemplative expression. "Now look who's getting sweet on who!"

"Give me a break! Look, I'm still investigating both of them. As far as I'm concerned, they're both a threat to this town and The Business. I don't trust either of them."

Nicole placed her hands on the table. "I want to see him."

"Who? Peary? Why do you want to see him?"

Any playfulness in Nicole's eyes disappeared. "Since when do I have to answer that question?"

"Since right now. I'm in charge of security, and we're in a high alert situation."

Wells reached over to the file and started to thumb through the papers and pictures, avoiding direct eye contact with Nicole.

"I just want to ask him a few questions."

Wells looked at Nicole. "About his eyes?"

"Yes, if you must know. I want to know about his eyes."

"I wouldn't trust his eyes. They can lie."

Nicole looked directly at Wells. "Perhaps that's the difference between you and me, Jeff. I think his eyes will tell us everything we need to know."

19

Peter sat by Sheila's bed, unaware that just a few blocks away his future—his life—was being discussed at the highest levels over beer in a pub.

He let out a breath of air with a deliberate slowness, as if the gentle rolls of his warm oxygen might revive her. Sheila was beautiful, even as bandages covered her head. He knew the sandy blonde hair could practically glisten in the sunlight. Any second, her eyelids would open, and those bright blue eyes would sparkle again. In another month, they would be laughing about the whole bizarre experience at the Georgetown Pub. Peter smiled at the thought of lifting two mugs in the air and toasting their narrow escape from death.

His smile disappeared as he looked again on the body, lying in front of him. He knew she was alive because the heart monitor kept bleeping every second or half-second. They had some machine hooked up to her brain, yellow, orange, and red blobs oozing from one part of her head to the other. Fred said that was a healthy sign; lots of brain activity meant her chances of recovery were good. Not 100 percent, but good.

He reached down for her hand. "Come on, Sheila," he whispered. "Come back."

Peter rested his head on her shoulder, careful not to push too hard against her neck, and closed his eyes.

***

Peter didn't look up when he heard the knock at the door. He wanted to keep listening to Sheila, feeling the steady rhythm of her body, responding to her breathing. She was going to open her eyes any moment now. He was sure of it.

Nicole Klaas entered the room anyway, but paused once she saw Peter's back, as if unsure of what to do.

"Hi Fred," Peter said, still focused on Sheila. "Any news?"

"Ummm," Nicole stammered, "I don't know. Fred didn't give me an update before I came in."

Peter sighed but didn't turn to face the new body in the hospital room. He had hoped Fred would return. He wanted a familiar face, not a new one to learn. "That's okay. It looks like not much has changed. I'm sure you need to do your hourly check on her vital signs. I won't get in your way."

"Umm, thanks."

Nicole stood behind Peter, watching him, careful to let him be with Sheila undisturbed. She watched as Peter's fingers caressed her sleeping hands. Nicole shifted her weight, aware of the intimacy she was witnessing by virtue of her anonymity.

Nicole opened a file folder, rubbed a wet spot into the thick paper and looked down at several photos. Peter had a scraggly beard and an ambitious look.

"No change in her status, huh?" Nicole asked after a few more moments.

"No." Peter's head bobbed up slightly, as if the voice sounded familiar, but not well-known enough to give it his full attention.

"I presume you've met with your lawyer." Nicole stepped closer to the bed.

"I guess everybody knows everything in this town," Peter mumbled. "I guess the entire nursing staff has a file a foot thick on me by now." Peter still didn't turn.

"I wouldn't worry too much about Sheila," Nicole said, positioning herself at the foot of the bed, patting the footboard with her hand. Peter moved again so his back still faced Nicole. He was sure the smoke detector was going to go off any minute, if this nurse kept patronizing him.

"Seriously," Nicole insisted. "She's getting better. Look at her charts and the monitors." Nicole found herself saying these words in a sympathetic voice, and she grimaced. She hated it went people treated her like this, making her feel as if she were some flighty airhead who needed to be protected and supported during this crisis or that. "Look, her blood flow is improving. She has significant brain activity. See, it's right here on the last scan. Fred takes good notes, but Dr. Patten is one of the best in the world. The MRI is showing good results…"

Her voice trailed off as she realized Peter was ignoring her. Nicole stopped as blood started to rush into her cheeks. Then, she calmed herself. "It's obvious you care about her—"

"Look, nurse, are you going to give her meds or not? Otherwise, can you just get out and leave me alone?"

Nicole smiled and shook her head. "I would if I was a nurse, but I'm not. And I think we should talk—somewhere else."

Peter wheeled around and was startled by the woman in front of him. She was definitely not a nurse. She carried herself with commanding authority, even though she seemed to be about Sheila's age. Was she another security guard? Another agent sent by Jeff Wells to pry more information from him?

"I didn't think anyone but hospital staff was allowed in here—except for that pest Wells."

"Wow," Nicole responded with subdued playfulness, "I think I'd rather be a nurse."

Peter shook his head and pivoted back to Sheila. "So, who are you? Security?"

"Can we go to another room?"

Peter shrugged his shoulders.

"I'm asking, okay? Maybe I should just call Wells, and he can escort you into the conference room."

Peter dipped his head into his forearms as he shook his head. Then he turned to let Nicole lead him away from Sheila.

***

The conference room was Spartan by corporate standards. The walls were the same sterile white plasterboard that boxed him into the hospital room one floor up. Six chairs circled the rough wood of an oval table big enough to seat eight. Large video monitors, their screens black and silent, seemed to play the role of sentinels, watching over the players below.

Nicole signaled for Peter to sit in one of the chairs around the table and motioned to a pitcher of water and two ceramic mugs sitting in the center. He reached over and poured water into a mug, then lifted it to his lips. He was surprised at its cool temperature, but grateful for the soothing effect on his throat. Nicole sat across from him, a folder secure in her arms.

Peter lifted his arms as if to say, "Okay, I'm here."

Nicole chuckled. "I'm just someone with an active interest in your case."

Peter's skepticism was obvious. "Another lawyer?"

"Guess again."

"Great. Is this fill in the blank or multiple choice? I'll warn you though, you're better off with fill-in-the-blank. I don't know what words you're looking for, and I barely broke 1800 on my SATs."

"I know."

"You know? Is there anything this town doesn't know about me?"

"Well," Nicole said, "that depends on how you define town."

"You know, I'm pretty sick of this place. I don't even know what you want from me. I don't even know how I got here. My lawyer says I'm at the North Pole, which was my goal—I think—but this isn't anything like the North Pole. This is a town. I don't remember a lot from my accident, but I was way past any town this size on the map. I was on the ice cap, and there are no towns on the ice cap."

Nicole nodded. "You're right. There are no towns on the polar ice cap."

"Stop with the riddles! You've got lawyers, doctors, nurses, bartenders, and paramilitary security guards. You all speak English, but no one will answer my questions." Peter stopped, embarrassed by his rant. He paused and then looked straight into Nicole's eyes. "Look, I know you can't let me go. I don't know why, but I don't have a lot of choices. Can you at least tell me where the hell I am?"

"Well, this is a little cold for hell…, look, I know this situation must be frustrating—"

"You don't know crap, lady. Look at you—you just waltz in here past the guards, don't even announce yourself and start buddying up to me. What's going on here? Did you ever think that if you tell me what's going on I could help you?"

Nicole looked down at the folder. "Sorry." She hadn't really considered the rudeness of entering the hospital room without an invitation. This was business.

Peter looked at her, his expression betraying a newfound clue. "Everyone else needs to go through a gazillion security checks and clearances before they come into my room. You just walked right in."

"Look, Mr. Peary, I'm sorry... really I am... but we can't let you walk freely just yet."

"Ron Cutler, my attorney, said you guys were bound by rules. But you seem to play pretty fast and free with them. In the Lower Forty-Eight, no one would put up with this."

"That's not quite true," Nicole said. "They keep people in jail all the time when someone is placed under arrest, even if they don't know whether they've broken the law or whether they have enough evidence to prove the case. Don't forget, your situation is complicated by the fact you were hurt. We invested a lot of time and care in getting you healthy. Would we have done that if we didn't want you to get healthy?"

"I didn't have much choice," Peter reminded her. "I was unconscious."

"Yes, so compassion led us to give you aid. We have given you the best medical care available. We even went beyond what was prudent and necessary."

"Humph. No one told me about that. But giving me medical aid out of humanitarian concern doesn't mean I have to do your bidding. I'm not a slave or an indentured servant. It's one of those humanitarian principle-type things that came along after the Civil War."

Nicole shook her head. She began a short pace along one side of the conference table, and looked up at the blank video monitor. "Mr. Peary, you are not bound to do our bidding. You are restrained, temporarily, until we can verify that you are not a security threat. The situation is temporary, and your freedom is restricted because we are under a Level Three Alert. This is the only time we've had a situation go this long at this level."

Peter didn't respond, letting his silence concede Nicole's point. But it just didn't make sense. "I want to get back to Sheila."

Nicole looked at him. "She's pretty."

"She's a friend," Peter said, his focus turned to the folder pinned under Nicole's arm. He closed his eyes and let his shoulders slump. A

103

calm overtook him for the first time since waking up in the hospital. Perhaps even before then. He wished he could remember more about who he was, what he did, and what he cared about.

Peter opened his eyes and turned his face toward Nicole. She was pretty, too. But her attitude suggested a serious and contemplative temperament not so much different from Sheila after she started graduate school. Nicole's clothes were loose fitting, but Peter could still tell she had a trim figure. She must work out; she seemed too cool under pressure to drop pounds from anxiety.

Peter's muscles began to tighten up. He struggled to keep his face relaxed as he started to put the pieces of this disjointed puzzle together. She had to be someone important, or else she wouldn't have been let in… not with the way Wells treated him. Cutler hadn't had time to go before the judge either.

Peter straightened up and looked at Nicole with fresh eyes. She was dressed in casual business attire, like the tech geeks in the computer lab: a white turtleneck and tan pullover sweater with chino pants. The hiking boots fit well into the outfit. Her unkempt hair did a good job of hiding her natural attractiveness, but Peter could see it nonetheless. "Can you at least tell me your name?"

Nicole blinked. "Oh, of course." She extended her hand. "I'm Nicole Klaas." Peter reluctantly shook her hand. He was surprised at the strength of her hand shake. She would get along well with Sheila. Or they would fight like stray cats.

"And what do you do, Ms. Klaas? Other than barge in on people, imprisoned in hospitals."

"Hmm. Believe or not, that was more polite than I expected. Probably more polite than I, or we, deserve, although the circumstances are a bit unusual. I don't expect you to give me the benefit of the doubt."

Peter shook his in agreement.

"Hopefully," she added, "you'll think differently by the time you leave. Anyway, I run a local business. Sort of an import/export, wholesale trade-type thing."

"What things do you trade?"

Nicole hesitated. "I shouldn't tell you this," she said at last, then cast a mischievous smile, "but we'll just have to erase your mind if we think I've told you too much."

Peter didn't get the joke. "After what I've been through, it wouldn't surprise me," he scowled.

"Oh, Mr. Peary, I'm sorry. That was a bad attempt at a joke."

"Excuse me for not laughing."

"Right, right," Nicole looked down at the folder and fumbled through some papers before finally turning her eyes back to Peary. "We've been under so much pressure lately. We're trying to sort a lot of this out."

"You know, I really don't care. My best friend is lying near death right now." Peary was puzzled by Nicole's apparent weakness. Everything about her told him she was stronger, more determined than this. This must be part of some interrogation strategy.

Nicole jerked her head toward Peter. She opened her mouth, but hesitated. Then she made a decision. "Mr. Peary, I don't think you give a damn about Sheila Livingston."

Peter fired a glare at Nicole. "Ms. Klaas, I don't think you're in a position to judge anything about me or Ms. Livingston, certainly not our relationship."

Nicole pulled the file from under her shoulder and opened it. "Right. Let's get down to business, then. Mr. Peary, if you want out of here with your memory intact, you need to answer a few questions. And it better be the truth."

"Is that another attempt at a joke?"

"No. You don't seem to realize that you are considered a real threat to this town and its people."

"Oh, I know that," Peter said. "It's kind of hard to miss. Have you talked to Fred? How about Rowdy or Cutler? I don't suppose you've run across this macho, He-Man, soldier-type named Jeff Wells, either, huh? Who would have thought that someone trying to find the North Pole would be a threat! Ho, ho, ho."

Nicole repressed an urge to slap Peary for the swipe at Wells, deciding the best strategy was to ignore his sarcasm. "Until you are cleared, we're not going to let you go anywhere. You should understand that fully now, after your little sojourn to the pub."

"I'm a little wiser now," Peter shot back, his eyes glimmering with expectation.

"Wells lost you once. He won't do it again."

"We'll see about that."

Nicole noticed Peter's voice was crisper, more cutting. She looked at him. She saw the glimmer. No, his eyes were on fire! She nodded, as if finally coming to an important resolution. "I don't think we have to worry about that at all. You won't go anywhere until Ms. Livingston is fit to travel. And we're not going to let her travel, even if you and she are cleared of being a threat, until we are sure she is going to recover."

"What makes you think I won't just jump out a window and take off again?"

"Ms. Livingston."

Peter hesitated at the shift in Nicole's negotiation tactics. She no longer suspected his feelings for Sheila were superficial. She knew he cared for her. A lot. "That didn't stop me before."

"You didn't have much of your memory back. And, you didn't know where she was or what physical condition she was in."

"I thought you said I didn't care about her."

Nicole smiled, a satisfaction warming her insides. She nodded her head. This was going to get interesting. "Or, the fact the windows are sealed shut."

20

Nicole lifted her shoulders up and pulled the folder close to her chest. The last few minutes of verbal sparring had ignited the fiery, determined look she saw in the old photo. That was the man in her file. But his attitude was the playful challenge of an adventurer, of someone on a quest.

Nicole's gut was telling her Peter wasn't a spy, or a threat to the town, or to NP Enterprises. She trusted her gut when she was working on the third-generation NP software package with Rowdy, and it paid off in spades. Running the business didn't give her enough time to think of her gut, let alone use it. But could she risk being wrong? The livelihood of more than 20,000 people across the globe depended on her making the right decision—now.

"I think Wells pegged you wrong."

"Great. Are we playing good cop, bad cop now?"

Nicole ignored him. "Dr. Patten thinks Sheila will fully recover."

"Who's Dr. Patten? What would a hick doctor at the North Pole— if that's really where we are—know about treating this kind of trauma? I've seen this kind of injury more than once. Most people don't recover."

"This isn't Mount Everest."

Peary's eyes shot up. "I see you can read newspapers."

"Sheila's condition isn't too complicated for someone trained at Johns Hopkins, who practiced internal medicine for twenty-five years, was a lead surgeon at Massachusetts General for ten years, and chief of surgery for five years before coming up here."

"You're kidding!" sputtered Peter, unable to keep his own surprise checked. "Why would she come to this God-forsaken place? If this is the North Pole, no one in their right mind would want to come here, except on a lark. Certainly, they wouldn't want to live here."

"Were you on a lark, Mr. Peary? Is that all you think your life has amounted to?"

The question caught Peter off guard.

"I didn't think so," Nicole snapped. "Two thousand people live in this town. Everyone except you and Sheila are here of their own free will. They choose to be here, and, for the most part, they don't leave. In fact, we don't have any problems recruiting people to live and work here."

Peter shook his head as he struggled to grasp the implications.

Nicole looked down at the folder again. "Can you tell me in your own words what happened? How did you end up here?"

Peter looked at her. "My lawyer said I shouldn't talk to anyone."

Nicole struggled to remain patient. She took a deep breath and pulled the folder closer to her chin. "If you answer my questions, you have a better shot of getting out of here. If it's the truth, I weigh in on your side. And that counts for a lot in this town."

Several moments passed before Peter finally lifted his hands as if to invite her questions. "Shoot."

The folder drifted away from Nicole's chest, as if Peter's acquiescence had pried her arms apart. "Okay. Let's try this again. Why did you stop exploring?"

"What do you mean? I'm exploring now. That's how I got into this mess."

"After the Everest incident, you stopped. Why?"

Peter diverted his eyes to the tabletop. Everest. Why Everest? What did Everest have to do with getting him out of here? Didn't they know about how he suffered? He lost his best friend. Wasn't that enough?

"Peter," nudged Nicole, "I read your file."

"The file's not me."

"I know. That's why I'm asking these questions. I want to know you better."

"Why are you so interested?"

"It's part of our investigation. It's the only way we can clear you."

Peter nodded. "The investigation. It all comes down to the investigation. When do people matter?"

"Huh? People always matter, here."

"No, they don't." He looked toward the door that kept him from going back to the bed that held his best friend. "We're just a 'threat,' to be handled accordingly. Even Rowdy is considered a threat. How do you explain the fact security is everywhere? You can't walk down the street without thinking one wrong step will give you a one-on-one with Wells' thugs. Get out the security manual to find out what procedures we go through to get rid of us!"

"It's not that way—"

"It's exactly that way." Peter's voice raised memories, crisp images and thoughts flooded into his brain. Mt. Everest was bone-chilling cold when they started the climb from Camp IV along the Southeast Ridge. The view of the south peaks was stunning when they reached The Balcony at 27,600 feet. He thought the real danger would be the cornices and avalanches as they headed toward the Summit, trying to beat the other climbers to Hillary's Step. He had gone over the procedures in meticulous detail, laying out each contingency. But Mother Nature had other plans. Peter's breathing became shallow as he remembered friends, disappearing into the squall. One… two… three… four… five.

Peter lifted his face to look directly at Nicole. "You want to know what human is?" He thrust his finger out at the file Nicole was holding. "Look in that stupid file of yours for a father of three kids—two boys and a girl, all under fifteen—who's not coming home because of a mistake you made. Look for the feelings and emotions you have to deal with as you watch your best friend fall thousands of feet off a mountain, knowing he will never be there to give you a good idea, to coach you, to listen to how you've really screwed up your life but tell you to keep going on anyway. One mistake. One mistake and you fall three thousand feet to your own death."

Peter stood up and lifted his hand to his head, running his fingers through his hair before rubbing his eyes.

"Human is waking up one morning and finding one of your teammates had walked out into the blizzard and disappeared. Human is knowing that nothing will ever bring those people back; their lives wiped out in a matter of seconds and hours, creating a black hole in the hearts and lives of each of their wives, children, lovers, parents, and friends. Human is seeing your best friend lie in a bed and waste away, because you dragged her out onto this desolate landscape to jumpstart your career again. Human is knowing all this resulted from a decision you made, and all your experience couldn't keep it from happening. Not then, not now."

Peter walked over to the door that could take him back to Sheila's bed and placed his hands on the cool wood. He longed for the touch of her hair, the warmth of her cheek, the strength of her fingers clasped inside his.

Nicole stood up and walked over to Peter, pulling the folder up to her chin. "Why wasn't Sheila on Everest that day?"

Peter's shoulders slumped as his head fell into the palms of his hands. He had caged the demons of Everest. Anger welled up in his body. "Back off. Leave me alone. It's all in the past."

Nicole wavered.

Peter stood and whirled to face her, hands clenched in a fist as the snow fields of Everest overwhelmed him. "How dare you! How dare you judge me!"

Nicole stayed by his side, holding back the urge to open the door and leave. She lifted her hand and touched his arm. The skin under the wool shirt was relaxed, the anger subsiding as fast as it had risen. "It wasn't your fault. You couldn't have predicted the storm on Everest, or the crevice that split the ice to send you here. The current of the Beaufort Gyre turns the ice cap one revolution every four years, and that creates stresses on the ice that no one can predict. We live with that reality every day."

Peter let his head rest on his forearm, allowing the wall to hold him as secure as an embrace from Sheila.

"Before Everest," Peter confessed, "my so-called life had purpose. I was the best; no one had accomplished what I had. Everest was going to put me on top of the world. Nothing could go wrong. We had prepped for everything. We had trained. We had an experienced guide. I had paid top dollar to get the best Sherpas. It was my test. I would be able to lead people to their summits after I made that trip. But it was Everest. How could I lead people to their dreams if I couldn't also keep them safe? How could I lead them, unless I knew they would see their wives, boyfriends, girlfriends again? Or see their children graduate from high school, get married, and have kids?"

Peter lifted his hand to rub a tear into his cheek.

"Ironic, huh? Sheila refused to go on the Everest trip because she thought I was obsessed with it. I wanted to leave my mark on the world. Everest showed me the folly of all that. The futility. This trip to the North Pole just confirmed it. I killed my best friend—again."

Nicole looked away and stared at the blank, white walls. She turned her eyes back to the once-indomitable explorer and adventurer. "Peter, I need to show you something."

She pulled his arm toward the door, but he resisted. "It's okay, she's not going to wake up while we're gone. She's getting better, but she hasn't recovered that much yet."

"What about the guard."

"I'll take care of him. As long as you're with me, it will be okay."

"Where are you taking me?"

"You'll see. It might help explain everything for you."

Or prove you are the threat we fear you are.

21

Getko couldn't help pacing. It was all coming together so well. The most recent report just confirmed what he had suspected all along: a money laundering operation was in full swing in Miami and Los Angeles. But these people were clever—the cleverest he had ever run up against. The Bimini drug connectors and disruptors weren't even this slick.

"Boss, here's the latest from the task force." Joy plopped the thick folder of new analysis and computer readouts onto Getko's desk. The files tottered for a moment, forming a rounded mushroom on top of the stack of other files cluttering the oak desk.

Getko waved his hand over the stack, as if pushing an invisible folder off the top. "Do I need to read it?"

"Of course." Joy tried to keep her snippy tone hidden, but she doubted she was very successful.

"Give me an overview."

Joy let her eyes roll under the blink of closed eyelids. Getko was watching her, his hands behind his back, standing so that his suit was in no danger of succumbing to an unwanted crease or fold. Joy opened her mouth to ask him about his formal dress, but stopped. She turned her eyes back to the stack of reports. "The reports are consistent with the others."

Getko closed his eyes as he gave his head one crisp turn toward the window, then re-set his attention on the junior analyst. "Where's the money leading?"

Joy tapped the top folder, but paused, as if her next words held her career in the balance.

"What's wrong?" Getko snapped. "Is there anything that contradicts your previous reports?"

"Umm… no… not really."

"Not really?" Getko snatched the top file up from his desk, triggering another folder to slide off the stack and began to thumb through the papers inside.

Joy turned to the window. The winds had died down outside, and rain created a light pitter-patter on the office glass. But nothing beyond the 14th Street Bridge was visible. The overcast skies were still depressing, and Joy began to think about Vero Beach again. She sighed and shook her head. "I just have this feeling we're being misled by the data."

"Come now, Joy. You've been tracking this data for months. I thought we had been through this. You've seen the logic of the money flows. We have the account numbers. We have the surveillance tapes. We've got agents in Miami and Los Angeles ready to swoop down and arrest them at any minute."

"What?" Joy tried hard to contain her alarm. "Are you sure that's a wise move?"

"I've got two teams of agents and local law enforcement ready to arrest more than two dozen players in this laundering scheme," Getko continued, ignoring her protest. "Man, these guys are clever. I haven't seen a web this complex since 1988."

Joy's mind raced. She looked at the stack, as if trying to burn a hole into it to locate some clue or recommendation for stopping Getko.

Getko smiled. "Just one thing." He looked over to Joy, the muscles in his face twisting his lips and jaw so that his head looked crooked and misaligned. "I don't understand the midgets."

"What?" asked Joy, dumbfounded.

"The midgets. It's like the midgets are a front for some organization."

"You mean the little people?"

"Yeah, whatever you want to call them. I swear half the people on the surveillance tapes are midgets—oh, excuse me, little people. Can you imagine? What kind of weird exploitation is going on here? Perhaps we can throw a civil rights violation or two into the mix, along with money laundering, drug trafficking, and drug possession."

"Look, Agent Getko—Miles—don't you think we should review the evidence one more time before we pull the trigger on Jamaican Snow?"

"I've been reviewing the evidence for more than a year. We've got everything we need. You've seen the evidence yourself—we've linked $10,000 deposits, multiple ownership of accounts, conspicuous consumption, and spending in vacation areas—all fronted by the toy industry!"

"Yeah," said Joy, "but we don't have any evidence of drug dealing."

"Sure we do. Follow the money. Look at the pattern of money and bank accounts. It's a classic fit. The pattern hasn't changed one bit since my bust in 1988."

"Miles," Joy said. "That's just a pattern. Look, what if these are legitimate cash businesses? What if they're a legitimate franchise or chain of stores, perhaps even with a big presence in Miami and Los Angeles? We would expect to see the same pattern of deposits and withdrawals, particularly if they pay most of their employees and investors in cash."

"Really, Joy," Getko said, his eyes lifting his eyebrows as he chided her. "You almost sound as if you're in the enemy camp."

"No, no, sir, you're misunderstanding my point." Joy lifted her hand to her mouth as she scrambled to think of a way to show she wasn't working against Getko or his operation. "It's my legal mind working—I just want all the T's crossed and I's dotted."

"Hmm." Getko looked at her with noncommittal eyes, then nodded. "I guess those Georgetown law degrees can get in the way of clear thinking."

"Yes, sir," said Joy, diverting her eyes to the desk and its stack of papers again.

"Joy, I've been at this a lot longer than you have." Getko's tone was gentle, almost nurturing. "I know in my gut that something's going on here—in Miami or in Los Angeles—that's illegal. The pattern is too consistent. I know these cartels; I know what they want and what motivates them. And, this is text book. Besides, if these businesses were legitimate, you would have uncovered the evidence in their incorporation papers or filings with the Securities and Exchange Commission."

"Not if they're private companies."

"But they do export/import. International businesses leave a paper trail with the departments of commerce or customs. Your investigation didn't find anything on these companies with ties to the North Pole."

Joy stood in front of her supervisor, keeping her body still.

Getko gave a slight shake of the head as he waved his hand to dismiss her, saying, "I've got to brief the higher-ups in a few minutes."

"Then, you should let me continue to play the devil's advocate." Joy seemed to gasp for air as she interjected.

Getko nodded. "Okay. That's a good way to keep me sharp before meeting with Colson."

"Where do you want to start?"

"Start from the beginning when the DEA initiated the investigation a year ago."

"Great," said Joy, a hint of glee in her voice.

Getko's spirits revived as he prepared to engage his most talented junior analyst and future agent. He stepped over to his desk and picked up a legal pad, brushing invisible dust off with his hand as he prepared the first page for his pen.

"Mr. Administrator," he said signaling the beginning of the mock briefing. "The CTF has assembled enough information to engage Operation Jamaican Snow. The investigation began twelve months ago when we identified three transactions in excess of $10,000. The transactions were moving cash from a Miami bank to the U.S. Virgin Islands."

"How did you detect these transactions?" asked Joy, assuming the authoritative deliberateness of the agency's deputy administrator.

"Our computers tracked transactions through the Federal Reserve Bank. We have special arrangements with the Southern District, based in Atlanta, to monitor transactions at suspicious banks. The transactions were flagged using computer algorithms developed just for these kinds of operations."

"How did you target these banks?"

"We didn't," Getko said, smiling. "The computers flagged the transactions. We didn't use any personal information."

"Did you get judicial permission to track these transactions?"

"It wasn't necessary. The computers just flagged the transaction based on patterns. They didn't access any of the individual accounts or tap into otherwise confidential or private information."

"How did you identify these individuals?"

115

"It turns out the identification process was easy: the people making the withdrawals were midgets—err, little people."

"How did you determine that the transactions you flagged were illegal?"

"We sent a team of investigators to the banks and interviewed tellers and bank officials. We identified the individuals making the transactions using security video footage and then used our agency database to make positive IDs."

"You didn't answer the question. How did you determine the source of the cash was illegal?"

"After identifying the individuals, we searched our databases at the DEA, FBI, CIA, and Interpol. In each case, the individuals had Social Security numbers, which allowed us to track their credit histories, drivers' registrations, home addresses, and employment histories. All public information in various state and local government databases. From this investigation, we found that the individuals identified in our investigation did not have any record of home addresses or employment histories for the past five years. Thus, we determined they were employed out of the United States, but they did not have passports issued by the U.S. Department of State."

"What is the basis for determining that their activities were illegal?" Joy looked at Getko and stepped closer to him.

Getko cocked his head to let her know he picked up on her attempt to ramp up the pressure. "Once we identified the individuals, we tracked their activities. They traveled from Miami to the Caribbean. They spent four days in a remote resort area near Port Elizabeth. This is a known courier point for Venezuelan drug traffickers who serve as middlemen for several Latin American drug trafficking organizations."

"Association isn't enough to prove a link," said Joy.

"During this period," Getko continued, "the CTF identified and confirmed three separate, unauthorized flights by private pilots into a remote airstrip on the back of the island. Within three hours of the last flight, the suspects returned to Miami and boarded a plane to New York City."

Joy's jaw dropped, as if her next words were stuck on the back of her tongue. That information wasn't in her files!

Getko's gaze was now hard and direct, gauging her reaction to this information. Joy stepped back and drew her shoulders up straight as she kept her focus on Getko. "That still doesn't link them to the North Pole."

Getko snorted a smile as Joy regained her authority in the interview.

"The suspects changed planes at JFK in New York and flew to Montreal. Then we tracked their activities to a flight to Anchorage (via Calgary). The Alaska branch office of the FBI tracked them to a bush pilot. When the bush pilot reappeared, the suspects were not on the plane. The last known point of the plane according to FAA controllers was fifty miles east of the North Pole."

"What happened to the suspects?"

"We are confident they are part of an elaborate drug trafficking ring with a hideout on the polar ice cap."

"The polar ice cap?" Joy asked, raising her hands as if to say, "Really?"

"Yes, the polar ice cap. It's brilliant. The CTF would not be expected to look for a laundering ring in the arctic. Over a period of nine months, we tracked three dozen similar movements by groups of people. Six months into the investigation, however, we realized the trips were starting in Los Angeles, in an area of the downtown commonly referred to as Toytown. The subjects passed through Toytown and then moved on to Miami and then the Caribbean islands."

Joy was stuck. "Okay, Agent Getko. Why move now?"

"We've accumulated enough information to establish a pattern of illegal activity forming a triangle. The North Pole is the peak of the triangle and, we believe, the nerve center of the entire operation. Los Angeles serves as the point of first contact for couriers, using immigrant communities in L.A.'s film industry and Toytown as a cover. Securities and cash are then moved from banks in L.A. to banks in Miami. There, the money is withdrawn and laundered to drug dealers in the Virgin Islands, using resort vacations as cover."

Joy's head popped up. "But why move now?" Her heart skipped as she realized this might be the key to stopping Operation Jamaican Snow. Getko would have to answer this question, to get authorization to mobilize the interagency forces.

Getko hesitated, then said, "We have evidence that their operation may be dismantled soon."

Joy drew in her breath. Getko noticed her lull, and the sparkle in his eyes showed he was reveling in the trap he had sprung.

"What evidence?" Joy demanded, dropping any pretense of the mock briefing.

"Someone in the arctic operation has uncovered parts of the CTF investigation."

Blood rushed to Joy's brain.

"It's only logical," Getko continued, training his stare into Joy's eyes. "They have to move their operation quickly to avoid detection. Moving on Operation Jamaican Snow now is critical to shutting this drug triangle down."

Getko's face radiated. Joy was stunned. How could all this have happened without her knowledge? Why couldn't she pick this up through her own investigation? He must have a mole!

"Thank you, Joy!" Getko said. "You've done an excellent job prepping me. Colson will have no choice but to go along with my plan."

Joy turned toward the wall. She wanted to scream. If Getko had any inkling she wasn't on board with his plan, she would be filing papers in a back office—DEA's Fox Mulder without any benefit of aliens, extraterrestrial cases, or files she could label with a big X!

Getko shoved his memos and papers into his briefcase and grabbed the thick file of evidence Joy had given him. "Joy, you've been great. I'll definitely make sure your file reflects the brilliance and diligence of your work." He looked up at her and smiled, silently signing off on her promotion. Then, he left the room.

As the door clicked closed, Joy sank into the closest chair, her hands holding her head to keep it from hitting the floor. What would she do now?

22

"We can't afford a failure."

The deputy administrator's tone was firm and authoritative. It wasn't a warning; it was an order.

"Yes, sir. I understand," said Miles Getko.

"Jesus, this is risky. How confident are you that the base of operations is at the North Pole? The North Pole! Of all places, Getko! What do I tell my kids? That Santa Claus is a drug dealer?"

Getko almost smiled at the thought of turning such a popular myth on its head. "That's the beauty of their scheme. No one would think that Latin American drug gangs would run their operations through the polar ice cap."

"It's still hard to believe, and I've seen the evidence, nearly a year of work by your analysts burrowing in the bowels of this building. How could they maintain an outpost up there? It's an ice desert. Nothing lives up there."

The deputy administrator's physical size gave him a naturally tough edge, something that had helped him win confirmation in the U.S. Senate. No one believed a former, all-pro football tackle couldn't also be a hard-charging, drug law enforcer. But Getko had seen his boss's softer underbelly before, and he had never been convinced of his commitment to putting dealers in jail. Was he really going to put this operation on hold because of a myth?

"Satellites and remote sensing have identified sporadic breaks in the intense cold and evidence of a possible human settlement," said Getko, laying out the photos of the earth from 1,500 miles above. The two men leaned over a knee-high table, peering over the images. The administrator looked awkward as his gluttonous gut unfurled over his belt, and he tried to keep his butt secure in his overstuffed office chair. His situation became more precarious with each photo Getko laid down, explaining the plot and the plan, as charts overran the photos in their race to consume the table top. Getko kept calm, barely containing his anxiety over the stakes if he failed. He had to overcome his boss's reluctance to commit to Operation Jamaican Snow.

Success was far from certain, but he knew millions of dollars in cocaine and marijuana off the streets would make it worth it. This operation was based on more than a hunch. He remembered the same warm, confident feeling he had during the Bimini Triangle operation. He looked at the satellite photo. Each image registered readings that showed irregular patterns of heat, often bursts in two or three locations around the North Pole.

The EPA scientists couldn't explain their source, although they speculated that the bursts represented methane gas breaking through cracks in the ice cap after being released from the ocean bed more than a mile below the surface. Another theory was fissures in deep-sea volcanoes, breaking through the Arctic Ocean floor. Given the shifting nature of the ice cap, they said it was almost impossible to pinpoint the actual source. The cracks closed up too soon for in-depth monitoring of the sites. Remote sensing and sonar had identified what appeared to be a hollowed out area about fifty miles east of the North Pole. The area was huge, about two and one half square miles, but the same staff scientists thought it was an optical illusion, unique to the environmental and climatic conditions of the polar ice cap. Besides, they hadn't found convincing evidence of continuous human activity.

Getko didn't buy it. He was trained in detecting the illusive patterns of people who didn't want to be seen or caught. After working the drug beat for almost twenty years, he specialized in identifying ways humans adapted to new and different environments. No drug dealer wants to be seen. Drug dealers could be the cleverest of all— they had to be to survive. If he had waited for statisticians and scientists to confirm the drug trafficker settlements in the Caribbean ten years ago, he never would have busted that cartel. He scanned the photos one more time. It was time to move and move fast.

"The whole scheme seems pretty weak," Getko's boss said, picking up a photo with two white splotches with black circles drawn around them, each with a label that said "anomalous burst."

Getko's breathing quickened. Colson could nix the entire operation with the wave of a finger or the stroke of a pen. He could even close down the CTF with the same pen.

Getko leaned on his left hip, quietly shifting his right foot under the table to loosen his muscles. He sent his brain searching through different scenarios with lightning speed, evaluating each case based on its sales potential, its impact on the size of the operation, and the score. CTF would become very well-funded, indeed.

Joy sat nearby, content to be ignored, as she waited for Getko to ask for more data, charts, or other material that might be needed at a moment's notice. Perhaps Getko had spent too much time in this room, she mused. He seemed unphased by its elegance and corporate veneer. She was intimidated by it and couldn't wait to get back to the secure, but open, cubical-like, teamwork area several floors below. A few blinking lights on a computer monitor seemed very comforting right now.

Getko laid down the outlines of the plan, emphasizing the resource needs for Operation Jamaican Snow: agents, officers, soldiers, arms, helicopters, and weatherized equipment, essentially anything that would be needed to win a fire fight at God-knows-what degree below zero. All his one-page form needed was the deputy administrator's approval.

Joy watched the deputy administrator spar with Getko as he moved through his presentation. Colson steadily rubbed his chin with his right thumb and forefinger, elbow on his right knee, and his left hand resting like a pillar on his left thigh. Colson was asking all the right questions, but Getko held his ground and answered each question with precision and facts. Some of those facts were pulled from her files. Others were pulled from… who knows where?

Stranger still, Joy thought, Colson seemed to be overly concerned with the political fallout that might accompany Operation Jamaican Snow. Of course, that seemed to befit a political appointee's demeanor and pedigree. These were people accustomed to fine tailored suits and policy discussions over lunch with "all the president's men." It was a consequence of the system of lobbying and counter-lobbying that appeared to grow the bank accounts of Congressmen and their families.

But Colson seemed worse than most appointees. He had a law degree (about as rare as cappuccino in Washington, D.C.), but no real experience in law enforcement. In fact, despite his cleanly shaven face, carefully groomed, brown hair, a football player presence, and a gruff demeanor, she couldn't find anything of substance in his background that would qualify him to run the DEA, or the investigative unit of any other federal agency with a law enforcement function.

Her own illegal background check on Colson revealed a pure "Blue Beltway" career: hot intern on Capitol Hill, special assistant to the director of the National Office of Drug Control Policy, chief counsel to Congress' special task force on drug control, and a lot of travel to drug trafficking hot spots. He seemed to have a particular affinity for the Caribbean and the warmer Latin American countries, too.

Getko was sitting like a minnow in Lake Superior, as the deputy administrator listened to every word and tracked every point on the images. Colson's office was immaculate and uncluttered, not at all like Joy's office, where she could disappear behind piles of reports, data readouts, and notes. Most people didn't know she worked at a 1940s-era metal desk—the design now emulated in wood and sold for lots of money by a Swedish furniture maker—and rows of metal filing cabinets, when she wasn't following blinking lights on that computer monitor in the control room.

But the administrator's office was different. Even her chair, like the one the administrator sat in, was thick, heavily cushioned, and uncomfortable. She glanced quickly near the conference table to make sure her two legal briefcases were in easy reach. Bookcases lined the walls of the deputy administrator's office with legal codes from key states and the federal government, but she was sure he didn't use the personal library very often. At least she could look out the picture window with a penthouse-like view of the Pentagon, as she waited out Getko's plea.

"It's still a pretty weak case," Colson said, tiring of Getko's argument. Joy's ears perked up. Was he going to reject Getko's request?

"Sir," Getko said, almost pleading. "We have a year of painstaking work poured into this case. You can see the money trail: North Pole to L.A. to Miami to North Pole. We've got two dozen people ready to sweep L.A. and Miami, but we need the nerve center in the North Pole for it all to work."

Deputy Administrator Colson was shaking his head again. "I see a pattern, but the dots don't connect nearly as easily for me as they do for you and your team." Colson glanced over to Joy, who sat waiting for orders from Getko. For a brief moment, their eyes connected, and Joy directed them down to the folds in her map. Why did he do that? Doesn't Miles want the chart showing the Triangle yet?

Colson's tone changed. "No, Miles, I'm not seeing the dots at all." Joy's heart sped up. "If this blows up, the president will feel the heat. And it's my job to protect the president."

"Joy," Getko said. "Give me the chart of the L.A.-Miami transactions." Joy flipped through the folder marked CHARTS, grateful to have something to do, and handed them over.

"Here sir, let me show you some of the data we collected."

"Wait a minute," Colson said, leaning back in his chair and lifting his hand to stop the presentation. "You've got to appreciate our situation. What you are asking for is unprecedented in DEA history. In fact, nothing like this has ever been contemplated outside the plot for Ice Station Zebra. They probably haven't even dreamed this up for James Bond, but that's probably because their writers are still stuck in the 1980s."

Joy smiled at the quip but quickly painted a businesslike expression across her face.

"There's a downside to this I don't think you fully appreciate," Colson said. "This is a very expensive operation. We have staff in Southern California and in the Caribbean. We don't have the agents up north. We would have to re-assign staff and agents from the FBI and Customs Service. You're also asking for Special Forces, right? That's going to mean the involvement of a Four Star in this operation, and I really don't want generals poking into our affairs. How do we explain this to the Canadians? Russia's going to have a field day with this at the United Nations if word gets out. The budget for this operation alone, if it goes according to plan and doesn't degenerate into a shooting war, will run at least $100 million. How do we know we'll get a pay off? How can you be so sure that this is the nerve center of this operation?"

Getko didn't skip a beat. "Sir, this discussion is feeding right into the plans of the drug traffickers. We've been asking these questions, too, and we wouldn't be here unless we felt we had answered these questions adequately enough to justify such a large reallocation of law enforcement dollars, staff, and resources. These guys have put up an amazingly complicated operation. They want to keep us guessing, to question ourselves, to paralyze us with doubt so that we won't take action."

Joy shook her head in disbelief.

"Maybe so," Colson said, lifting up the folder marked FINANCIAL REPORT: MONEY LAUNDERING: L.A. & MIAMI. "But you need to understand the risks. If this mission fails, it could jeopardize the budget of this agency and every other operation for the remainder of this president's administration, and probably the next. The DEA will effectively be shut down for a decade, reduced to arresting drug users for possession, and going after street-corner dealers."

Getko hesitated, blinked twice, and then refocused on Colson. "On the other hand, if we're right, we will make a major dent in the world drug trade."

Colson closed his eyes. "How do you know? Remember when we busted up the Medellin and Cali cartels in the early eighties and nineties? Cocaine processing just shifted to Guatemala and Venezuela. We busted up the Middle Eastern heroin market only to see it shift to Thailand and Cambodia. When we shut down trafficking through Miami, the drug runners shifted to Texas and Southern California. How can I authorize a multimillion dollar operation with no real evidence it will make a dent in drug running?"

Joy sat back in her chair. This might be the end for Operation Jamaican Snow.

"We don't have a choice," Getko insisted.

Of course he has a choice, Joy protested to herself. He can pull the plug on the operation at any time. Surely Colson could see that. After all, he's a political animal, and politicos stop risky operations all the time.

"Explain," Colson ordered Getko, miffed by his aggressiveness.

"This is the Drug Enforcement Administration," Getko said. "We are charged with enforcing the drug laws in this nation. A key component of that is stopping the supply of illegal drugs entering this country. Our mandate does not say: 'reduce the supply of drugs when the budget allows for it.' The mission is general, and the political foundation for our tactics is solid. Almost all states allow for aggressive law enforcement when it comes to drug trafficking, even seizing property they believe was used during the commission of a crime, when the link has not been proven beyond a reasonable doubt. We have an office established within the executive branch whose sole purpose is to coordinate federal, state, and local resources to maximize their ability to achieve this mission."

"I know all this," the deputy administrator fired back. "Remember Getko, I wrote most of those laws."

Good, thought Joy. He was becoming impatient with Getko. This meeting should end soon, and they could all get back to real detective work.

"Yes sir, I am very well aware of that, but we have to consider the very points you raised. First, drug traffickers are nimble. They are masters of disguise. They also have no values of any relevant kind. They would front their operations through their grandmother's church basement if they thought they could get away with it. So, a North Pole operation would be exactly the kind of cover we would expect the cartels to shift to, given our success in the Caribbean.

"Second, as good as the state and locals are at pursuing the drug war, some things will always be federal. This is one of those cases. The operation is international and requires resources no state or local law enforcement agency could front."

Joy's hopes ebbed as she watched Colson's face hang on Getko's words.

"Third, if we don't stop this triangle, another agency will step in. The long-term effects on the DEA would be debilitating. Do we really want the customs office to control drug investigations? Do we want Interpol to become the lead agency? We have the experience, expertise, and leadership to wage this war here. Operation Jamaican Snow will solidify our position. If we fail, we have plenty of evidence to back up this operation. The risks of not authorizing Jamaican Snow are far greater—operationally and politically—than not pursuing it now."

Getko's boss sat in silence, digesting the entirety of his argument. Joy's heart fell into her stomach. She didn't have to hear Colson give Getko the verbal authorization, or see him sign the memo authorizing joint force to begin mentally preparing for the mission that would radically change her life. The fact that she knew the outcome before anyone in the room weighed heavily as she collected the folders and walked out.

23

Getko was giddy with excitement as he approached the elevator. "What a great victory for the CTF." He turned to Joy and grabbed her arm. "What a great victory for you and your team!"

Joy didn't say anything. In fact, she wasn't sure she heard him, his voice distant and faint in the echo chamber she had sent him to in her brain. Her head twirled with thoughts of a disaster—the world economy, foreign policy, interagency operations, international partnerships—all disasters that could tumble from the fateful decision made today.

"Joy?" Getko stepped into the elevator, pulling her by the elbow. The meeting had lasted well past 6:00 p.m., and they were alone. "What's wrong? This is a great opportunity."

Joy remained silent, as if she had left the world of the DEA and U.S. Department of Homeland Security.

"Perhaps you should stay in the home office on this one," Getko said as the elevator beeped past floors.

"No!" Joy startled herself by the outburst, and the look on Getko's face suggested he was far more surprised than she. "No," she repeated in a more subdued voice, shaking her head. "No, I'm sorry Miles. I was just thinking of Jamaican Snow—we've got a lot of work to do."

An electronic beep signaled the end of the ride. The elevator doors opened and Joy scrambled to lug her briefcases stacked on her dolly over the elevator threshold and into the hallway. She felt like a circus clown as she tugged at the dolly, banging cases against the doors and walls as they made their way back to Getko's office.

"Okay, let's create an operation checklist," Getko said, once they were in his office.

"When will the funds be authorized?" asked Joy.

"Overnight. Once Colson gave the verbal okay, I started the paperwork. I already have the authorizations underway at Homeland Security and the Canadian Embassy."

Joy's head shot up. "When did you start that?"

"Planning," Getko said, smiling, pointing a finger to his head. "Planning and forethought, Joy."

Joy's shoulders slumped; the operation was well ahead of their timetable for rolling out. Why hadn't she anticipated this?

"Come on, Joy," Getko said, noticing her ambivalence. "We are about to embark on an adventure that will make your career in this agency! Trust me, I know; it happened to me."

"Oh, I know," Joy lied. "I'm just having trouble shifting gears from research to operations."

Getko nodded. "No problem. I know it's tough, moving from the cubical to the field. But it's exciting!"

Joy was puzzled by Getko's special interest in her. She was the computer nerd, not the action figure that springs into motion when her button is pushed. She liked the agency-issue gun slung in her shoulder holster under her jacket, but her only experience with firing it was during safety training at the shooting range. Ten rounds every other month. She practiced to keep herself familiar with the gun. Now, she didn't relish the idea that she might have to use it and began to doubt her enthusiasm for going into the field.

"Let's go over the satellite photographs," Joy said, pulling out several large pictures. Pointing to a big "X" on the photograph she said, "Here's the North Pole."

Getko traced his finger from the North Pole to three dots about fifty miles east. "And here are the heat readings." He tapped the three spots, which traced a triangle of about two-and-a-half square miles south by southeast of the North Pole.

"But those heat points are transient," Joy pointed out. "How can we be sure that is where their base of operations is?"

"The hot spots are transient but consistent. They appear too often to be random."

Joy bristled at Getko's invocation of a statistic term. "Statistically speaking?"

"Expertly speaking. I've talked to polar climatologists, and that's their opinion."

Joy looked at Getko. "Why didn't you tell me about this? This kind of information is critical for our assessments. We can't make recommendations unless we have all the information."

"True." Miles began to write in a notepad. "But I had the information."

"I'm supposed to make recommendations to you based on evidence," Joy said. "I can't do that without having this kind of information."

"Joy, I'm the one ultimately making the decisions around here. I use the information as I see fit. If I feel it's in the best interests of the investigation to withhold some information from my investigators, I'll do it. It's my responsibility, not yours. Got that?"

The one thing Joy couldn't do was turn off the defiance in her eyes, but she knew she had better button up. Joy reached into her file case, glaring at Getko in a visual show down, and pulled out her notepad.

"Your sources tell you these hot spots are human made," Joy continued. "Why do they disappear?"

"We couldn't figure that out. The climatologists really couldn't explain it. It took us a while before we figured it out." Getko searched through another pile of black and white pictures and picked up two showing little people. He pounded his fingers on the two pictures.

Joy picked them up. "One's in L.A., and the other's in Miami."

"Right," Getko said. "Then, we saw these." He picked up two new pictures. One picture had five or six little people in it; the other included a mix of taller people and little people.

"Toronto," Joy said.

"Exactly," Getko confirmed. "Guess where these little people are going?"

Joy looked perplexed. "Oz?" *Does he really think drug traffickers are in a global conspiracy with little people?*

Getko grinned. "Anchorage."

"Anchorage?" Joy felt the beat of her heart quicken.

"Joy, look at the pattern. These little people are making the deposits, spending the money, and flying all over the country, including Anchorage. But we weren't able to track them once they got to Anchorage. They just… disappeared."

128

"They can't just disappear."

"Somehow they do! We don't know how or where they go."

Joy could feel the muscles in her arms tense, and she became self-conscious of what seemed like slow-moving fingers as she thumbed through the photos. Miles knows something. "So, what's the connection?"

"The North Pole!" Getko exclaimed, throwing up his hands. "The key is the North Pole! They aren't on the ice—they're below it!"

"Miles! Do you know what a stretch that is? You just admitted you didn't know where they went. We don't have any independent confirmation of their final destination or location."

"Joy," Getko said, bringing his fingers together to make a tent, or a prayer, as he peered at her over their tips. "Think outside the box. Look at your own data. Here are the bank accounts and the transactions. Look at the connections. The amounts tell the story. The money comes into seven separate accounts at the L.A. Bank from deposits by Ebson and Associates. Each is logged as a deposit from a different toy company in Toytown. Most of the money—89.5 percent according to your calculations—stays in these L.A. bank accounts. Then, we see a pattern of three withdrawals of between $5,000 and $9,500 over three days, each drawing from a different account."

"Right," Joy said, thumbing through the spreadsheets, then pushing the hair out of her eyes. "But note the withdrawals are not connected to the Miami accounts."

"Yes, they are," Getko said. "The deposits in Miami are made about three days after the last withdrawal from the L.A. bank."

"But the deposit amounts are different."

"But the total deposit is within 10 percent of the total withdrawal from the L.A. bank," Miles observed.

Joy shook her head as she looked at the different sheets of papers with numbers and transaction amounts.

Getko dropped his hands to the table. "How much do you think it would cost for three people to travel to Miami?"

Joy's eyebrows raised in sudden recognition: "Between $2,000 and $3,000, depending on if they took the train, flew, or rented a car, and what kinds of hotels they stayed in."

"Right," Getko said, relief allowing his face to relax. "The money goes into the Miami bank, using one of another seven accounts and is wired to the Caribbean. Unfortunately, since it's an off-shore account, we can't track it."

"I don't get the North Pole connection," Joy said.

"Our surveillance has tracked the little people from Miami to New York, then on to Toronto, and then Anchorage," Miles continued. "Each has an airline ticket purchased in advance, presumably from a travel agent in the islands. It's not online because our Internet surveillance hasn't been able to find the transactions."

Joy looked at Miles, trying to hide her disgust. "Those searches are illegal."

Miles set his jaw. "This work is necessary."

Joy checked herself. "Okay Miles, suppose this is in fact a classic money laundering case. What's the connection to the North Pole?"

Miles pulled more satellite photos onto the table, laying them over the expanding clutter. They plopped onto the pile as if to emphasize the final step in his logic. "Look at these maps. Note that the most intense hot spots are in the same place each time."

Joy's heart sank. Miles had connected the dots all too well. She looked up at the dates on the satellite photo and compared them to the photo from Anchorage. "Twenty-four hours. Are they all within twenty-four hours of each other?"

"Yes," said Miles, his voice edging up with excitement.

"Are the patterns the same for the L.A. deposits?" Joy's head continued to spin.

"Bingo."

Joy drew in a deep breath and let it out slowly. "It's very clever." She looked up at Miles. "But it's still circumstantial."

Joy stepped back as she felt Getko's anger rise behind his desk, knowing she had pushed him too far. She clutched a folder of satellite photos, as if they were a shield.

"Joy, I'm taking you off this case."

"Miles, you can't!"

Getko's eyes seemed to bore a hole through Joy's forehead. "I can do anything I damn well want to with this task force!"

"No, Miles, that's not what I meant!"

"You're dismissed." Getko waved her off toward the door. "I don't want you as part of this operation any longer."

"Miles, no, please; I've worked so hard on this project—six months!"

"Joy, I can't have someone on this team who doesn't believe in the mission."

"But I do!"

Getko turned to her again. "Joy, I can't have anyone on this team who doesn't believe in me."

Joy stood in numbed silence. She looked down at the photos, and with deliberation, refiled them in her briefcase. She gave a short, heavy sigh. She looked up at Special Agent Miles Getko. "I thought you brought me on board to question you, to make sure every decision and plan was carefully thought out. That's the role I thought you had given me. I'm sorry; I must have misunderstood your directive."

Getko was silent. She was right.

24

The hallway was just as sterile and cold as the first time Peter escaped into it, but this time, as he followed Nicole out of Sheila's hospital room, he didn't mind. He looked for Wells, half expecting him to jump out of nowhere and handcuff him, but nothing seemed to disturb the air. Two men stood outside the door, but Nicole clearly had more pull than Cutler. Peter cast a quick glance toward Sheila's room as the door clicked shut.

"Don't worry," Nicole said, although Peter didn't even look at her. "Sheila will be fine. We aren't going too far away."

A guard outside the door dutifully lifted his hand. Peter noticed that the first guard, a burly man of almost six feet, had been replaced by a dwarf. His small size didn't seem to diminish his presence. He projected strength, aggressiveness, and command. Peter had the clear feeling this dwarf could take out an entire platoon of Army Rangers with little effort.

"It's okay, George; Mr. Peary's coming with me. Can you tell Jeff for me? He can track us with the remote sensors."

The guard looked suspiciously at Nicole, one arm by his side and the other tucked behind his back.

"What?" Nicole asked. "Do you want a note from my mother?"

No, Peter mused, *but maybe a note from Jeff Wells would work.*

"You know my orders, Ms. Klaas. Mr. Peary is not supposed to go anywhere without the written consent of Mr. Wells."

Peter struggled to contain a smile, but he thought the hair on the back of Nicole's neck was standing on end. George didn't seem to notice. Or care. He stood his ground, eyes focused on Peter. Peter couldn't see a gun or other weapon, but he had the sense that weapons probably were not important to George's job. He could probably take down anyone he wanted, anytime, with or without weapons. Peter's mind raced. Now that he thought of it, he hadn't noticed weapons on any of the security guards. Not even Wells. For some reason that didn't make Peter breathe any easier.

"George," Nicole said, her tone steady. "Who does Wells work for?"

"NP Enterprises."

"Well?"

"Ms. Klaas, with all due respect, I work for Mr. Wells."

Nicole paused, mouth open, then laughed. "Yes, you do. And I'm not forgetting that. But George, I need to take Mr. Peary some place urgent. As you can tell, I am not being forced to go. Mr. Peary doesn't have any weapons. And, as you know, there is nothing in his file or psychological profile that gives him the power of mind control or hypnosis."

Peter fumed. Has everyone read his file?

George chuckled. "I know Ms. Klaas, but you know I have my orders."

"Yes, George, and I will tell Mr. Wells that you are performing your duties exceptionally well. I assure you, this is perfectly fine. NP Security will be tracking every move."

George didn't move, but his eyes softened. "Well, okay, Ms. Klaas. But I'm going to report this to Mr. Wells right away."

"I would expect nothing less," Nicole said. "Thank you, George."

The pair moved down the hall, leaving George at the door as he tapped a message into an electronic device Peter assumed was a phone or PDA. Soon, they had turned the corner and were out of George's sight, but Peter had the distinct sense he was being watched, followed, or tracked anyway.

As they walked down the corridor, Peter noticed the now-common mix of normal sized humans and dwarves. As best he could figure, about one-quarter of the hospital staff—nurses and doctors—were dwarves. Why didn't he see more of them in his regular life? Had they all moved to this desolate outpost?

"What's with the little people?"

Nicole smiled, guiding him by his arm. "You'll get used to them. They're our greatest asset. Of course, most would rather not be here."

"I thought you said everyone was here of their own free will."

"They are, but for many dwarves, like most people, they would rather be in sunny, warm climates like Miami, not the frigid North Pole."

Peter sent a skeptical glance toward Nicole. "Why are they here?"

"We offer them more opportunity here than they can get south of the border."

"How could this place offer them more opportunity?"

Nicole stopped and looked at him in disbelief. She shook her head, as if talking to a grade school child. "Peter, when was the last time you saw a little person?"

Peter's unfocused expression was enough for her to conclude the answer was *never*, and she pulled him forward again.

"Exactly," said Nicole. "To most people, like you, little people are invisible except for Christmas, Halloween, and in the spring."

Peter nodded. "Spring. Tornado season. *The Wizard of Oz.*"

"Right. If you're a little person, the first thing someone thinks about is a hoard of Munchkins, looking in wonder at a naïve, little girl dropped down in the middle of their town after a horrendous storm. All the little people gather around Dorothy, staring in some sort of metaphysical awe, as if they can't understand that physics killed the Wicked Witch, not some supernatural power vested in a teenage girl from Kansas—or her little rat of a dog."

"That's a little simplistic. Most people don't judge people based on how they are depicted in a movie, especially one as fantastical as *The Wizard of Oz.*"

"Tell that to Julia Roberts, Madonna, Jennifer Lawrence, Halle Berry, or any other celebrity!" Nicole's gait slowed as she thought. "Most people don't form an opinion about an entire class of people based on how they're projected onto the silver screen. No, the images themselves reflect those prejudices. The prejudices define the characters, not the other way around."

Peter continued to follow Nicole, his thought slowing his pace, as the doors to hospital rooms seemed to fade into the walls.

"How many times do you see dwarves projected as anything other than weird little people, just one step or job away from the circus?" She continued, a tinge of bitterness lacing her words. "Did you see *The Wolf of Wall Street*? They used little people as human darts. Seinfeld had a decent character for a few episodes, but those parts are few and far between. Mini Me was a literal shadow of Dr. Evil. When was the last time you were treated by a dwarf doctor? Lawyer? Can you honestly tell me that you wouldn't instinctively question their competence if you did? Most people would have to rationalize their way out of their prejudice. Sort of like a man seeing a woman doctor."

Peter's cheeks flushed as he thought of his first reaction to Fred and his exchange with Ron Cutler. "Come on, Nicole, that's not really fair. There aren't that many dwarves around, so you can't blame most of us for being a little skeptical. It's normal."

"Exactly." Nicole's frustration clipped her words. "You don't see dwarves around in your everyday life; they're not 'normal.' So, it's easy for the prejudice to keep little people at bay, and everyone can rationalize their way around it so they can sleep at night."

"I still think you're a bit harsh."

"Maybe, but I work with these people every day. Most everyone here is creative and hard working. And, honestly, I get a little angry thinking that some of the world's best software engineers, business owners, doctors, lawyers, all manner of professionals and laborers, have to come all the way here, to the North Pole, to get respect. Even then, they get respect only here. Once they leave, they go back to fighting for it every day of the week, every time they cross the threshold of a new office building."

Peter walked in silence for a few more minutes, hoping the cool air would calm Nicole's attitude once they were outside. "Thank God for the Internet!"

Nicole laughed. "Yes! The Digital Age is giving them opportunity and freedom that they couldn't buy with all the money in the world in the Lower Forty-Eight."

All the activity Peter had seen around the town began to make sense. The pieces of the puzzle weren't so jagged after all. This wasn't a fairy tale. This wasn't an illusion or a dream. This was a working city.

Peter chuckled. "There are 'elves' at the North Pole."

"Yes, Peter, there are elves at the North Pole. But they aren't the elves of myth. They are real people, with real skills, real aspirations, and real needs. They didn't just appear here. Everyone has their own history, their own story. They are here, like all migrants, in search of opportunity. If opportunity isn't here when they arrive, they make it. You've met Rowdy if you need proof of that."

"They aren't elves," Peter said.

Nicole smiled again. "I think you're beginning to get it, Peter R.B. Peary. No, they most definitely are not elves."

25

Peter and Nicole descended the hospital stairs without speaking. Could Peter be for real? Nicole couldn't help but feel warm inside as she opened the door and they stepped into the cool, dark air.

Peter now saw the darkness enveloping the village in a new light. This was a full-fledged city operating under the arctic tundra. But how? The ice wasn't that thick. How could they go undetected like this? He still wasn't sure if he was ready to ponder the enormity of this achievement, but it was coming together, slowly.

"Thirty thousand," said Nicole after they had left the building and started down the frost-covered sidewalk.

"Thirty thousand?"

"That's the U.S. population of dwarves, as best we can tell."

Peter looked around. The streets were busy again, and he could see dwarves and others bustling in and out of shops. This time, all the activity had a bizarre normalcy. That worried him—he seemed to be developing an affinity for this weird, mystical place.

"Hah," he said chuckling in a low voice. "It seems like every dwarf in the world lives here!"

Nicole laughed. "Sometimes it seems that way. My company estimates that about 10 percent of the adult dwarf population in the U.S. works for my company, or their employment is directly tied to businesses in this town. Most appreciate the opportunities they have and don't want to risk exposing it. Besides, we pay well. That's the benefit of a billion-dollar global enterprise!"

She glanced over at Peter, letting her hair fall to the side of her face. "Stock options help. If anyone blows the whistle, their pension and income become dust. Or, more like melts away."

Peter grinned. "This is incredible. But how?"

Nicole caught her breath. "No one really planned it. It just happened."

Peter shook his head. "This is way too fantastic to 'just happen.' None of my expeditions 'just happened.' We had to plan to the most finely grained detail. Wasn't this someone's vision?"

Nicole snickered. "My great-grandfather, Nicholas Klaas, really didn't like people. That's why he moved to Alaska more than one hundred years ago. He was Dutch. We never could figure out why he even married. It was probably just because he was expected to. He lived off the land and made wood carved figures that adventurers would buy to take home as souvenirs."

Peter thought of the jewelry, smocks, and scarves he had bought during his first expeditions. He bought their wares even though he knew it didn't make them rich, and the smiles on the faces of the children and their parents felt sincere when he paid them.

"My grandfather, Nicholas II, was a bit more social. He had kids and stepped up the wood carvings. First, he made toys for his kids, including my father, Nicholas III. Then, he found the Alaskan adventurers would buy more of his toys and animal figures to take home to their families and kids. Pretty soon, that's all my grandfather was doing. He opened a shop in Nome and sold enough stuff to keep the family afloat financially. Then, my father took over. That's when things got interesting. We got too big, but my father really didn't want to have to deal with anyone, especially the Alaskan state government. So he built a few shacks on the polar ice cap and started our town."

Peter shook his head even faster. "Don't you think you're missing a few steps?"

Nicole tossed Peter a curious look, like her story was the mundane history of a third grade textbook.

"Nicole, this town isn't just like any other town—it's under the ice!"

Nicole laughed. "You mean not all towns are under the ice?"

Peter was surprised at how comfortable he felt with Nicole. Once they left the hospital, the weight of expectation and escape seemed to lift. The town seemed to have an energy all its own, despite the darkness and cold. "How can you have something of this size and not be seen? This town is the size of Ridgeway or Bear Creek. It would probably rank in the top fifty biggest cities in Alaska."

"We would be fortieth," Nicole said. "We're actually bigger than the city of North Pole, which is a real suburb of Fairbanks."

"So you survive based on identity confusion with a suburb?"

Nicole laughed. "Let's just say our technology is a bit more advanced than most towns."

"You mean a Klingon cloaking device?"

Nicole's laugh was more like a howl this time as she envisioned the Star Trek species burrowing their space ships under the ice. "Not quite. It's actually a lot more basic than you might think. Think of our town as living in a giant igloo. The ice is a very good insulator. Our buildings are tight and super well-insulated. We really don't have much of a heat signature. We don't heat the outside, for obvious reasons, and all our energy is contained in the structures."

"But the ice is not that thick. It's just ten or thirteen feet thick."

Nicole lifted her hand to Peter's shoulder and gave it a gentle squeeze. "The ice ridges can be as high as sixty-five feet. Our buildings are very modest. They are human scale. We need twenty feet of clearance. Basically, a few very big refrigerators powered by water turbines in the right place can keep the ice solid enough to hold us and generate enough energy to keep the town alive, as long as the buildings are engineered to distribute the weight properly."

"You have very talented engineers."

"Someone else's prejudice is our gain in talent."

Peter walked in silence, mulling over Nicole's revelations, still unsure he could absorb the magnitude of what he was seeing with his own eyes and hearing with his own ears. "This is fantasy."

Nicole's smile was silent but could be detected nonetheless. "I don't work in fantasy. A few years ago, it was science fiction, but we're in the now."

Peter's brain whirred with thoughts and impressions. "Why the secrecy?"

Nicole stopped in front of a two-story building that seemed to take up an entire block. The building didn't have any identifying information and just a few windows that seemed to be covered and boarded up. "Here we are," she said, acting as if she hadn't heard the last question.

***

Nicole pulled a glove off her hand and pressed her thumb up against a finger pad on the wall. A yellow light flashed above the pad, and Nicole leaned forward. "Nicole," she said into the wall. The yellow light turned red. Nicole seemed confused.

"Jeff!" Nicole roared as a frenzied red light blinked on the touchpad. She turned away from the door. "He changed my password again!"

Peter couldn't keep from smiling. "A real practical joker!"

His smile disappeared once Peter realized what the practical joke really meant—Nicole wouldn't be able to show him the secret. He sighed, letting his eyes roll back into his head as he leaned back.

Nicole seemed more embarrassed than upset.

"Do you know what he changed the password to?" Peter asked, regretting he asked such a stupid question as soon as he uttered the last word.

Nicole looked at him and shook her head. "Yep." Nicole punched new numbers into the pad, pressing her thumb against it after each sequence. She sighed. "Well, I guess I don't have much choice." She stepped up to the door again and pressed her thumb onto the finger pad. The yellow light began to blink, and she moved her face close to the wall. She whispered a few inaudible words, careful to keep Peter at a distance.

"Come on Nic," Peter teased. "What am I going to do with your password? I don't have your thumb."

"Or my voice. Or my breath. It uses voice recognition, the thumb print, my DNA, and the password."

She sighed. "Okay, close your ears!" Nicole closed her eyes and said, "St. Nic, Inc.!"

The flickering light turned green, and a steady hum from behind the door clicked open the lock. Her faced tightened as she clenched her jaw. "I hate it when he plays tricks like that on me."

No you don't, Peter thought. *You love it.* Otherwise, he wouldn't play them on you.

Now, however, that was the least of Peter's concerns. They were going into a building that used state-of-the-art security technology. Something very precious was inside these walls, and he was about to find out why Nicole Klaas and Jeff Wells were going to such great lengths to conceal it from everyday people.

26

Peter struggled to sort through his emotions as he walked through the door of the nondescript, unnamed building. He was a prisoner, and each step seemed to take him deeper into his prison. Yet Nicole was driven by a sense of justice and compassion he hadn't seen in someone for a long time, perhaps ever. Perhaps the answer lay in this building, but he couldn't see anything that looked like a clue as he passed over the threshold. Like the others, the building was encased in two floors of wood siding. He could now see that the cloud cover he thought was obscuring the night sky was in fact the ceiling of the gray colored ice of the cave, protecting the town.

Inside, Peter scanned the hall for evidence of the secretive work conducted inside its walls. The halls were frugal, even in comparison to the sterile design of the hospital. The light was dimmer, and Peter figured that added to the dullness of the atmosphere. He looked forward. The pathway was short, ending at a security post about 100 feet away. A head bobbed up from the desk, as if waiting for them.

Within seconds, Nicole and Peter were facing yet another dwarf. The guard wore a uniform this time, and Peter could just make out a patch on her arm with three big letters: "NPS". A long sleeved white shirt covered her arms, while a navy blue, traditional, high-neck turtleneck sweater seemed to crop her face. Her brown hair was pulled back in a ponytail. Her expression wasn't quite as severe as George's, but Peter knew she was looking at them with equal suspicion.

"Good afternoon, Nicole."

"Hello, Juanita. This is Mr. Peary. He'll be my guest inside today."

"Yes, ma'am." Juanita looked at Peter then deployed her eyes into a search of every pocket and crease of his clothes. "Mr. Peary, may I have your thumb please?"

Peter extended his hand, and Juanita guided it into a small box and pressed it up against a smooth plastic touch pad. Peter felt his finger settle in a rounded, depressed groove. Juanita punched a series of buttons. A plastic card popped out.

"Here you go," she said, inspecting it for defects before handing it to Peter. "Clip it onto your shirt pocket and make sure it's visible at all times. Not that it matters. We can detect it under just about anything a normal person would wear. We just like to see it—to avoid any 'complications.' It expires in four hours."

Peter looked at the card and turned it over in his hands. His picture was emblazoned on the left side. On the right side was a dark plastic square. In between were vital statistics: birth date, height, weight, eye color, occupation. "How—?"

Juanita just chuckled. "We have ways!" she said with exaggerated eyes and mocked seriousness.

Nicole smiled and shook her head, as she started to pull Peter past the guard post and toward another door. "Don't worry. It's all information in the public domain. We didn't violate your privacy. Besides, the information on display disappears once the chip on the card expires. The black square is your finger print. You'll need to run it through a scanner at each of the doors."

"This is all a bit too James Bond."

Juanita scowled at Peter as he passed her station.

Nicole cast a tolerant smile toward Juanita and sent Peter a smirk with the roll of her eyes. "Juanita's been around as long as I have. We practically grew up in this building. She's seen the system work—and fail."

"Yeah, Mr. Peary, don't think you can stray too far without Nic. The pass has a sensor that tracks every move you make in the building. We know where you are every second."

"Don't think about throwing the ID away, either," Nicole instructed him. "By touching it, you activated a chip that allows our computers and security system to track you through a map of the heat your body gives off. Each person has a unique heat signature that our computers trace in real time. It works particularly well in this town, because temperatures are cool enough that even small differences in heat are magnified under the ice."

Peter's head was spinning. "You seem to have it covered."

Nicole's smirk melted as a frown purged the mirth from her eyes. "We've had our share of near-death experiences."

Peter approached another door behind Juanita's security post. Nicole passed her ID through the scanner, and they entered another corridor. This one was much better lit, and Peter could see doors on both sides of the hallway. They were also numbered, and some included names with titles for directors, managers of operations, software development, global and domestic distribution, personnel, legal affairs—all manner of departments and functions for a large corporation. He wondered if those doors led to offices, other corridors, or new chambers.

Peter and Nicole walked. And walked. The corridors seemed endless, more like a maze than a route to a final destination. At last, they approached an unmarked door. Nicole scanned her ID and then signaled to Peter to scan his. Peter raised his eyebrows.

"It needs both of us to scan the cards." Nicole looked at him, bemused as he fumbled with his ID card. "It's tactile and visual. It also has a subordinate, audio function that matches voice to our security database. It can only prevent an unauthorized person from getting in, not confirm a person is legitimate. That's what the ID card does."

Peter didn't understand, but containing his excitement at finding out what was on the other side of the door was becoming an emotional burden. At first, he couldn't figure out which end was up. Then he saw a glowing arrow, pointing in one direction and slid the ID card through the scanner. Nothing happened.

"Try it again."

Peter slid the card a second time. Nothing. He hoped Nicole couldn't see his cheeks flush with embarrassment. How hard could this be? He used these stupid cards all the time at the dorms at Georgetown and in hotels! He thought Nicole was laughing at him even though he couldn't hear her chuckles.

"Faster. I really hope it works this time." Nicole seemed serious.

Peter looked at her and hesitated.

Nicole encouraged him with a nod. "Otherwise the alarms will go off, and all of NP Security will be on us in a nanosecond."

"No pressure, right?" Peter swiped the card a third time. The red light turned to a blinking, yellow light. After another second that seemed like minutes, the light turned green, and the door opened automatically.

Nicole caught Peter's sleeve and tugged him over the threshold.

27

Peter squinted as he stepped into a well-lit chamber, forcing his eyes to blink as they adjusted. He continued blinking for a moment, unsure of whether he had stepped into a parallel universe.

Any semblance of an isolated town under the ice was gone. Two rows of computer monitors faced a picture window that looked out over another five rows of computer terminals in another larger room, at least five feet lower. Dozens of people—dwarves and average-sized—skitted about from monitor to monitor, checking numbers and talking. A few more minutes allowed the picture to sharpen. Each person had a remote ear piece, and they were talking into telecommunications devices, reporting whatever they saw on their screens. Some screens had tables of numbers that appeared to update in real time. Others had maps and graphics that seemed to track the movements of little dots, some blinking, some constant. On the far side of the big room, an electronic map of the world was fixed to the wall, a hodgepodge of blinking and constant green, blue, yellow, and red lights. Peter couldn't see any obvious pattern, but they were clearly tracking something. Thousands of lights lit up the map and the room.

Peter's head was spinning. "What is this place? NASA?"

Nicole laughed. "Not a bad image, but NASA would envy our ability to track our products and services. NORAD would be a closer analogy, but I really think it's FedEx on steroids."

Nicole must have recognized that her comment flew over his head like a flock of seagulls scattering at the twitch of the unfamiliar on a beach. "I know it's probably hard for you to understand. It's kind of mind boggling, the logistics and all."

Nicole's patronizing tone sent Peter's blood streaming into his heart, but now was not the time for him to let his emotions take over. He had to focus. He had to understand.

Peter struggled for something to say, but the lights on the map, covering the entire expanse of the wall drew him in, focusing his attention, almost like a hypnotist putting a client under his spell. The image was a monster, and he sensed the lights still couldn't convey the enormity of what he was seeing. The maps, the lights, the scrolling numbers—this was big. This was much bigger than anything he could have imagined. And he didn't understand it. He didn't think he would ever be able to understand it.

"Nicole," Peter said, his voice vague and distant, "I don't know what's going on here, but this is awesome."

Peter's eyes danced at the sight of the technicians running from machine to machine, jabbering in jargon he couldn't follow. He continued to turn back to the map, like each new glance gave him even more insight into the universe in which he had stepped. Each country seemed to have blinking lights. Other lights seemed to peg cities. Some he recognized—Delhi, Boston, Mexico City, Seattle, Washington, D.C. Something massive was going on inside the room, and his senses reveled in the lights and images with a comfort and ease he had never experienced. The term "global" didn't capture his sense of awe. Galactic? Universal? Peter had never dreamed, seen, or sensed anything like it. The closest thing he could think of was the NASA control center that he toured as part of a special program for prodigies like himself. But he understood that. The processes, the software, the programming—it all made sense—at NASA. In this room, staying grounded was nearing impossibility. This was extraordinary, probably unique and un-replicable or replaceable, in this world at least. And they thought he was a threat to this? How could he possibly destroy this? He couldn't even understand it, let alone devise a plan to destroy it—and he knew he wouldn't want to even if he could.

Nicole stood without saying a word, as if unsure of what to say. The wonder in Peter's eyes was obvious. They sparkled with the same intensity as the photograph on Mount Everest.

"Well," she said, trying to gather her thoughts to hide her own surprise. This was supposed to be an analytical tour, not a spiritual revelation. Her gut told her bringing Peter into this room was the right thing to do. His concern for Sheila was not opportunistic. His connection to Sheila was deep. His spirit was....

Nicole practically screamed in her head. *How stupid!* "Ummm, this is... well..."

Peter was oblivious to her intervention. "Nicole," Peter said, eyes still directed toward the wall-size map. "What are you doing here?"

The question forced Nicole to step backward as if hit by a lead pipe. The answer—tracking the delivery of toys—seemed so trite she couldn't bring herself to say it. "I... uhh... why is that important?"

"I don't get it. Why are you doing this?"

Nicole stumbled, as she turned the question over in her mind. Did he mean NP Enterprises, or her? No one had asked her that question before. Everyone just assumed she would be here, stepping into her father's footsteps. "Uhh, we're adding a little sunlight to the lives of more than 100 million people."

"That's a marketing pitch for one of my expedition brochures."

Nicole turned away from him, embarrassed she didn't have a better answer. She looked at the numbers flowing across one of the giant screens. "We're up 30 percent from last year."

"What do you mean, 'up 30 percent from last year'?"

"We're growing," Nicole pointed out. "We've set growth targets of 20 percent per year in our strategic plan."

"Strategic plan? What plan? What are you talking about?"

"Okay, uh, sorry. I guess it's not that obvious. We live and breathe this every day, and we haven't had to explain it to many people. Every business has to grow. We set out strategic goals for the company—"

"What company?"

"NP Enterprises."

"NP Enterprises?"

"Yes," Nicole said impatiently, "NP Enterprises. North Pole Enterprises."

"Wait, hold up. What does NP Enterprises do?"

"We're a turnkey distribution company." Nicole looked at Peter as if she were pointing out the obvious. "We keep the global supply chain intact. What do you think all these computers are here for? The map?"

She could see the understanding finally sink into Peter's thinking as his brain continued to process everything around him. Distribution. All those lights and numbers were tracking packages and parcels. Logistics. Peter looked again at the terminals and operators buzzing into their audio remotes. They were connecting manufacturers to wholesalers to retailers. The operators were talking as they touched their screens, dragging icons from one location to another. Each operator was busy tracking movements and blinking lights and used a finger—sometimes three or four fingers—to move shipments from one location to another. In a daze, Peter picked out a glittering light on the map just as an operator touched a point on his screen. The light stopped blinking and moved on the wall map. "So, you're a very cold version of FedEx? But this is big. Way bigger."

Nicole's jaw dropped. What had she done? What if Wells was right, and Peter was an agent with the DEA, or—even worse—the Treasury Department?

"Umm," Nicole stammered, nodding as much to herself as she did to Peter. "This was a mistake. Come on, I'm taking you back to the hospital."

"No, you aren't."

"Uh, yes I am. I can call security, or you can come without my prodding."

"What? A dwarf is going to throw me out of this building?" Peter said, regretting the words as soon as he said them. He was sure George or Juanita could take him any day of the week.

Nicole turned to him, anger boiling through her glare. Peter closed his eyes, bracing for a slap in the face or a punch to the gut. Nicole cocked her hand, ready to sling it full force across Peter's cheek.

Nicole pulled her hand back to her side, aware that scores of eyes were bearing down on her. The expression of every technician in the control room seemed to ask her for an explanation for what they were seeing.

"Come with me," Nicole ordered. She didn't wait for Peter to move. She grabbed his arm and pulled him toward the door. Peter didn't resist, still overwhelmed by what he had seen. Nicole only hoped that he still didn't understand the full scope of what was inside that room. Peter's ignorance was her only hope. It was NP Enterprises' only hope.

28

The slam of the door behind them jolted Peter back into reality. They were back in the hallway, and she was pulling him. The draw of the room held him, like a tractor beam. For the first time he was resisting the forces tearing him away from this cave. He felt himself accepting the ones trying to keep him here. And he wanted answers to even more questions now bubbling over and clouding his brain.

"Hold on," Peter said in a soft voice that surprised even him. But Nicole continued to pull him toward the exit.

Peter planted his feet, bending his knees to use the force of his body to keep her from pulling him further. The move worked, forcing Nicole to a standstill, although she didn't look at him.

Peter looked toward the walls even though he knew he didn't have to worry about seeing her face or expression. "Look, I'm sorry. I was overwhelmed. The room—the control room—it was fantastic, incredible! I'm sorry. I may not have reacted appropriately."

"Mr. Peary, I will not tolerate anyone disrespecting my employees, my friends, or my family."

"Family?"

"Of course! What's wrong? You don't think big people and little people intermarry?"

"Well, of course they do," Peter lied; he had never thought about that before.

"This isn't the South," Nicole chided.

"The South isn't 'The South' anymore."

"*Touché.*" Nicole paused. She turned to Peter and leaned against the hallway.

Peter turned toward her. "Nicole, I'm sorry. I didn't mean to be disrespectful. I was a bit overwhelmed." He paused. "I want to know more. Can you answer a few questions?"

Nicole shook her head.

"Why not?"

"This was a mistake. I shouldn't have brought you here."

Peter stepped toward Nicole, placing a gentle hand on her shoulder as she looked toward the ceiling. Peter thought he could see the glisten of a newly formed tear. "Nicole, what are you afraid of?"

"It should be obvious." Nicole lifted her hand to wipe away the tear. "You're not as smart as I thought you were."

"I'm the same guy that was in the hospital room. The same guy you ordered your staff to heal—"

"I didn't order them to do anything!"

"I don't believe that!"

"Everyone stays here on their own free will. I don't own anyone. I can't tell anyone what to do. They are free to leave anytime they want!"

"Like me?"

"You're different."

"How? I'm human like them. I bleed like them."

"You didn't agree to come here," Nicole said. "You say you are here by accident, but I don't know that."

Nicole was too embarrassed to admit that Peter may be smarter, or at least cleverer, than she was. If he were DEA, she had magnified their problem beyond calculation.

Erase his memory, she thought. Well, she thought they could. But the procedure would be unprecedented. She would have to talk to Patten about setting up the paperwork. The legal details would be a nightmare. What if Cutler found out? And what would Rowdy think? Good Lord, this was going to be high profile, a real challenge to her leadership, but it had to be done. Her miscalculation had left her and NP Enterprises no choice.

"Nicole!" Peary yelled, seeing he had lost her attention. Her eyes snapped back to focus on him. "What's going on?"

"It should be obvious by now," Nicole said, stepping away and crossing her arms.

"I don't get it; spell it out."

Nicole looked toward the ground. If they could erase his memory, why shouldn't she tell him the truth? Wouldn't that be the real test of

151

whether Peter was a DEA agent? She continued to lean against the wall and angled her head up toward Peter. "Let's work through this. Where are you?"

Peter shook his head and let out a frustrated exhale. "I'm under the arctic ice cap."

"And we call this place...?"

"The North Pole."

"What did you see in that room?"

"Computers. Dozens of computers, maybe hundreds."

"And what else?"

Peter thought for a moment, a tightening in his chest making his growing annoyance harder to ignore. "An electronic wall map of the world."

"Okay, Mr. Explorer Man. Try to shake the cobwebs from your brain and use a little deductive logic."

Nicole pushed herself off the wall and squared her body in front of his. "Okay, Peter R. B. Peary. Let's try some word association."

Peter threw up his arms with a flailing, exasperated suddenness. "Shoot!"

Nicole lifted her forearms and hands as if to carve out a block of air for the first set of words. "North Pole," she said, using Peter's left arm to hold the air in place. Moving his hands to the right, she said, "ice." Peter shook his head.

"Little people: elves," she said, moving her hands from left to right again.

This preschool playgroup was just about all he could take. Then, Peter stopped. He shook his head, eyes hardened by sudden recognition.

"Computers: Reindeer."

Peter's jaw dropped. *Could this be...?*

"NP Enterprises: workshop."

Peter's jaw opened as his brain finally made connections that would short-circuit his most expensive laptop.

"Saint Nick," he said under his breath. "Saint Nic. Oh, Jesus. What are you telling me?"

Nicole placed her hands on his chest and gave him a gentle pat. "Yes, Virginia, there is a Santa Claus."

Peter felt like a little kid who had just discovered a new set of roller blades under the Christmas tree, the kind he had bugged his parents about for nine months, nonstop, and had given up hope of ever getting when he was eight. Or a Red Ryder® BB gun.

"But… how?" he stammered.

"You saw it," Nicole said.

"No, I'm beginning to see, but I still don't know how you achieved this."

"We couldn't do it without the microchip and the Internet."

"How long have you been doing this?"

"My great-grandpapa didn't get very far." Nicole stopped, unsure of whether to start. No one from the outside had ever been told the full story. Perhaps the time had come to spill the tale so entrenched in her family history and childhood. "He didn't come close to building this town. My grandpapa, Nicholas II was the one who really started to put the vision for this together."

"That still doesn't explain this." Peter used his arms to demonstrate the sweeping nature of the operation he had just seen. He straightened his shoulders. "This didn't just come out of the ether."

Nicole took in a breath. Peter was softening her, drawing her in. She felt lighter, relieved. He didn't know her story. Any of it. "We didn't get anywhere until my father began experimenting with personal computers. The microchip put us in business. Jack Kilby at Texas Instruments really did deserve the Nobel Prize as far as we're concerned.

"The first part of the plan expanded our craft business to sell to the Lower Forty-Eight. Then Dad started sending the carvings and toys to charitable organizations in the Midwest to make sure kids had toys for Christmas. They began to use us as a clearing house and our network expanded. Then, we started experimenting with distribution systems and the Worldwide Web to connect charities, so we became a network and a clearinghouse. By 2000, we were networking with more than 5,000 companies and charitable organizations in the Lower Forty-Eight. Dad still made toys, but we couldn't make enough, or pay for them. So we networked. We coordinated. Most of our toys come through L.A. where we work with hundreds of toy import-export companies."

"How do you pay for all this?" Peter asked.

Nicole laughed. "Toys are our currency, but not the source of the wealth that distributes them."

SR Staley

"How can you afford to pay all these people? The hospital? The doctors?"

Nicole couldn't resist keeping a broad smile from cresting her normally, corporate, poker face. Peter was startled by the beauty produced by the smile. She needed to smile more often.

"Well, I guess I can take credit for part of that," she said, struggling to subdue the pride behind the smile. "We developed a new software system—NP2000—capable of handling large volumes of transactions instantaneously while accurately tracking logistics to very small and remote destinations. Rowdy perfected it, sort of added a business sense to the whole concept and got it to market. So, now 90 percent of our revenues are in software sales and consulting. That lets us distribute our toys for free or coordinate our efforts through individual donors, organizations, or charities. We're networked with 100,000 organizations, service providers, and charities across the globe."

"Consulting? Other people know about this racket?"

"No. The Internet provides us with anonymity. We can transfer funds electronically, and all our business is transacted off the Web. We 'ghost' the homepages through another software system we developed. We don't sell that one though—security issues."

"Boy, the defense department would like to get their hands on that."

"We're more worried about the Department of Homeland Security," admitted Nicole.

Peter looked into Nicole's eyes. "You still don't see it, do you?"

Nicole's confused expression told Peter what he needed to know before she confessed it with her words. "See what?"

"You have no idea what you've accomplished."

Nicole looked at the door to the computer room. "Sure I do. I work with it every day."

"You don't see it." The sparkle in Peter's eyes seemed to illuminate the hall. "You've really created something here. You've pushed beyond the limits, beyond what anyone could have imagined possible. This is a *real* North Pole."

Nicole paused. Tears thickened above her cheeks, and she brought a hand to her face to catch them. Her father had done this. Her father had created the real North Pole. She had lost sight of the power of her

154

father's vision. She had it when she and Rowdy were blasting out the code for NP 2000, but she lost it when her father died.

Peter grabbed her arm and pulled her back toward the logistics center for NP Enterprises. He swiped his card then found hers and swiped it also. The doors opened to the same bustle of activity they had left. "Look at all the people that depend on you to keep this enterprise healthy." He opened the door and let Nicole immerse herself in the energy of the work she, her father and mother, her grandparents, and her great-grandfather and his wife had created with sweat equity.

Blood roiled through Nicole's veins, invigorating her, igniting her. This feeling had been gone for too long. She missed it. She needed it. This feeling is what sustained her working on code into the early hours at MIT and allowed her to accept the CEO responsibilities for NP Enterprises. The energy sweeping her body and brain gave her a new glow.

Peter moved his hand to Nicole's. "Nic, you've really built something here. Yes, Virginia, there is a Santa Claus. And her name is Nicole Klaas."

Nicole no longer held back the tears as the legacy of her family and father's work swamped her. She swayed, as if plucked by a gentle, but strong breeze, locking onto Peter's hand to steady herself. He pulled her closer. "Look," he said in her ear, directing her eyes to the giant map. "That's what you do. It isn't all numbers; it isn't all managing this and managing that. It's providing something people really want and need. It's providing a livelihood to all those people in this room and outside. It's the foundation for everything and everyone here."

Nicole's brain was clear, her thinking fresh, her body poised. She saw the beauty of the world generations of Klaases had toiled to develop. She saw the vision in action. The blinking lights reminded her of the hundreds of thousands of children that would benefit from that legacy, and the enterprise she had built with Rowdy. She shook her head, this time with a broad smile, and looked at Peter—a washed out explorer was responsible for her rebirth.

Unfortunately, she would have no time to embrace it.

***

The vibration from Nicole's cell phone jumped all over her skin as it went off, jolting her back from the dreamy world Peter had created for her. She snatched the phone from a front pocket in her slacks and peered into the glowing screen.

"Oh, God," she said. She turned to one of the men in the computer room. "Level Four Alert! Secure the room and the building!"

A red light started flashing, sending the room into frenzied activity as fingers dashed across screens.

"What… what's going on?" asked Peter.

Nicole shot a glance at him, anger and doubt sweeping the mirth from her face. "Come with me."

29

Sheila opened her eyes, letting the mist of the drops administered by the nurse clear. She blinked to regulate the light. She had waited what seemed like hours to make sure no one was left in the room.

The coma had been easier to fake than she thought. They knew she wasn't brain dead, but months of training at The Farm ensured she could suspend herself physically, even while her brain registered every sound and conversation in the room. She knew all that Asian philosophy and training would come in handy, and the psychologists merely taught her to channel it in the right way. Peter got her started, and the CIA helped the DEA finish it.

Peter Peary. What an idiot! How could she have ever loved him? But Getko was right. He was the perfect patsy. Sheila shivered inside at the thought of Peary's hand on hers.

She blinked again and let the light pull her into full awareness. Guerilla training began to kick into gear. She closed her eyes again and focused on her breathing. Adrenalin clears the mind and the veins faster than any drug the CIA had ever given her, but that wouldn't help her think clearly. She needed to calm herself to clear the neurological highways so her thoughts would travel with speed and accuracy.

The nurses had told Dr. Patten she wasn't going anywhere soon, so now all Sheila needed to do was to make sure no one rearranged furniture while she played opossum. Was there a guard outside the door? Probably. They weren't stupid.

The Agency had been tracking their movements for months. God, they had a complicated network—Bahamas, New York City, North Pole, Los Angeles, Miami, then that North Florida backwater of

Tallahassee. From the Bahamas, all the tell-tale markings of the South American drug connections were there. This was her ticket to real power in the Agency. This was Getko's ticket. They would become the power team, reestablishing it as the pre-eminent white collar and drug enforcement arm of the federal government. Now, she had to play the cards out and not make any mistakes.

Sheila had waited, avoiding any movement that might betray her consciousness. She was fine as long as they didn't run a brain scan. Sheila tried to tamp down the excitement. She felt so alive. All her experience as an explorer, all the times pulling people off an icy ledge and mountainside, all her training in law enforcement, and the Armed Forces Experimental Activity training at Camp Peary, were building toward this moment. In a matter of minutes, she would be able to assess the operation, break out of this concrete hospital prison, and give Getko everything he would need to destroy this operation.

She began to outline her strategy. She would wait a few more minutes before making her move. Then, she would have to double-check her clothes. She wasn't sure what was left after that fall. The fall! Did they take her boots? They could take all her clothes but not her boots. Getko would be waiting for her signal. Without her boots, she couldn't signal him. Was her homing device still working? Where were her clothes?

Sheila felt the panic rise with the adrenalin as she lay on the bed. She had to make sure her clothes were still here. She needed her parka and her boots. The gloves weren't that important, but she needed those boots. And her coat. She began to shift in her bed.

"Ahhhh," she moaned, her eyes closed to mere slits between the eyelids. She pursed her lips to keep from making another sound. They might have this room bugged. Or, videotaped! She closed her eyes quickly, then opened them a crack to scan the walls and ceiling. What was that in the corner? A round black dot was visible near the ceiling. That would be the perfect location for a video camera, she reasoned. Right out of the Agency handbook. She would have to move to escape from the hospital and get into the streets. If she could get outside the building, she could fade into the woods, or hide out in the alleys or an abandoned building. Then, she could work from within to guide Getko's raiding party in for the kill. Yes, that's what she needed to do.

A noise outside the door kept Sheila from moving any further. The door knob turned and Sheila's eyes snapped shut as she let herself fall back into the bed. Relax, she told herself. She began to breathe deeply, moving her consciousness deep into her body. Inhale deeply. Now, exhale. Remember how relaxed you felt at the end of the exhale, she instructed herself. There. Start at the top of the head, then move to the eyebrows, then the nose, then the lips… all the way down to your toes. Within moments, she was completely relaxed again, letting the movement in the room soak through her body, into her brain. Every sound, every movement registered as an unconscious data point.

"I don't know what Dr. Patten's going to do now," said someone in the room. It was a man's voice.

"I'm sure she'll do a full physical and mental assessment later this afternoon," said a woman's voice.

"Do you think she'll be able to handle it?"

"I don't know. Let's see."

Sheila heard footsteps approach her bed. The rustle of papers on a clipboard told her they were checking her recent history. Now, they were writing something on it.

"Fred, why don't you take her vitals?"

Small heavy steps approached Sheila's bed. Gentle hands took her pulse and blood pressure. Fingers moved to eyebrow and her closed eyelids. Yeow! Sheila screamed to herself silently—the light was blinding.

"Wow," the man's voice said.

"What?"

"You should see her pupils react to light! They're faster than anything I've seen on conscious patients! Are you sure she's not conscious?"

Deep, shallow, steady breaths, Sheila chanted to herself. That would also control her panic. What would she do if they found out she was fully conscious? Should she open her eyes now and try to act as if she just woke up? Or should she overpower them and make a break for it?

"Let's look at her charts," the woman said, now concerned. Both sets of feet shuffled to the bottom of her bed. Now would be a good time; she would have the complete element of surprise.

"Nothing here," said Fred. "No signs until now that she was coming out of it."

"We better tell Nicole ASAP."

"I'll track down Dr. Patten."

Nicole heard the clipboard drop and the two nurses left the room.

Who was this Nicole Klaas chick? She was in charge. Sheila figured that out from the security guard conversations. Her business was no small enterprise, but Peter was too thick to realize that. Of course, the other one—Jeff Wells—was the one smitten by Nicole, not Peter. Sheila doubted Nicole knew anything about that though. She had run into his type before, tough on the outside but too much of a wimp to face it straight up. Wells and Peary would be fighting soon, if they hadn't already, because they were exactly the same. Sheila clucked as she shook her head.

Sheila turned her attention back to her current dilemma. There was no time to lose. The nurses had already figured out she was conscious. As soon as they told Patten and Nicole, the gig would be up. She looked up at what she thought was a video camera. It really didn't make much difference now what it was. She had to move. Now.

Sheila scoped the hospital room. She saw the washbasin, the other bed, the counter tops. There, she thought, eyeing a metal closet close to the door, and under the suspected video camera. That's where my clothes must be.

Sheila swung her feet to the floor and tested her weight. Dizziness immediately swept through her head and she paused. She didn't have time for this. If she didn't move now, she would be caught, and the entire operation would be jeopardized. Forcing herself to her feet, oblivious to the cold draft sweeping through her hospital gown, Sheila grabbed the handrail and pushed herself upright. The dizziness was still there, but it wasn't quite as unsettling. She pulled herself toward the metal closet, letting the rail take her full weight.

Leaning up against the cabinet, she opened the closet door.

"Thank God," she muttered under her breath. Her sweater was there, as well as her pants and long underwear. She crouched on her knees: socks, gloves, shirt. Everything was here. They were clean. At least these people are considerate, she thought.

The boots! Where were her boots? She pushed through the clothes, feeling desperately along the closet floor for her boots. Toward the back she brushed up against thick rubber. What was that? Sheila let out a deep, gratifying sigh. They were there.

She pulled the boots out to look at them. Yes, these were hers. Or were they? Something seemed different about them. She looked at the soles. "Damn!" she said. The soles were hardly worn. The boots were the same brand and size, but they weren't hers. They had bought new boots for her! She looked up at the other clothes, touching them, feeling them, looking at the tags. All the clothes were new; they had replaced all her clothes.

What did that mean? Were her clothes so badly damaged in the accident they couldn't be used? Or did they discover the homing device and miniature radio in the inside lining? Sheila quickly examined the lining. They had replaced that, too. Where were her old boots? In a dumpster? Or a laboratory?

Fatigue gave way to unnatural strength as Sheila let the adrenalin pump through her veins. She had to get out. She had to get word to Getko. She needed a plan. Sheila jumped into the winter clothing and surveyed the room for anything she might need. No gear, it must be stored somewhere else; she couldn't find any equipment. She walked over to the cabinets and washbasin and started opening drawers. She scooped up two roles of tape, some gauze, and scissors, stuffing them into pockets.

Sheila pressed her ear up against the door, straining to hear any sound from the hallway. Nothing. She was convinced a guard was posted outside her door, but she couldn't hear a sound. She placed her hands over the door knob and turned. The door nudged open, letting a sliver of the hall's light into the room. Sheila peered through the crack for any sign of life. Nothing. The guard must be out of sight.

Sheila glanced around for a clock but saw nothing. How much time had passed since the nurses had come in? Had they notified Patten, Klaas, or Wells? She scanned the room again for something she could use—anything—but the room was clean.

With the deliberation and authority of a trained agent, Sheila opened the door. The guard, slumped in a chair half-awake, didn't have time to react before Sheila's cast and fist on her good hand made contact with the side of his head, knocking him unconscious to the floor, his body falling with a loud thud. Her eyes darted up the hallway, gratified to see it empty. What luck!

She scrambled for the exit at the end of the hall, dashed into the corridor, and loped down the steps to the first floor. The halls were busy with people, some in hospital gowns, most in heavy winter clothing; Sheila melted perfectly into the crowd as she pranced nonchalantly into the cold, ice-tinged air.

***

The frosty air was invigorating. The hospital room's sterile environment had been suffocating, and Sheila thought every minute she lay in that bed drained ounce after ounce of energy from her. Now she was out, free from the hospital, and able to move about again. It was so easy!

Sheila moved into the darkness toward what appeared to be the main street. The place seemed a little off kilter, even weird, and nothing like Getko or the briefing team said she should expect. This was a town, not an isolated den for drug dealers and their contraband. Anger rumbled inside her as she thought of how the cartels had funded such an active place right under the noses of the DEA.

The town practically hummed with activity. As she walked up the boardwalk, she soaked in the different stores—clothing, hardware, even an electronics. It was extraordinary. Drug dealers were taking their business to new heights. Sheila felt the tingling excitement of expectation as the idea of bringing the entire town down through a DEA sting began to soak in. Who could put this kind of accomplishment on their résumé?

But something was still off. She couldn't put her finger on it. The streets were loaded with people: men, women, and children. That's it. Children. That was what made this place so different. She had been debriefed on the drug-dealing villages in South America. Those villages functioned like normal towns, relying on subsistence agriculture or a cash crop like cocoa beans. The children and families were essential to maintain this environment. The real power derived from its largest revenue raiser—the clandestine drug trade and its drug money. No one was safe from the cartels, not even the children; they were an equal opportunity corruptor.

Sheila seethed with anger as she watched families stroll down the street as if everything they did was normal. In each window, Sheila saw the fruits of a vibrant drug trade—clothes, stereos, CDs, restaurants, all supported by the Bahamas connection. She had to shut it down.

Think, she said to herself. *Think. You need a plan.* She looked up, as if hoping a plan would come down from the heavens. And it did. She knew exactly what to do.

"Excuse me. Are you okay?"

"Huh?"

162

"Are you okay?" repeated a soft, little voice.

Sheila glanced in the direction of the voice but didn't see anything. Of course, she thought, it was a child's voice, so she looked down.

"You look like you're lost."

The girl was very small, about two and half feet, maybe shorter. Sheila's instincts told her a two-foot-high child couldn't be much more than three years old, but the question was well formed and enunciated clearly. This wasn't a three-year-old... or a four-year-old. The girl's words suggested ten or eleven.

"Umm, maybe I am a little," Sheila answered, trying to play innocent.

"It's not surprising," the girl said. "When I got here, I couldn't find anything. Can I help you?"

Sheila smiled at the innocence of the girl's concern. Now she was going to help her break up the town. Of course, the little girl would be helped; she wouldn't be forced to live in a criminal town any longer.

"Yes," Sheila said. "I need some help, and you may just be the person that can help me. My name's Jane."

30

Nicole trudged through the frost without slipping an inch as Peter struggled to keep his balance. Each time he seemed to slacken, she grabbed at his jacket and tugged him forward.

"Where are we going?" said Peter, still bewildered by the sudden change in mood and events. Nicole ignored him.

"We've got to meet Jeff Wells."

"Why? What's going on? What did the message say?"

Nicole ignored him and hauled him along. Peter didn't have much choice; he was convinced that any attempt to escape NP's security was fruitless. He didn't have a chance without proper winter gear, a map, and a compass. The activity in the streets and everyone on high alert turned a fruitless attempt into a pointless one.

They crossed a frost swept street. People walked fast and with purpose along the sidewalks. A few snowmobiles gunned down the streets. The pace had picked up everywhere in the town. The North Pole wasn't moving at the happy pace of busy elves before Christmas. The motion was edgy and urgent. Something was wrong, and Peary had a strange feeling he was a big part of it. He just wished he knew how, and not knowing made his heart seem heavy and burdened.

Peter stopped in an alley and twisted his arm from Nicole's grip. "What's going on?"

She looked at him with a cold, mechanical expression. "There's been a security breach." She then added under her breath, "I hope you're not it."

Nicole led Peary up the back steps of one of the few brick buildings in the underground city. Pulling off her gloves, she pressed her thumb into the security scanner and spoke softly but clearly into the hidden speaker, carefully lining up her retina with the soft light scanning from a rectangular plastic plate mounted on the outside wall. The door opened, and they entered a long and wide hallway. People were moving quickly from one room to another as the pair made their way down to a solid, metal door halfway down the hallway. Nicole turned the handle and walked in.

"What's he doing here?" Wells was standing next to a computer terminal as a NP Security guard pounded on a keyboard, and pictures clicked across the computer's monitor. "Where have you been?"

Nicole knew the question was rhetorical. To Peter, the tone seemed all too much like the accusatory question of a suspicious lover.

Wells looked at Nicole and then over to Peter. His eyes hardened. "What the hell?"

Nicole shook her head. "It's not Peter. I've been interrogating him for the last two hours. Your security breach didn't occur until twenty minutes ago."

"Nice guess," Wells said, "but it was an hour ago. I wanted to isolate the location before paging you."

"Peary couldn't have caused the breach." Nicole hoped her executive tone could disguise what was really hope in her voice.

"Don't bet on it," Wells snapped, slapping a computer read-out and map at her chest. "Check these out while I get an update from the outer perimeter."

Nicole looked at the pages before her. The stages of the alarm were tracked along with the events, so she could see the progression from security Level Zero to security Level Four. One more level would indicate a direct attack. This was uncharted territory. Nicole didn't need to read the details. All the information was in the first line of the printout, the event that pushed the town into higher alert.

"She's gone," Nicole said, turning to Peter, her expression expecting an explanation.

"Who's gone?"

Nicole held her breath for a moment. "Sheila. She escaped from the hospital."

Peter's mouth opened, but no words came out for several moments. "What? How...? What...? When...?"

"The guard was found unconscious outside the door. A nurse found him, but the concussion was pretty severe. We're not sure if he'll make it."

"How?" Peter muttered. "She was still in a coma when we left."

Nicole shook her head with disgust. "She was screwing with us. She must have been conscious most of the last two days to overcome one of Jeff's guards. George was probably thinking she was in a coma, too, and got lazy."

"She's probably disoriented. She wouldn't know where she is," reasoned Peter, his expression blank and tone listless.

Nicole looked at him as if asking, *Is he really that naïve?* "Maybe, but the best approach is usually to ask if you can leave before you jump someone outside your door and leave them for dead."

Wells re-entered the room. "New report. We've identified what looks like an attack force south of Snow Field Five."

"Who are you mobilizing?" asked Nicole.

Wells cast a cynical look her way. "Not a professional army, that's for sure. I've got about twenty-five trained security personnel right now. I think I can muster 100 reserves from the town. I've already called Rowdy. He's shutting down the factory and dispatching his workers to their stations."

"What about the evacuation plan?"

"We're sending the kids home and we sent e-mail instructions to families to prepare for an emergency evacuation. They'll be…" Wells turned toward Peter.

"He'll stay with us," Nicole assured him. "He's clean; he can't contact anyone outside."

"They'll be evacuated out of one of the northern exits. We also may send some under the ice cap. The escape subs have already been notified. We have one ready to dock. The other two might take a couple of hours. I don't think we have enough time."

"I don't understand," said Peter, shaking his head.

Wells walked up to Peter, within an inch of his nose. "We are now at Level Five Alert. We're under assault. Our intelligence now says that about fifty agents from the DEA, Immigration and Naturalization Service, and contract assault troops are advancing on our town on the ice above. My guess is these are former Special Forces personnel hired by the DEA for their operation. Given their pace and organization, they aren't hunting polar bears. For your sake, you better not be part of it."

Peter looked at Wells. "Believe me Mr. Wells, I am not. After what I've seen in the last two hours, I would pick up a phone right now and call it off if I could. But I have no idea what's going on here."

Wells glared at Peter. He broke his stare and then thumped Peter's chest with his hand. "I hope you are telling the truth."

Nicole backed closer to one of the walls, head dipped in thought, an invisible barrier between her and the security personnel bustling about. "Jeff, we need to divert them."

"We can't afford a battle. Even one gun shot or letting one or two outsiders in could destroy everything," he said.

And that's when it hit them. All the defense preparations for the town were worthless. They couldn't risk a real battle underground; any shot would expose the town, NP Enterprises, and the entire operation. The town was so fragile it could barely survive one intruder, let alone an army. Peter proved that even before Sheila escaped.

"We need to evacuate," Wells said, resigned to what seemed like the inevitable. "Let's leave this town vacant, make it a ghost town."

"We don't have time," Nicole said. "We need a diversion. We need to buy time and throw them off the trail."

"Look at the map," Wells said, using the mouse to move an image of a topographical map of the arctic ice cap to a widescreen mounted on the wall. Wells pointed to several gyrating dots moving towards a point that was obviously their town. "Their pace and direction is too deliberate. Somehow, they figured out where we are. They're heading right toward us." Wells looked at Peter. "Someone must have told them."

"Wells," Peter said, frustration and anger pulsating his voice. "How could I have done that? I've been cleaned of any transmitters, radios, or other electronic devices. You know that."

"The FBI, CIA, the DEA have all sorts of ways of monitoring their agents," Wells said.

"I'm an explorer!" Peter lifted his hands for emphasis. "That's it."

"Yeah." Wells taunted. "A washed-up explorer who's afraid he can't keep people alive in his expeditions. Sounds like a snitch to me."

Peary lunged, punching Wells' jaw before Nicole and the security guards could restrain him. Wells fell, sprawling backward from the power of the sucker punch. Peary struggled to pull himself free. "I'm not FBI!"

Wells pulled himself from the floor, rubbing his jaw, glaring at Peter. "I deserved that for not taking you more seriously. I'm slipping."

"You asked for that," Nicole scolded Wells. "I don't know if Peary's FBI, but he hasn't been communicating with anyone outside. He's been with me since we left the hospital."

Wells sent a sharp look at Nicole.

Nicole walked over to Wells and lifted her hand to his cheek. "He's seen everything. He knows, but he hasn't told anyone; he hasn't had time."

Wells relaxed once he felt the cup of Nicole's hand on his jaw and the soft sweep of her thumb over his cheek. He lifted his hand to hers, letting their eyes say the words they no longer had to speak. He nodded.

Wells turned to Peter. He continued to rub his jaw, but his eyes softened. "Your strength must be coming back. I guess anyone who denies being part of the feds that hard might be telling the truth."

Peter relaxed.

"But I still don't trust you." Wells turned to the two guards, holding Peary's arms. "Don't let him out of your sight until this is over."

"Okay, boys, let's get back to work," Nicole said. She went over to the computer and pulled up a layered map of the ice cap that showed both the surface and the town below in three dimensions. "These forces can't be FBI," Nicole said. "We're outside U.S. national borders. Only three non-defense agencies operate outside U.S. national boundaries: CIA and the DEA."

"That's two," Peter said.

Nicole looked at Peter. "The third wouldn't waste their time on us."

"Why not? The map shows dozens of law enforcement of some type headed in this direction."

"That's just it," Wells said in a near-relaxed tone. The fight must have released pent-up tension. "The third agency doesn't have a legion of personnel. We've only been able to identify two dozen members, and only one person below the president and the security advisor in the entire federal government who has any authorization to direct them. They focus primarily on burrowing moles deep inside target organizations to gather intelligence and carry out political assassinations. The agency is so secretive they don't have an official name, just a code word: Velvet Glove. We're too small time for Velvet Glove. They have bigger targets than international toy distributors.

"Besides, we know the guy running this operation: Milosevic Getko. He's dangerous because he's ambitious. I'm amazed he got this far. His last major success was busting up the Bimini Triangle about ten years ago. If you had asked ten months ago if this guy was capable of pulling this off, I would have said he is washed-up and wouldn't have a snowball's chance in Hell."

"You seem to make a habit of underestimating 'has beens'," Peter said.

Wells looked at Peter, "Getko at any rate."

The two guards tightened their grip on Peter, but he stayed focused on the map.

"What do you think?" Wells asked Nicole.

"You tell me," she said after a brief, contemplative pause. "You're the security expert. We hire you to have the answers."

"CIA's interested in espionage. This operation is more about contraband. My bet's with the DEA."

"I'd rather deal with the CIA," said Nicole. She didn't say it, but her skin crawled at the idea that Velvet Glove might be part of this operation. "Look," she said after a few moments, "I think I see a way out of this. It's a long shot, but it should work if we move—fast. When I was a little girl, I played in the tunnels south of town. We were originally going to build a telecommunications facility down there, but with Rowdy's business booming, it never took off. So, all we have down there is about two miles of ice tunnel."

"How does that help us?"

"What the map doesn't show," Nicole continued, tracing a long line south of town with her index finger, "is the escape tunnel at the end that goes to the surface. It's about 1000 feet long and can hold several hundred people if necessary. It's big enough for our security people, particularly your elite recruits, but small enough that the feds can't send all its forces down the hole at once. It's only about six feet in diameter, so even the dwarves in our reserves should make quick work of any average-sized person on the attack. In theory."

She looked at Wells and read his skepticism. She took her finger and traced it down the tunnel to a point marked, "exit/entrance." "We can go up the emergency tunnel, start a skirmish, and lead them down into the abandoned tunnel. We can close it off, keeping the exit open

169

while sealing the tunnel off from the rest of the town. That should at least buy us enough time to evacuate the town and destroy the equipment. No one will have a chance to see the town. If we're lucky, they'll just leave, and we can get the town up and running again a month or two after this blows over."

"Man, that's a long shot," said Wells, shaking his head.

Nicole looked at him. "It's the only shot we've got."

Peter peered over the map and suddenly burst-out laughing. Nicole and Wells looked at him, raised eyebrows framing their blank expressions.

Peter pointed to the dot on the map where the south tunnel reached the surface, his face alight with a smile. "That's Point Gamma."

Nicole and Wells looked at each other. "Point Gamma?"

"That was the rendezvous point for my expedition to the North Pole. That's where Sheila and I were supposed to camp before the ice split, sending us into the crevice. We were supposed to check in with the Alaskan Coast Guard station there. We were supposed to camp right on top of your escape hatch!" Peter became quiet as the absurdity of the coincidence faded. "We never made it."

"What a coincidence," Wells said, signaling to the guards to step closer to Peter. "A little too much coincidence for my taste. Peary, you're not helping your case here."

"I don't know," Nicole said. "He said that was where he was supposed to check in. They didn't make it. They couldn't have given the DEA the signal to go ahead. If anything, they would have stopped the operation and assumed something had gone wrong."

Wells scoured the map. Nicole was right. If Peary couldn't have signaled the DEA, Livingston couldn't have either. She was still in her bed at the medical center. Even if she wasn't in a coma, she couldn't have sent a signal to the DEA. Who gave the signal? Wells' heart fell into his stomach at the thought of a mole inside NP. He looked up at Nicole. "Jesus, Nic, do you know what that means?"

"How long will it take for the DEA to get here?" Peter asked, looking at the moving dots on the screen, failing to catch the exchange between the two.

"At their current rate," Wells said, "we have about eight hours before they get to the outer perimeter. If the diversion works, everything has to be ready in six hours."

170

"Does anyone else have a better idea?" asked Nicole. No one responded. "Okay, let's go. I'll give the orders to Rowdy, Dr. Patten, and the other directors to follow procedures at Level Five Alert."

31

The wind whipped over the ice dunes as Getko huddled with his senior staff around a map. Getko pulled his arctic parka, stretching the yellow letters DEA across his back. He looked up, taking note of the four former Special Forces officers and the official representative of the Canadian government. Scores of missions targeting terrorists in Iraq and Afghanistan had chiseled workman-like expressions into these veterans of the Devil's Brigade, the 7th Special Forces Group garrisoned at Eglin Air Force Base. Getko was counting on their experiences with surgical strikes to make this wintery assault a success. Getko's eyes passed over the gold oak leaf cluster signifying the rank of Major Mark Hutton (Retired), the chief advisor to the detachment, secreted to the North Pole to assist him with Jamaican Snow.

"A little north of Pensacola, right Major?"

Hutton chuckled. "Not to worry, Agent Getko. We'll do our job. We've been itching for something to do since winding down from Afghanistan. Drug dealers are just a more pragmatic form of a terrorist, and they don't change their stripes or their tactics because they moved from the jungles of Central or South America, to North America. I'll admit, we didn't include a North Pole scenario in our usual training, but that's why I'm here. We adapt. It's my job."

"Good to hear," Getko said.

"I don't get it," Joy said, looking at the map laid out in front of the group. "How can you be so sure we're going in the right direction?"

"Extrapolation and a careful reading of our intelligence," said Getko, with a dismissive air. He looked at Joy, then Hutton.

"We don't have much to work from," Joy said.

Getko straightened his back. "We had more than enough to commit the DEA's resources as well as our Special Forces friends. You know how dangerous the cartels are."

"I could use a little clarification," Hutton said. "We've got the coordinates, but this place is like a desert. Any additional information you can provide will help the operation go more smoothly."

"Simple," Getko said, turning his gaze back to the map. "Our last communication with Special Agent Livingston was here." He pointed to a point fifty miles south of the North Pole. I think we can safely assume that is where the drug traffickers operate the clandestine trading post discovered by Livingston and Peary and took them hostage. Since we haven't heard from them, we can assume that the drug dealers have either killed them or found their bugs and destroyed them."

The agents nodded in agreement, but Hutton seemed to take in the information without emotion.

"So why are we sixty miles southeast of the North Pole?"

"Our satellites have picked up scattered, seemingly random heat readings at these three points." Getko let the tip of his forefinger tap a triangle on the map, about two miles from each other. "That area is about a square mile. Those points are the likely exits for the drug dealers from under the ice. Each time the door opens, it releases heat, which is picked up by the satellites through remote sensing. These readings were classified and only forwarded to me." All three points were about ten miles north of their current position and southeast of the North Pole. "We head for those dots, we get into the lab and ice warehouse, and we destroy them."

"They must be pretty well guarded if you are calling us in." Hutton's voice was firm, but the demand for more information from Getko was obvious.

Getko nodded. "We believe they have at least twenty-five or thirty cartel soldiers working this facility."

"Something seems odd," Hutton said. "If this operation is as sophisticated as you say it is, we're probably going to run into a lot more people than that."

"We haven't found any evidence of large caches of armaments or large numbers of bodies moving from the exits. In your surveillance of the L.A., Miami, Jamaica, New York connections, have you seen any of the suspects carrying guns?"

"No," Joy said, realizing the salience of the observation. "None of our surveillance has found any sign of any weaponry."

"They're a pretty cocky bunch," said Getko, a sinister tone creeping into his voice. "They are so stuck up on their own cleverness, they can't even contemplate someone figuring out their operation. Who would think a cocaine and heroin trade would be taking place underneath the arctic ice cap?"

Heads in the huddle nodded.

Hutton looked up to Getko. "We'll get the job done on the ground. Or under the ice if necessary. What kind of infrastructure do you expect us to see?"

Getko hesitated, knowing that he was stretching the bounds of plausibility. "It's hard to tell, Major. The ice this time of year is reliably only ten feet thick, maybe fifteen in places. Like the mountains of Central and South America, we expect the caves to be low and narrow, with spaces carved out to warehouse the drugs. We have someone working from the inside, and we believe the tunnels are about five and a half feet square. Since this is ice, we'll have to keep our fight to small arms. Explosions will destabilize the ice and could end up drowning the entire assault force."

Hutton shook his head. "I don't like it. Sending your men or mine into that kind of an environment is like putting them in a shooting gallery."

"It's not that much different than clearing out the caves in Afghanistan," Getko said. "Just be more careful."

Hutton looked at Getko with a hard stare, as if trying to decide how far to push his point. "So you don't expect any permanent structures below the surface?"

"No. The ice is too unstable. I suspect they have winter tents and gear, but nothing permanent. It's like living in a giant igloo. I don't think anything could live down there for long, and they are probably ready to evacuate at a moment's notice. They wouldn't risk putting anything more permanent together."

Hutton seemed satisfied. The pieces seemed to be falling into place. But Joy still felt something else must be going on. Getko was holding some information back. Did Sheila start reporting back to him on another channel? Could Sheila have planted an undercover agent without Joy knowing about it?

"How far are we away from this southern-most entrance?" Getko asked one of the agents.

"I would say we're four hours out," said an agent, burrowed deep in a parka. "The vehicles are running well. We've got plenty of fuel, and the choppers got us much closer than we anticipated."

"What about getting back?"

"That's a bit more problematic. If we have prisoners and contraband, we'll need more equipment."

Getko wasn't worried. Once the drug traffickers were arrested and the drugs seized, he would have all the resources he needed. This was going to be an international bust of unprecedented magnitude—all orchestrated by the master of the Bimini Triangle.

"One thing, Agent Getko."

"Yes, Mr. Gaston."

"As the official liaison of the Canadian government, I must warn you that violence must be limited. My government granted permission for this operation based on the principle of minimal force. You should make sure your special agents are not trigger happy."

"Don't worry, Pierre. Everything is under control. Our agents are trained to hold their fire except in self-defense. For all intents and purposes, that means they must be under fire before they can fire their own weapons. Your advisors are under the command of our agency, correct Major?"

Hutton nodded.

"Their role is purely advisory."

The Canadian looked at the soldiers. "They seem pretty well armed for being advisors."

"We're going into a hot zone," Hutton said. "We'll keep our distance, but we're here just in case something goes wrong."

Getko nodded. "They understand this is an international law enforcement operation, not a military one. We've got all the checks in place."

"I understand that." Gaston's response was slow to emphasize the deliberateness of his words. "Your agents are very well armed. They have assault rifles, repeating rifles, and pistols. Some of the units even have grenade launchers."

"That's true," Getko said. "We need to remember what we are up against: These are hardened drug dealers. They are terrorists, but very pragmatic about human life. They will not hesitate to shoot, and shoot to kill. These weapons are for our own protection in case they don't surrender. They learned their tactics from the jungles of South America. We can't expect them to take prisoners. They would rather die than be captured by us. Anyone taken prisoner by them should expect to be tortured or killed."

Joy wanted to interject, but didn't.

"Alright," the Canadian acquiesced. "Remember my report will be complete and objective. I won't cover anything up."

Getko clapped his mittened hand on Gaston's shoulder. "You won't have to, *mon ami*. In a little more than twelve hours from now, you will be standing with me at an international press conference proudly describing your country's role in eradicating one of the most extensive international drug operations on Earth. It will be a great moment in U.S.-Canadian relations."

A body emerged suddenly next to the huddle. Getko looked up to take a piece of paper from the messenger, reading it silently.

"Hmm, that's strange," he said, then nodded with a smile. "Ahh, excellent." He looked up as if only now becoming aware that the others were waiting for his orders. He waved the paper. "We just received another satellite reading. A series of three long heat releases were discovered." He pointed to a point on the map south of the designated entrances. "Here."

"But that's not one of the entrances the satellites identified earlier," said one of the officers. The new spot on the map seemed to change what had been a triangle into a square.

"Correct," Getko said, his voice perking up by the opportunity to once again demonstrate his analytical skills. "And it's closer. It's a new entrance. They must have created a new route. It follows the pattern we saw earlier; each of the heat spots emerges in succession. Some of the earlier ones, the ones furthest north, have been dormant for months."

Getko clapped his gloves together. "This is excellent. As far as these drug scums know, we still haven't figured out their pattern. They'll even be more relaxed, thinking they have some time before we put the patterns together and come after them—if they're even thinking that far ahead. We still have the element of surprise!"

Joy was puzzled, too. Why would they risk exposing a new exit? She was pretty sure the element of surprise was gone, but she couldn't figure out the three long flashes of heat at a new site. This did not bode well at all.

The wind let loose a deafening howl as the men folded the map and directed their flashlight beams toward the mass of agents and soldiers. The mini army heaved forward, rested and ready for what they could only guess would be the strangest battle they had ever witnessed.

32

Jeff Wells opened the door to the howling arctic wind first, forcing himself out into the dusk of the ice desert. *This defines the word "desolation,"* he thought as he helped Nicole and Peter up onto the ice. Gusts pummeled the intruders, nearly pushing the small band of defenders back into the haven of their cave. Fortunately, enough snow covered the surface, giving them sufficient traction to move forward.

The bracing wind whipped around Peter's head, and for a moment he thought it might tear the nose and cheeks right off his face. Peter lifted his arm to shield against the gnarling wind and flying ice crystals, his heart racing as anxiety raced through his body. Within seconds, the panic was pushed from his mind, calming his body to the point the sub-zero temperatures were as tolerable as the hot sun on a Florida beach in July. The arctic snow fields were not strangers, but known enemies with familiar weaknesses that he had defeated before. Peter stood at the entrance to the tunnel leading to the underground village, a comfortable normalcy taking over his body for the first time since he woke up in the hospital.

"Come on, come on," Wells cajoled. "The remote sensors on the satellites are already picking up the opening. The longer it's open, the easier it will be for them to get a definite read and fix on our activities."

About a half-dozen NP Security officers were on the surface now. Peter's body guards were still below. He would be even more of a fool to try escaping now. He would be dead in hours without a map or compass and no real fix on the invading army of law enforcement personnel.

Nicole pulled her parka around her face to check the wind, then signaled Wells to proceed.

"Alright," Wells said. He turned to a short, stocky man next to him. "Alright Fred, lay it out for us."

Fred? Peter peered into the parka of the little person in front of him.

"Yipperdo," said Fred, instantly sensing Peary's bewilderment. "What? Didn't think I could handle more than one job?"

"No, no," Peter said, smiling. "You're a nurse!"

"That's my day job," Fred said. "When I'm bored, I go chasing bad guys with Mr. Wells. And we make snow angels. And play tag with polar bears."

"Okay, okay," said Wells, "get on with it. Peary's here as an observer. He's not calling the shots, so move on."

"They're coming from the southeast," Fred began. "They should be here in about two hours. We couldn't get a reliable fix because the weather was interfering with our ability to tap the satellite feed. At their current pace, we'll need to divert them in about fifteen minutes. We'll do that by opening the door to let heat out. Our intelligence is pretty clear that the main way they're tracking our whereabouts is through remote sensing satellites—basically, the same technology we're using to track them."

"How many men will you use?" asked Nicole.

"Men?" asked Fred somewhat flippantly. "We've got a couple of ladies, too, ya know."

"Yeah, right!" The quip had broken her train of thought. "You know what I mean."

"Yes, ma'am." A broad smile illuminated the inside of Fred's parka. "Anyway, we're going to station an outpost of reservists about two miles out. They'll start a diversion, using flares and fireworks—leftovers from last year's Fourth of July. Boy, did that throw the U.S. Air Force into a quandary! You should have heard the radio cackle when they saw their screens light up with those babies—imports from Tennessee, you know. Anyway, good thing *Fail Safe* was a movie because—"

"Okay, okay, okay," Wells said, throwing his hands up. "Fred, get on with it! You're our most senior reservist in the security force. We've got work to do down below, and we don't have much time."

"Yeah, right," Fred said, casting a sly glance toward Nicole. Nicole shot a piercing eye his way, and Fred straightened up. "An ice dune provides great cover. The main point is to slow them down by using the pyrotechnics to create confusion and caution. The weather is too bad for them to call up air reinforcements—a real break. A couple of helicopters or scout planes would make this whole project more difficult. Good thing for us the feds decided to make their assault in darkness. That gives us the same kind of cover they're counting on."

"Fred," said Nicole. "How will you get back to the tunnel? Won't they open fire?"

"The strategic beauty of stature!" exclaimed Fred. "Little people are hard to see in this environment, especially with our winter gear on. We've got three snowmobiles we're bringing up from one of the northern scouting posts. We'll use them to get to the ridge and back here."

"Three? Why three?" asked Nicole. "They're four-person vehicles."

"Do you want to hear the plan, or are you going to second-guess me?" asked Fred, irritated at Nicole's question.

"Answer the question," ordered Wells.

"The snowmobiles are rated for four people, but they aren't very flexible fully loaded. We need the extra space for the pyrotechnics going out to the ridge, and we need to be fast and nimble getting back. Their equipment will still be loaded, so they'll be a little slower, but on the way back we might need the extra space for people if one breaks down."

"What about the snowmobiles when you get back here?" Wells queried.

"We'll have to leave them here," Fred said, keeping his impatience in check. He hated running security by committee.

"Isn't that a bit dangerous?"

"Why? They're just snowmobiles. We have scores of them."

Wells looked at Nicole in alarm. He could tell by her blank face that she had no idea where his question was going. "Come on guys, use your heads. If you leave them here, the feds'll get them."

"So what?" said Nicole. "We'll need to leave them here to draw them down into the tunnel."

"Yes, but that's the point. You leave them here. What's special about the snowmobiles? These snowmobiles?"

"They're modified," answered Peter suddenly. All three turned their heads toward him. "They're modified," he said again. "I heard them down on the street. You've adjusted their carburetors for running lean underground. Most of them are calibrated for speed in clear weather in a controlled environment—"

"Exactly," said Wells, pleased that someone finally caught on.

"That's a problem," Peter continued. "You bring those snowmobiles up here under these conditions, and you won't go anywhere. They'll freeze up in minutes."

Fred stood in depressed silence, then clicked on his two-way radio. "Zebra One to Zebra Three, Zebra One to Zebra Three, do you copy?" He looked over at Peary. "*Ice Station Zebra*, what a great movie."

"You and Howard Hughes!" Wells quipped. "Get on with it."

"Zebra Three; go ahead Zebra One."

"Has anyone calibrated the snowmobiles for surface conditions?"

The radio was silent, but everyone thought they could hear the yelling and finger pointing going on more than a mile to the north under ice and snow!

"Uhh, roger Zebra One. We might be delayed a few minutes."

"Ten-four. Re-estimate rendezvous at plus-fifteen minutes."

"Roger, Zebra One. Out."

"You've got another problem," said Nicole, almost in turn.

"What now?" asked Fred, rolling his eyes.

"You have to destroy the machines when you get here."

"Why?"

"The feds'll seize them as evidence and take them back to Virginia for analysis," said Wells. "They'll look at how they're maintained, their hours of operation, wear and tear on the runners and treads, and verify every suspicion they ever had about our town. They'll be back."

"Damn!" said Fred, slapping the air with his arm. He paced a few feet.

"You won't have time to go back to the northern entrance," said Wells, trying to reason an answer. "We wouldn't want to risk it even if we had the time. The plan will only work if they come to this point here. If they find the other entrance, we might as well give it all up and blow up the town."

Fred swung his arms, hoping the movement would loosen up his thinking. "No, no," he said, deep in thought. "There's got to be something I can do."

Peter looked at the machine. "Bury it in the snow."

Fred continued to pace. "We can't risk it. I've got it. We've got some flares that I can rig. We'll pre-soak some rags with gasoline and rig them with a slow fuse about twenty-five feet from the entrance. When the sparks hit the fuel tank, the whole vehicle will blow, but I'll tear apart some of the fireworks and seed the engine and underbelly with the powder just to be sure."

Peter's eyes lit up. "That should work. They won't be able to recognize anything from the engine as long as the powder ignites inside. The explosions will destroy any identifying marks or wear patterns on the engine parts. The only thing they'll be able to work off of will be the bearings in the wheels, but those are easily maintained and changed, so they can't conclude anything definitive."

Wells looked at Peter. Perhaps he was wrong about the explorer. Or, maybe Peter's just playing the game. They won't need the equipment if they have Peter as a witness. Still, his input seemed sincere, and Nicole had been with him all afternoon.

"It works on another level," he said. "If they see the equipment burning, they'll think they have us on the run. They won't have time to think it's a trap or some other ploy. If you time it right, Fred, and they see you go below the snow quickly, they'll follow the momentum you create. They won't want to risk stopping and losing the element of surprise."

Despite the cold and wind, the group began to move more easily, like old friends around a campfire.

"We still have a lot of work to do." Nicole reminded them.

"Right," said Wells. "Is your team fully briefed and ready, Fred?"

"Yep."

"Let's get the tunnel ready."

33

"Wells! Klaas! What in Gawd's name is going on?"

The nasal, Boston accent forced Nicole to groan under her breath as she and Jeff Wells assembled at the bottom of the ladder. "I'm not ready for her yet."

Two dwarves, one male and the other female, were approaching. They had sandwiched their snowmobile next to three other machines.

"What's going on?" said the man. "We've got everyone mustered for a Level Five scenario, and the families are evacuating, but nobody's filled us in. What's going on with my client? Have you charged him with anything? Is he under house arrest?"

"Calm down, Ron," Nicole said. "Your client has been helping us prepare the town for an assault."

"Assault? What assault?"

Alarm widened the eyes of the professional woman still in hospital garb next to Ron Cutler.

Wells hoped the urgency of the assault news might give him the leeway he needed to by-pass the community directors. "Dr. Patten, U.S. law enforcement agencies are advancing on our position. They are preparing to invade the town."

"What do you mean?" asked Patten as anger reddened her cheeks. "Why didn't you let the directoahs know about this?"

Nicole and Wells looked at each other as if saying to themselves, *This was exactly the kind of thing Jeff was hired to deal with.*

Wells put his hands on his hips and looked directly at NP Community Director Dr. Julie Patten. "We didn't know it was

SR Staley

happening until about six hours ago. We've been busy preparing our defensive plan and reviewing our Level Five procedures. I've been working closely with Nicole."

"That's no excuse," Patten barked. "This is a major threat to this town. Ouaa families and livelihood aww at stake. You shouldn't have done this without consulting us."

"There wasn't time," he insisted.

Patten pitched her finger at Wells. "Bullshit. You had enough time to pull us into a closed-dooa session and brief us. We ahh the directoahs of this town!"

"There wasn't time," Wells repeated, invoking a stronger, more authoritative tone. "Getting the directors together for a session would have wasted hours of valuable time that would have compromised our preparedness."

"What? Ahh you saying we waste youaa time? Is that the attitude you have with the people that pay youaa salary?"

"No, ma'am," Wells said, calming himself. "You know that is not what I meant."

"What ahh you trying to pull?"

"Nothing! Look Dr. Patten, you've known about Peary and Livingston since they got here. You knew they were a potential threat."

"And Livingston's gone! Vanished. And I didn't find out until two houaas after she had left."

"That was a mistake," Wells admitted.

"Bullshit, youaa trying to run this ship on youaa own, Wells."

"No, ma'am. I agree, you should have been notified immediately when Livingston was discovered missing. In fact, you should have been notified with me. There was a breakdown in the process."

"Youaa damn right there was a breakdown in the process. Wells, I don't know what youaa trying to do—"

"I'm not pulling anything over on you," he insisted.

Wells looked at Rowdy and Patten. "Look, you hired me to do a job—protect the town. We created contingency plans based on the type and level of threat. We're implementing those plans now. You need to let me do my job."

Patten crossed her arms as her jaw set. "Not at the expense of the directoahs' authority."

"This is my job," said Wells. "I'm doing it. I will not allow you to micromanage my company or the security of this town."

184

"We are not micromanaging," Patten spat. "We ahh making sure you follow the priorities of the town. In matters of public interest, you should report to the trustees at once."

"Patten," Wells said, dropping the pretense of respect, "the trustees approved all levels of emergency plans. Nothing has changed since the adoption of those policies. If you doubt whether I or my company can do the job, say so. Don't mask it in the crap about not having the authority to act. Do you want me to resign?"

Nicole stepped forward, placing a tender palm on his chest. "Dr. Patten. There was no attempt to exclude you or any of the other trustees. Things have moved fast over the past couple of hours, and it would have been unreasonable to call a meeting before deciding on a course of action." Turning to Cutler, Nicole said, "We have been implementing your L5 plans very quickly and efficiently."

Julie Patten turned to Nicole and stepped up to her, raising her hand and pointing to her chest. "Klaas... you've really bungled this. I can't believe youaa in bed with Wells. I know youaa family helped build this town—"

Nicole's expression hardened. "My family *built* this town!"

Patten's cheeks reddened. "Klaas, this town exists because the people make it woahk. Youaa family started it, but it's the people living and working here now that make this town. That's why we have the council. As far as I'm concerned, we've given you too much reign."

Ron stepped forward. "Julie, this is neither the time nor the place to bring these issues up."

"The hell it isn't, Ron. We need to assert authowity as leaders of this community. Why the hell do we have the Board of Community Directoahs if not to demonstrate real leadaaship in times of crisis?"

Ron shook his head and looked directly at Patten. "We have a board of directors to govern the town, not nitpick to death by saying 'yes' or 'no' to every detail. The directors don't exist to provide leadership in times of crisis, or micromanage our contractors. We can't solve these problems by committee."

Patten fumed, looking at Cutler like a traitor, as if to ask, *Are you really backing Wells and Klaas over me?* "Ron, don't take theaa side in this."

Ron's face fell. "Is that a threat?"

"Ron, we can't let them take ovaa the town like this. They don't know what's best foaa the town. We have as much right to run this

185

town as they do, and we can use the community directoahs to make sure that happens!"

"This is not about taking sides!" he shot back. "It's about dealing with a serious external threat to our existence. I don't know the details, but Jeff was hired to do a job, and by God, now we've got to let him do it."

"It's not just that," said Nicole. "Dr. Patten, you have made an incredible contribution to this community. That's why I and the rest of the directors appointed you to the Board. But let's not lose sight of the issue at hand. We have U.S. federal agents and law enforcement personnel converging on our town at this very moment. Unless we implement an adequate defense and evacuation now, everything will be lost. We won't have a town to govern. We won't have a business that employs 20,000 people worldwide. We cannot sustain the network that shows millions of children they count—that someone believes in them—that someone cares enough to sacrifice for them." Nicole looked at Julie Patten with the clarity of a laser. "There will be no haven."

"My God, Dr. Patten. Can't you see what is happening?"

The voice jarred everyone, and they looked at Peter, as if aware of his presence for the first time. His face was relaxed, his voice steady, and his eyes clear, despite the tense argument mounting between Nicole, Wells, and Julie Patten.

"Shut up," Patten ordered. "This is my town. Youaa not a citizen, and you have no standing. We will decide what is right and determine the best way to move forward. As the head of the community board of directoahs, I will make that happen!"

Nicole looked at one of the world's greatest and most skilled surgeons, perplexed and confused. "Her" town? She has a right to run this town? It's her community? What was Julie saying? That Nicole and Jeff didn't have an equal stake in this community and its survival? Rowdy's business—the one she co-founded—was thriving, creating new wealth and new toy distribution capabilities by the minute, but NP Enterprises was still the bread and butter of their underground arctic economic hive.

Patten looked around, saw the quizzical expressions of the others around her, and her shoulders dropped as her body adopted a calm exterior. "Maybe, youaa right," she said. "The pressure of the attack seems to have gotten to me."

Cutler looked at Patten and nodded with a deliberate steadiness. "Okay, Jeff, we're here. Bring us up to speed."

"May Day, May Day!" cackled the radio speaker, slung around Wells' neck. "Zebra One to Mole One, we have a breach!"

The group began whispering in urgent, alarmed tones as Wells and Nicole turned their focus to the radio. Wells snatched the transmitter and shoved it to his lips. "Zebra One, Zebra One, what do you mean you have a breach?"

The radio clicked, and the small group heard the pok-poking of automatic rifles in the frozen tundra above. "We've got a breach! I said we've got a—" An explosion cut off the report.

Wells and Nicole looked at each other alarmed. "Zebra One, Zebra One! Where is the breach? Can you read me? Where is the breach?"

The radio's static echoed ominously off the cavernous walls of the tunnel.

Nicole lifted her hand to Wells' shoulder as she looked at the silent radio. "Jesus, Jeff."

Wells grabbed the arm of one of his security officers. "Deploy to the southeast emergency tunnel entrance."

"Mole One to Home Town," Wells ordered into the radio.

"Home Town here."

"Did you here that?"

"Yes, sir. What are our orders?"

"Bring five units up to the tunnel entrance. Are the underground explosives in place and set to fire?"

"Yes, sir."

"Ready the fuse. Be ready to blow the tunnel at my command."

"Sir, what if people are still in the tunnel?"

Wells looked up at the group surrounding him. "Blow it on my order. I'll use the code words, Velvet Glove. When you hear those words, blow the tunnel and expedite the evacuation."

The group fell silent. He turned to Nicole. "Call Rowdy and tell him to complete the evacuation plans for the town." He turned back to Patten and Cutler, his expression making it clear they were to stay put. "Let's go," he said turning to Nicole and Peter.

Wells began to disperse rifles and pistols from a packed snowmobile, not completely sure they would know what to do with them. The reservists had never been tested. Now, he reasoned, they needed bodies. And directors' bodies served the same purpose as other bodies. "You," he said pointing to Cutler and Patten, "Pick up a weapon. We're going to need you."

Peter stepped up for his weapon. Wells hesitated. "I don't think so."

"Come on, Jeff," Peter said. "You need everyone on this. You have no idea what Fred is able to do. I know the plan, and you know I've got the guts to follow through with it."

"I'm not worried about whether you have the guts," said Wells. "Take the snowmobile and start moving men into the tunnel."

"Go ahead Peter," said Nicole. "Right now, that's the best way you can help this effort."

Wells' radio crackled and everyone looked at it expectantly. "Zebra One, Zebra One, can you read me?" The static grated through the air.

"I thought I heard him," Nicole said. "I'm sure of it."

"Zebra One, Zebra One. This is Mole One. Do you copy? Over."

Static.

"Let's move!" he barked.

Wells looked around. Patten and Cutler had already gone on one of the snowmobiles. He didn't have time to sort it through. They were probably at the entrance by now, waiting for him.

Wells signaled for Peter to bring the last snowmobile over, then he and Nicole climbed on board. He hoped they weren't too late. If the federal troops had broken through, he would have to blow up the tunnel. The lean whine of the engine kicked up as the three careened toward the tunnel entrance, drowning out the gunfight ahead.

34

The U.S. drug enforcement agents and their *advisors* took less than two minutes to route the NP security officers and reservists. They retreated as fast as they could, firing as they fell back to the tunnel entrance. Miraculously, no one had been killed, but two agents and four reservists with emblems displaying NP Security lay wounded on the tunnel floor. The area was thrown into further chaos when a snowmobile carrying two dwarves barreled around a bend in the tunnel and were thrown into the mêlée.

"Let's go! Let's go!" Getko implored, following the officers into the tunnel. "Get the medics down here."

Getko looked at the bodies, his hands shaking as if counting, then losing count. Blood soaked the ice a deep red in the center, fading to pink toward the edges as it crystallized. "Joy!"

"Yes, sir."

"What's wrong?"

"Nothing sir," Joy lied, the quiver in her voice barely audible.

"Where's Major Hutton?" Getko clicked on the radio. "Hutton! Bring up the other units for phase two."

Joy looked around at the other soldiers who were guarding the dark North Pole entrance. "How many should we bring down from above?"

"How many agents made it into the tunnel?"

"About a half-dozen. Two of them are wounded though."

"That's not enough. Leave two to guard the prisoners, and use the other two to recon the tunnel."

Getko stepped closer to Joy, just out of earshot. "What's the deal with the midgets?"

"They're not midgets."

"What do you mean? Of course they're midgets. Look at their size!"

"They're little people."

"Jesus, Joy, you're losing it."

"Hey!" yelled one of the dwarves, holding a piece of cloth over a glistening red splotch on another man's rib. The other man was average sized, wearing a butternut shirt with breast pockets and heavy winter slacks, and he clutched the hand of the dwarf as they tried to staunch the bleeding. The NP Security emblem was visible as they reached toward the wound in his side. Another NP security guard, a dwarf, rested against the tunnel, blood covering his hand as he held a leg with an injury less obvious.

"Are you going to help us?" the dwarf pleaded. "Or are you going to let this man bleed to death?"

Getko walked over to the dwarf, kneeling next to the wounded NP security guard. "What's your name?"

"Fred. Tom's the guy on the ground, and José is the one leaning on the wall. I'm a nurse, but I can't do much for Tom's wound without help."

Getko laughed. "A nurse? You've got to be kidding me. They send a midget nurse to fight us?"

Fred's expression lit up as he stood with a clenched, angry fist, prompting one of Getko's *advisors* to immobilize his arm. The bleeding man moaned as Fred lifted the pressure off the bandage. He gasped as pressure was applied back to the wound.

Getko ignored the fallen defender. "Oh, I'm real scared," he said, waving his hands lazily in the air.

Fred's eyes blazed, prompting Joy to pause and wonder for a moment, whether the heat might melt ice and make the tunnel collapse. Fred's fury didn't lessen. "You son of a bitch! What are you doing? Why are you here?"

Getko waved Fred's expression off. "I'll let the prosecutors and your lawyers work that out—if you make it to the states that is."

The wounded dwarf coughed. "What are you talking about? What prosecutors? IRS?"

Getko laughed. "The IRS will be the least of your problems! Don't worry; I've got medics coming. They'll attend to my wounded first, then to your friends. We don't give criminals priority health care."

Another dwarf, unarmed, approached Getko as another soldier lifted the point of his gun menacingly.

"We're not criminals," protested Ron Cutler. He looked at Dr. Julie Patten who stood nearby. He cast a disgusted look her way, then redirected his attention to Getko. "I'm a lawyer; tell me what the charges are."

"You're a lawyer? Right. Tell me another joke," Getko snipped.

"Harvard Law, class of 1985."

Getko laughed again at the thought that the little man in front of him could have gone to Harvard Law and then joined a drug gang. "If you'd gone to Harvard Law," he said, "You would have been smart enough to stay out of this crap. Excuse me if I find it a little hard to believe that these guys would waste a Harvard-educated lawyer on the front lines of this fight!"

Cutler was livid. "What are you doing here? What right do you have to come in here and invade our property like this?"

Getko grew silent. "What right? Now, do you mean what legal right or what moral right?" Getko glared at the diminutive attorney, measuring him up and down with his eyes. "How dare you question my authority? You are under international law, and we are here on an international mission."

"I don't believe it," Cutler said, the veins in his temples flaring as he struggled to keep his tone professional. "Show me a warrant from the World Government."

Getko hesitated. "We don't need a warrant in international territory. This is a joint mission with the blessing of the Canadian government."

"Then tell me what we are charged with."

"Shut up. You will have the details of the charges in due course. You know what you're guilty of."

"I don't," Cutler insisted. "Present me with the charges. I am the attorney representing everyone at the North Pole."

Getko waved his hand, as if pushing Cutler aside. "I'm not playing this game."

The wounded defender moaned again as Fred turned his attention back to the helpless man on the icy floor of the tunnel.

Cutler looked around, his eyes counting each person as his mind raced through calculations. "Please, help my friend. If he doesn't get help soon, he'll die." Cutler looked back to Patten, using his expression

191

to plead for her to do something. She stood still, resolute, just steps from the group.

"We've got to do something about the wounded," Joy said.

Getko looked around and then slid a casual glance toward Joy. "We've got medics coming. Get moving up the tunnel."

Joy joined two remaining agents and set out into the tunnel. After about five hundred feet, a bend obscured the long, cavernous interior.

Cutler bent down over the wounded dwarf, lifting the cloth from the wound. "Patten, get down here. José's got serious injuries."

Patten looked at Cutler, as if at first the words didn't register. Then she walked over to Fred and Cutler and kneeled down.

"What the hell, Patten?" Cutler whispered out of Getko's earshot. "These are our friends. You can't just sit back and let them die."

Patten looked at the bloodied, makeshift bandage. "What do you think they would do to me if they knew I was a doctoah? They'd kill me."

Cutler looked at Patten in disbelief. "Based on what? These aren't Nazis, or terrorists, or drug cartels. They could have killed us when we came around the bend, but they didn't. Why would they kill a doctor?"

"You heard the way that agent talked to you. He didn't believe you were a lawyer. Or Fred was a nurse. Why? Because youaa short. Look Cutlaa, I've spent my careeaa in their world. They won't give you a shot unless you point a gun to theaa head. I'm not going to put my life and profession in the hands of a high-stepper like Getko."

Cutler couldn't believe his ears. "I don't get it. There's something more going on here than we've seen. Now, step to it! We've got to help José and the others."

Patten began to examine the larger wounded defender as José continued to lean against the wall and gingerly hold his leg. As she applied pressure to different parts of his body, Tom's yelps and moans revealed he had several broken ribs and a broken ankle. The gunshot wound in his side was still bleeding, but a real emergency room was necessary to know how serious the wounds were.

"Tom," Fred said, stroking his arms and cheek, "What happened up there? We tried to contact you."

Tom blinked. "They must have moved in faster than we predicted. We almost had the pyrotechnics set when an advance unit appeared over one of the ridges. They must have had someone out on recon to track us down. Anyway, they got us before we were set up. We used

192

the pyrotechnics to keep them from closing in, but there were too many of them."

Cutler's eyes narrowed. "How many, do you remember?"

Tom shook his head. "Couldn't see them all," he mumbled.

Cutler looked up to José. José shook his head. "It all happened so fast." José tilted his head toward Getko. "They're professionals, all of them. We were outmanned and outgunned."

Cutler nodded and gave a slight jerk to his head. José sensed the signal to stop talking and closed his eyes. Cutler looked around, trying to keep from making his nervousness too obvious. Only Patten was close enough to hear anything. Cutler released the pressure on Tom's arm.

José opened his eyes. "Their snowmobiles were tricked up, so they moved real fast." José shook his head as he closed his eyes for a long second. "We were sitting ducks. We didn't have time to charge the explosives. All of us would have been killed if you and Dr. Patten hadn't surprised them, coming around the bend in that snowmobile. That woman agent, Joy, she's the one that kept the others from firing on you."

Getko and the DEA agents fell to the tunnel floor as gun shots rang through the corridor, followed by the crunch of twisting tin, and the snapping of hard plastic.

"What was that?" Cutler blurted, turning to Patten, Fred, and George.

"Must've been Wells and Klaas," Patten said without looking up.

Ron turned to her. "Julie, you don't appear too worried about our fates."

Patten turned her head away from Cutler, a weak effort to hide a subtle smirk crossing her face.

Cutler reached toward Patten's arm and grabbed it. "What?"

The sudden whine of snowmobiles drowned out all the words as a posse of machines rounded the corner of the tunnel and skidded to a halt. Nicole, Wells, and Peter were in the lead machine, several paces in front of three others that carried Joy and the federal agents, with guns pointed at the trio. Wells was holding his shoulder and Peter had an obvious limp as they dismounted the snowmobiles. Nicole's disheveled face masked any physical pain, compounded by anger and frustration.

"Well, well," said Getko. "What do we have here?"

An advisor with captain's bars knitted into his winter uniform stepped from behind the prisoners. "Looks like more foot soldiers."

Getko sized up the three average-sized people. "My, this haul is getting big. All we have to do is find the inventory."

Nicole's face tightened as she looked at Getko. "Inventory?"

"Please, young lady," Getko said. "I'm sure you know what inventory I mean."

Nicole looked at Cutler, then Patten, Fred, and José, her eyes glassy from tears.

Getko walked up to the new acquisitions, inspecting them like horses at auction. He clicked his fingers at Nicole and Wells. "I don't know you two." He stepped over to Peter. "But I know you."

"I knew it!" growled Wells. He lifted his fist toward Peter. Peter stepped to the side with a suddenness that made him slip on the slick tunnel floor, scattering his legs and arms as he fell. Two of Getko's military advisors leapt forward, catching Wells and pinching his arms to his sides, his fists secure in their grips.

"I can't believe it," Nicole said shaking her head. She looked at Peter. Something didn't seem right. "Jeff, I don't think it was Peter."

"Ah," said Getko, his expression perked up. "So, we have a name. Jeff!"

Wells ignored Getko and continued to stare at Peary.

"Jeff," Peter said, his eyes pleading. "I've never seen this guy in my life. I have no idea how he knows my name."

Wells pulled at the arms of the two soldiers, both several inches taller than he, but they flexed their knees to ground their position and keep him in check. Their grip remained firm; Wells couldn't move.

"His name is Peter R. B. Peary," said a woman's voice from behind Getko. Startled, everyone turned to see Sheila Livingston stroll into the group.

"Sheila, my dear girl!" exclaimed Getko, almost as surprised as the rest of the group. He walked over and gave her a bear hug. "So good to see you after so long. We thought you were lost for good."

"Sheila?" Peter's voice quivered. He looked around. Of the group, she was the only one without a gun guarding her or a soldier restraining her.

Sheila walked up to Peter, looking into his eyes, her expression cold. "You are an idiot." Peter blinked and pulled his head back like he was avoiding the contempt she seemed to spit in his face. "Don't

194

worry. You won't get tagged with the others. You were just along for the ride."

"I don't understand," Peter stammered, voice weakened by disbelief.

"You wouldn't," she sniffed, turning to Getko. "About two kilometers down the tunnel is a sight you won't believe!"

Getko's eyes sparkled with revelation.

"We've hit the mother lode," she said, unable to keep a toothy smile from breaking across her face.

Getko took in a deep breath and nodded. "Great work Agent Livingston."

"Agent Livingston?" cried Peter. "I don't believe it. All this time… this trip…. Oh, Jesus. No wonder you were able to get all those supplies so fast. It wasn't your grandmother's gift, was it?" The hurt in Peter's eyes began to overwhelm him, as his voice tapered into nothing. He looked up at her, sadness welling in his eyes. "You don't care at all, do you?" His knees weak, Peter sank to a crouch and let his head fall into his hands. "You don't care. You never did."

Sheila looked at him and rolled her eyes.

Nicole stepped toward Peter and placed a silent hand on his shoulder. The touch seemed to stir something in him. He pulled his head from his hands and looked at Sheila. "You have no idea what's happening down here."

"I know exactly what's going on down here," Sheila said, casting a look of disgust his way. "I can't believe you've let these people dupe you like this, but I knew you were all washed-up after Everest. God, you're pathetic."

Peter crouched, his sadness turning the corners of his mouth into a deep frown, a tapestry of her betrayal.

"Miles," Sheila said turning to Getko. "There's a whole town under the ice. It's incredible. They must have an operation ten times greater than anything we suspected. They have corner grocery stores, pubs, electronics stores, grocery stores. I think I even saw a factory!"

"Probably methamphetamines and coke," Getko said.

Nicole's eyes widened. "What are you talking about?"

Livingston stepped up to Nicole and thrust a finger at her face. "This is Nicole Klaas, CEO of the whole operation." She stepped over to Wells, the trace of her finger linking the two. "This is Jeff Wells, head of security for this God-forsaken ice fortress. You'll see it on the surveillance tapes."

Ron Cutler stepped forward. "Excuse me? What do you mean they run the place? That's ridiculous. This is a town. We have a board of community directors. I'm a director of this town and an attorney."

Getko looked down at Cutler, unsure of his next step, then stammered, "You are admitting to this?"

Ron's face flushed with anger. "I've worked long and hard to build my business in this town and in the Lower Forty-Eight!"

Getko looked at Livingston and then back to Cutler.

"How dare you accuse us of trafficking in drugs!" Nicole blurted. "This town has never trafficked in drugs."

Getko raised his face and hands in mock surprise. "Really? How do you explain this operation?"

Nicole paused as if weighing the impact of her next words.

Cutler snapped his gaze toward Nicole. "Nic. Don't say anything."

Wells looked at Nicole, his face calm and calculating.

Cutler pivoted back toward Getko, as if ready to throw a punch. "Don't say a word."

Nicole kept her eyes trained on Getko. "You have no evidence that drugs have ever been sold here, made here, or consumed here."

"Ahh, but we will soon enough," Getko huffed. "Agent Livingston, if these are the leaders, we don't need to wait. We've got everything we need right here. Use them as the point."

Dr. Patten lifted herself from a crouch over the wounded NP security guards and stepped forward. "Agent Getko."

"Yes, Dr. Patten."

A soft gasp consumed the tunnel as Peter, Wells, Cutler, and Nicole looked at each other.

"I think we've gone faa enough with this exercise," Patten said.

Cutler looked at Patten, a glimmer of hope relaxing his cheeks, only to be replaced with the taught muscles of fear, as he looked into the alarmed worry etched into the faces of Nicole and Wells.

"I don't think you're in a position to make that decision, Dr. Patten," Getko said.

"Agent Getko," Patten said again, using a more assertive tone. "You don't need to go further into the tunnel. I've got everything you need, one kilometer down the tunnel. Theaa's 100 kilos of cocaine in an ice cave. It'll only take a couple of picks with the ax to get it out.

You will also find ten pounds of meth and about 2 million dollaas in cash."

Getko nodded as if confirming old news. "Good. I knew drugs were down here. This is going to be a great success!"

"Dr. Patten," said Nicole, her voice low but determined. "We don't traffic in drugs. Where did those drugs come from?"

Patten looked at Nicole. "Then how do you explain the drugs in the tunnel? Did a polaa beaa burrow them theaa?"

Nicole leveled a steel look at Patten. "Julie, we've never had drugs in this town. There is only one way drugs could have gotten anywhere near here."

"My, how indignant!" Patten walked over to Nicole and looked into her face, anger giving the stare a hardness Nicole had never seen. "I think someone is hiding something."

Nicole nodded as she recognized the ploy. "The only person who could cover up those drugs was someone with the confidence and trust of the entire town—someone with the authority to order any kind of drug she needed for her profession—someone with access to the supply chain—someone neither Jeff, nor I, would ever suspect."

Patten laughed. "I can't believe it! I think that was a confession."

Nicole fumed. "I would never forsake this town or my family!"

"We couldn't have done it without you." Getko leaned down to pat Patten on the back. "When Sheila's homing device was lost, we knew it was up to you then. You were the only one capable of pulling this operation off for us."

"The mole!" gasped Joy.

Patten couldn't contain a broad smile. "Getko, why don't you take the agents down to the tunnel and get the cache. I'll watch these prisoners. It won't take you too long. They won't give me any trouble."

Getko nodded his head in agreement. "Agent Livingston, I want you to stay here with Agent Gault to keep the prisoners under control. I'll get the others. Let's track down the meth, coke, and cash!"

***

As soon as Getko disappeared around the corner with his small army of agents and advisors, Ron Cutler pointed his finger at Julie Patten. "Traitor!"

Cutler's accusation rang off the walls of the tunnel, igniting a rage in Patten that propelled her to within an inch of his nose.

"You set us up," Cutler said in disbelief. "You planted those drugs and led the DEA right to our town. You've destroyed everything we've built."

Nicole collapsed against the ice wall. "I can't believe it. Three generations of Klaas work, destroyed. Thousands of lives... jobs... good jobs... destroyed!"

Patten lifted her finger and trained it between Cutler's eyes. "You are the traitoa!"

Patten walked over to a snowmobile and pulled out a pistol. She walked over to Nicole and pointed it at her. "I'm not doing anything but reclaiming the rightful heritage and place for my people."

"Your people?" asked Wells.

Julie Patten's entire face flamed with anger. "*My* people—little people!"

Nicole looked at the North Pole's most respected senior surgeon in disbelief. "What do you mean? My family... Ron... Rowdy... you... we built this town."

"You took pity on us," Patten said. "We can't do anything without you or The Business—or Jeff Wells—signing off. We can't come and go as we want. Every vacation requires security clearance."

Nicole opened her mouth but closed it quickly. She raised her arm, letting her hand sweep around the carnage ten feet below the snowy surface of the Arctic Circle. "Because no one would believe us."

"Dr. Patten," Wells said, his voice low and deliberate, "you know why we have these procedures. NP Enterprises is a global business that doesn't operate inside any country's borders. If anyone knew what we were doing, they would try to shut us down."

"We don't need to be beholden to anyone," Patten said, shifting the barrel of her gun toward Wells. "We can run this business without you, NP Security, or the Klaas family."

"Julie, please." Fred's voice was consoling, not accusatory as he stepped toward her. "Nicole and the Klaas family have never short-changed you or anyone else."

Patten dismissed Fred with the flick of her hand. "You can't even see how the Klaases and her clan are manipulating you."

"She's been fair. NP Enterprises funds the hospital, the supply chain."

"NP2000 would be nothing without Rolf Hackett."

Cutler stepped over to Patten. "Julie, Nicole's father died. She was co-founder of NP Software. She had to take over NP Enterprises. We practically drafted her. Do you remember?"

"And what did she do? She left Hackett with half the enterpwise. She didn't give anything up. She doesn't let the hospital run on its own. It depends on Klaas money to run. The community should fund it, not her, or her business. He should have had it all."

Cutler shook his head. "NP2000 was her idea. Ask Rowdy. He'll tell you. She deserves half the business, if not more."

"I don't believe you," Patten yelled. "Rolf is better, smaater than she is. You are smaater than she is. You graduated from Haahvaad, Ron. Look how they treated you! You don't have the privileges of her kind."

Cutler shook his head. "Julie, please, be reasonable—"

"Shut up!" Patten looked over at Sheila. "I've had enough of these injustices. Weaa going to build a community for ouaa people, and we don't need any Klaases around—or former Navy SEALS to run our security. This is the end of the line. Right, Sheila?"

Sheila Livingston was looking at Patten, the barrel of her rifle having drifted away from Peter's chest to the ground.

"Right, Sheila?"

Patten's question seemed to refocus Livingston. "Umm, right." She brought the rifle back up to train its sites on Peter. "Drug dealing bastards like you don't deserve a place on this Earth."

Peter's eyes widened. "What are you saying? What are you going to do?"

"Peter, sometimes your stupidity amazes even me. We are in a legal no man's land."

The group stood silent as the realization that Livingston and Patten were ready to kill everyone connected to the North Pole. The cold air became damp and close, as the warmth of human breathing created a glistening, liquid veneer on the walls and ceiling. Every sound, no matter how small, seemed like it could echo for hundreds of miles through the ice-encased tube that now was going to transform the North Pole's emergency escape tunnel into a tomb for some of its most important citizens. Nicole's eyes closed as she waited out the final seconds.

"Put your guns down." Joy Gault's voice resonated through the tunnel. "Agent Livingston, Dr. Patten, put your guns down."

Livingston and Patten looked at the junior DEA agent. "Agent Gault, you are not authorized to give us directions. I am the senior agent in charge," Livingston said, her weapon turned back to Peter. "This is the end of the line."

"I said, put your weapons down." The metallic click of a hammer from a pistol echoed in the tunnel as Joy lifted the barrel of her weapon toward Sheila's head.

"Agent Gault, these people do not deserve to live. They deal in drugs. They infect our streets with violence and dependency. They enable the sale of drugs to our children, and they murder anyone who gets in their way."

"No, they don't," Joy's calm voice responded.

"I've seen their operation," Livingston insisted. "We've got all the evidence we need down in the tunnel. Right, Dr. Patten?"

Patten stood, her gun pointed at Nicole.

"No," Joy said. "You've seen a lot of trading, bartering, and banking. We've traced the transactions, but we've never seen any drugs trade hands."

"I don't have to," Livingston said. "I've seen enough. I don't need any more evidence."

"Sheila, you're wrong." Joy's voice remained calm. "We don't have the evidence. I know. We've been tracking it for almost a year."

"Agent Gault," Livingston snapped. "Does Miles know you believe that?"

"I've raised my objections."

"And?"

Joy paused, knowing her silence would reveal that Getko disagreed with her and validate everything Livingston now suspected. What would Livingston do to her, if she thought she was becoming a shell for drug dealers? "Miles dismissed them."

Livingston's face lightened. "I thought so!"

"Getko is wrong! We don't have the evidence to convict, let alone arrest them."

"Miles never would have allowed this case to get this far unless you had enough evidence to put them in jail. Right?"

The pistol in Joy's hands wavered. "I don't know," she admitted.

Sheila swiveled her gun toward Joy. "You sound like one of them. I'm not going to let anyone keep me from doing what's right."

Wells saw the furrow of the eyebrow, the subtle twitch of the finger on the trigger. "Agent Livingston, don't do this."

"Please, Sheila," Peter said. "You don't know what you are doing."

"Stay out of this!" Livingston snarled. "You don't know what *you* are doing. You don't know what *they* are doing!"

Peter drew in his breath. "You're wrong, Sheila. You've seen the stores, the kids, the little people. How can you say that's wrong?"

"You're done," Sheila said. "I knew it after Everest."

Everest! "That was a bad period."

"You were weak, and you didn't care about anybody. You let your entire future slip away because you couldn't get beyond that accident."

Peter looked at her. "I lost my best friend—"

"I was your best friend."

"I'm sorry, Sheila. I didn't realize I was hurting you."

Sheila drew in a deep breath. "Of course… of course… you were… selfish… self-centered. You didn't see what I invested in you… and then Everest. It's like I didn't even exist."

Sheila lifted the muzzle of the rifle, training it back on Peter's forehead. "And my father's death."

"I know I hurt you," Peter said, his voice hoarse. "I'm so sorry. I didn't appreciate what you brought into my life."

Peter turned to Nicole, then to Cutler and Fred. He looked at José, now unconscious on the tunnel floor. "But I know exactly what these people do and what they're doing. I've seen it. It's amazing. You're wrong Sheila. Put the gun down. Let me show you what they're doing. They are doing things for the spirit that we dreamed of doing with our expeditions. They are *us*."

Sheila cast a quick glance at Peter. Her hand wavered ever so slightly before firming her grip on the trigger. "You fool."

The tunnel flashed with the instantaneous firing of two guns, their roar drowning out any knowledge of who fired first. Sheila's body fell first, limp. Joy staggered backward, clutching her chest, as her pistol dropped to the ground. Patten swung her pistol toward Joy, a wisp of smoke visible, streaking in an arc toward her next target. Wells jumped, grabbing for the pistol as another shot burst from the barrel. Patten crumbled to the ground as Wells piled on top of her, pushing her into the ice, while Peter grabbed her gun. Nicole rushed to Sheila's motionless body as Rowdy scrambled over toward Joy.

"Livingston's dead," she reported.

"Joy's alive, but we have to get her to the hospital, fast. The others are in desperate need of help, too. Fire up the snowmobiles!"

"What about Getko?" Peter asked.

"My God," Nicole said. "They've had more than enough time to get to Patten's stash. They must be moving on to the town!"

Wells looked at Nicole and Peter. "They must have heard the shots, too. They'll be back here in no time."

Nicole shook her head. "I don't think so. This was part of Getko's plan, remember? He'll assume that Joy and Sheila started picking us off. That, ultimately, was the plan anyway. With the drugs, no one would question the circumstances surrounding the death of drug kingpins in a secluded hideaway in the Arctic."

Peter darted over to the remaining snowmobiles and pulled a rifle and bungee cords from the machine. He emptied the magazine and the bullet in the chamber.

Nicole looked at the wounded around her. "We've got to get them to the hospital."

"Nic, we don't have time," warned Wells.

Peter looked around the tunnel. "Then we need to stop the evacuation. People are going to die if we don't. We need someone to dispatch a doctor and medic. They need to get to an emergency room."

Nicole looked up the ladder to the surface. "Jeff, more feds are waiting to come down into this tunnel the moment Getko gives them the word. We have to find him and stop this madness."

Cutler perked up. "Look, you guys go after Getko. My legs can't keep up with you. Take the guns and stop them. I'll stay here until the others arrive, secure Patten, and we'll mobilize the reservists and track you down."

Cutler pulled a sliver of plastic from his boot. "Here, Jeff. This is my homing device. Keep it, and we'll track you down using GPS once I have the reserve units together, and I'm sure these guys are taken care of."

35

"Bimini Triangle," Special Agent Miles Getko said under his breath, "meet Jamaican Snow." Getko surveyed the five-foot-tall stash of drugs in hundreds of neatly, tightly wrapped, plastic bags. Patten was a good mole.

He had been suspicious of her at first, but she came through on each assignment, and her information was impeccable. This was exactly what the DEA wanted.

"Mark the contraband," Getko ordered.

"Should I radio the others?" asked one of the advisors.

"Not yet," Getko said, looking around the tightly packed ice cave. He looked down the tunnel, toward what he thought would be the town he had heard about. Patten didn't want him to go any further. He lifted his hand to rub his chin. Patten is a snitch, but this cache proved she was also a drug dealer. Something more, much more, may lie at the end of this tunnel.

"We're going to need them," he said, "but I want to do more recon down here. Let's move forward. I'm sure Agent Livingston has everything under control with the prisoners. I think we'll learn more with a smaller party than a larger one."

Getko led the few federal agents down the tunnel, putting them beyond earshot of the frozen entrance and odd gunshots.

***

Getko was sure of a lot of things that fateful day below the arctic ice cap, but the one thing he wasn't expecting was the site he witnessed as his assault party stumbled out of the escape tunnel and into the hollowed-out cavern that housed the village of the North Pole.

"I can't believe it," he murmured, eyes widening with disbelief.

Fewer than fifty feet away was a road bordered by two-story buildings, leading into what appeared to be a town square. The band walked forward, covering several hundred feet in a deliberate march. The buildings closest to the walls appeared to be residential, two-floor townhouses, emptying into small front yards, with sidewalks following narrow, sand marked roads leading to even more houses. They skirted the outside perimeter until they came to a large circle with a two-lane road extending further into the darkness. The streets were deserted.

"Sir?"

The heavily armed advisor, outfitted in winter combat gear crouched to his knees as he scanned the roofs, windows, and walls. Five agents and advisors created an arc around Getko as he stood surveying the spectacle.

"Where is everyone?" asked another advisor.

Getko looked around. "Let's go into town."

"On the road?"

"I don't care how we go," Getko said to the voice. "I think they would have fired on us if they really wanted a fight."

"Sorry, sir," the first advisor said. "It looks like a trap to me. I think we should call up reinforcements."

Getko stood for a few more moments, taking in the scene. He shook his head. "I don't know, captain. Something's different about this place."

"Drug cartels are pretty brutal."

Getko cocked his head. "Exactly. This is not a brutal place."

Getko stepped forward, examining the buildings. "Look at these buildings. They've been here a long time." Getko stopped at the foundation of one of the structures. He ran his hand over the railing porch elevated by about six inches above the ice. The rail was simple, but the finishing was exquisite. His fingers traced a subtle bevel in the wood that was ornamental. "I would say this woodwork was handled by craftsmen. Real carpenters and masons. These buildings are not temporary; they've been here a long time."

"I don't get it," the advisor said, keeping the tip of his rifle up, a laser site skipping from window to window. All the openings were closed up. "The town appears deserted."

Getko nodded. "Abandoned... or in hiding. My guess is hiding. We would have been able to detect an exodus on the scale of this town."

The soldier pulled the stock of his rifle up to his shoulder, and then issued commands to his team. "I don't have a good feeling about this. Smith, eyes up. Turk, eyes on the ground. Gonzalez, eyes on the windows and doors."

The patrol advanced along the road, split so they could watch the opposite side of the road with ease. Getko shook his head, mumbling, "I don't get it."

"Halt!"

36

Miles Getko looked at the pair of little people standing in the middle of the road, as if blocking the armed agents and soldiers from moving forward. The two were even stranger and more out of place than the rows of apartments and businesses that lined the street under dozens of feet of ice. It didn't make sense. Nothing made sense.

"I would like you to turn around and leave." The man made his request with a calm voice as he pulled a little girl close to him. Fear kept her arms around his waist, as they stared at the assault group.

"Are they going to go, Daddy?"

The man lifted his hand and placed it gently on her head, stroking her hair.

The lead agent and soldier kept their weapons trained on the father and daughter. The other three continued to scan the floors and windows of the building.

"Who are you?" Getko's voice was curious.

"We live here," the man said. "We would like you to go."

Getko looked around. "Where is everyone? This place is a little big for the two of you, isn't it?"

"This is our home. The others have left, afraid of you. I would like you to leave so we can get back to our lives, our business."

Getko shook his head. "We're not going to let drug runners operate out of this… town."

The man laughed. "Drug runners? You think we're drug dealers?" The man's laugh bellowed down the roadway, bouncing off the walls of buildings and the ice walls of the village. "This is the North Pole! We don't deal in drugs."

Getko continued to shake his head. He looked to his right and left, as if he had to verify that his patrol was real and next to him. He lifted his hand to his head like he was creating a wall to ward off a headache.

"Daddy, I'm scared."

The man looked down at the little girl and continued to stroke her hair. "Sshhsh, Virginia, it'll be okay."

The man stepped forward, giving a slight pull to the hand of his daughter.

"Stop," Getko said. "Don't come any further."

The man smiled. "Are you kidding me? I'm four feet tall! My daughter is under three feet tall. Where am I going to hide a weapon? What good would it do me to even have a weapon? I'm out numbered."

"Improvised Explosive Device, IED," said the advisor next to Getko. "Stop right there, or I'll have to shoot you both."

Getko stood, looking at the man and his daughter.

"Please," the little person said. "Let's be real here. Where am I going to put an explosive device?" He opened his jacket showing nothing but a cotton shirt. The jacket opened easily and lightly, obviously not weighed down by anything. The man took his jacket off, turned around, and put it back on.

"Now the girl," the advisor said.

The man sighed. "Come, Virginia. Let's take off your jacket to show the soldiers that we don't have any bombs on us."

The little girl let her father take her jacket off, then gently spin her around twice. He put her jacket back on.

Getko looked at the soldiers again. "Okay," he said, "you can come closer."

"Thank you," the man said. "My name in Rolf Hackett. I own a business down here. This is my daughter."

Getko motioned for the soldiers to stay back, and he walked up to Rolf. He extended his hand. "I'm Special Agent Miles Getko, U.S. Drug Enforcement Administration. I'm in charge of this operation."

Rowdy took Hackett's hand. "I wish I could say I'm glad to meet you, but you are about to destroy an enterprise that gives millions of children hope every year and employs thousands of people in a productive enterprise."

Getko shook his head. "I don't believe it. This town is incredible... no one could ever have imagined something this grand under the ice...

SR Staley

how is this even possible? But there's no way this place employs thousands of people."

"Well, you're right in the strict sense. This town is home to about 2,000 people, many of them little people like me, but our operations employ 20,000 people worldwide. My company alone employs nearly 1,000, and we have 200 working right here."

Getko shook his head. "We found drugs just 500 feet back in that tunnel."

Rowdy cocked his head. "Not our drugs. We don't manufacture drugs. We don't distribute drugs. We don't sell drugs. We don't use drugs."

"Then what do you do?"

"We make software."

Getko laughed.

"And we make sure toys get to kids and families who need them," Rowdy continued.

"Really? You distribute toys. Millions of toys to millions of kids? I guess right behind these two-story buildings is a whole new chamber of endless warehouses, storing all these toys? And then a massive factory for making them? What, you think you are Santa Claus?"

Rowdy smiled. "You don't believe in Santa Claus?"

"You are trying my patience, little man."

Rowdy scowled. "I would watch your tone, Agent Getko. This can end well, or it can end badly."

"It's your choice. It's no skin off my back if this ends badly... for you."

Rowdy shook his head. "But what about my daughter? Are you willing to sacrifice her?"

"You are the one sacrificing her. I am doing my job."

"In that case, your job is to destroy the livelihood and hopes of tens of thousands of people."

"My job is to rid this world of drug-trafficking scum like you. I don't know what lies you've filled your daughter's head with, but we've seen the drugs, and we are going to destroy this town."

"Please, Agent Getko. That would be an extreme measure, and completely unnecessary. Let me show you what is really here, and then you can make your decision."

Getko hesitated.

Rowdy continued. "Look, I am unarmed. I am not going to do something foolish in front of my daughter."

Getko nodded, then motioned the agents and soldiers to turn their guns down. "But keep a careful watch out. We don't know if anyone is just waiting for us to let our guard down."

"Don't worry, Miles. Can I call you Miles now that you're not going to blow my head off?"

"Daddy!" Virginia tightened her grip around his leg.

"Sorry, sweetie. I didn't mean to scare you."

Getko looked around at the buildings. "How can you do this? The ice is only ten feet thick, maybe thirteen. There is no way this town can be here."

Rowdy chuckled. "Yet it is. That's the paradox, isn't it? Let's just say we have a lot of science embedded in this business."

The high-pitched whine of snowmobiles emerged from behind Rowdy, as the beams from headlights pitched and ebbed behind him. The machines appeared to be coming up a side road several hundred feet behind Rowdy and Virginia.

The soldiers trained their weapons in the direction of the sound, two of them dropping to the ground while the other three scampered to the sides to take advantage of rails and porches.

"It's okay," Rowdy called. "I recognize those vehicles. They won't do anything unless you do something stupid."

Getko shifted his gaze from side to side as he tried to assess the sudden change in circumstances.

"You are going to have to trust me, Agent Getko," Rowdy said. "As you can see, this town is much bigger than your small patrol. Even with your automatic weapons, we could easily overrun you faster than zombies at midnight in the woods if we were here in regular numbers. We have no intention of harming you."

Rowdy continued to look at Getko and the soldiers as two snowmobiles rounded a corner, paused, and then headed casually toward the cluster of DEA agents, advisors, and two little people. As they approached, the figures of two people on each snowmobile appeared. Each rider in the back seat had a rifle, but they were pointed up in the air as the snowmobiles cautiously nudged up to Rowdy.

Getko's face flushed white as he recognized the riders.

"Put your weapons down," ordered Getko in a feeble voice.

Jeff Wells climbed off the back of one of the snowmobiles, while Nicole Klaas slipped her leg over the other one. Peter stayed at the controls of one while Ron Cutler kept his hands ready on the handles and throttle of the other.

"Relax, Agent Getko," Wells said. "We have no interest in hurting you or anyone else."

Nicole slipped up next to Wells and put her arm around his waist, and then lifted her hand to his chest. "We would like to end this peacefully."

Getko crossed his arms and looked at them. "I don't think you should be giving me orders."

Wells smiled. "I'm surprised you haven't guessed that you are not in control any longer. You could shoot us, but you wouldn't last long down here."

"Where's Joy?"

"She is attending to the wounded. She's doing what's right."

"I'm doing what's right."

Nicole stepped forward. "I don't think you are, Agent Getko. I think you are doing what you thought was good for you."

"This is a drug trafficking haven."

Nicole shook her head. "No, I'm afraid it's not."

"I saw the drugs."

"You saw the drugs that Julie Patten planted." Nicole's expression remained calm and firm.

Getko kept his arms crossed and cocked his head toward Nicole. "That's not true. The cache was too large."

Nicole looked at Getko with a hardened stare. "Why do you think that cache was so far away from the town?"

Getko's expression softened.

"Why didn't Patten tell you to continue past the stash of drugs? She could have told you about the town, but she chose not to."

Getko shook his head. "It doesn't matter. The drugs were there, just like she said. I have no reason to doubt her. I've been working with her for months to uncover this plot, this den of evil."

"And it's already cost one of your agents her life!"

The words stunned Getko.

"Sheila Livingston is dead," Nicole said in a somber voice. Peter let his head fall into his arms on the snowmobile.

"She died in the line of duty."

"Did she?" Nicole's voice was edgy, as anger began to tinge its timbre. "Did she really die in the line of duty?" She lifted her arms and turned a full circle. "Can you see this? Is this the type of place a drug cartel would build? We have been here for nearly fifty years! We gain nothing from putting this at risk."

"It can't be," Getko mumbled.

Peter lifted his head from his arms. "Show him."

Nicole looked at Wells, who shook his head.

"Show him," Peter said. "I believed, but only after I saw it."

Nicole's expression softened.

Peter nodded. "Believe Nicole."

Getko looked at Peter. "Believe what?"

Nicole looked at Wells. He nodded. She lifted her hand to his face and kissed him, and then turned back to Getko. "Follow me."

37

Agent Miles Getko let the folder marked OPERATION JAMIACAN SNOW fall to his desktop. He sat in his chair behind the large oak desk and looked at the cover, deep in thought, oblivious to the snow falling outside his fourth floor window.

Agent Joy Gault followed a few minutes later, carefully closed the door and sat in the chair in front of his desk.

"I don't know," Getko said, shaking his head. "No one would believe us. No one would believe me."

"What do they have to believe, Miles?"

"That an entire town exists under the polar ice cap."

"You swore you wouldn't tell anyone."

"No one would believe me if I told them."

"We... they trusted you."

"And I will keep my promise."

Joy nodded. "Thank you."

"It's amazing, isn't it?" Getko moved his hands gently over the folder. "How did you keep it a secret for so long?"

Joy smiled and diverted her eyes to the window, snow settling softly over the roads and sidewalks of the city of Arlington, Virginia. "I had never seen it, but I knew about it. I figured it out after visiting a cousin one summer. I guess I listened a little too closely to her stories of life in the northern reaches of the polar ice cap."

"You were their mole," he said, lifting his eyes to meet hers.

"I was a protector." She looked at Getko. "I believe in what we do in the department. I want to work in the field. I want to fight crime."

She paused. "But that's what I want to do: fight crime. Nicole Klaas is not a criminal. She's a hero; I think… maybe even a Saint."

Miles laughed. "A saint who runs a global enterprise, completely off the grid, employing 20,000 people."

"And giving millions of children and their families hope, at least once a year." Joy's smile broke into a broad grin.

Getko lifted the folder. "And as far as the Department is concerned, Operation Jamaican Snow was a wild success—$48 million dollars in seized drugs."

Joy nodded. "At least that's off the streets, right? You'll get your promotion. Another task force."

"Perhaps." Miles looked out the window. "But I've learned to like the snow, and even the ice. Maybe I'll turn that promotion down and just stay right here. I've had a good career. Maybe it's time for me to just do my job rather than create a new one." He turned back to Joy. "Besides, I think I might have some friends about fifty miles east of the North Pole that might be able to use my advice now and then."

"Yes, sir," Joy said, lifting herself up from the chair. "I guess I need to get back to work."

***

As the door closed behind her, Joy reached into her suit coat jacket and pulled out her phone. She opened the most recent photos in her queue of more than 1,000 pictures. Number 1,075 revealed Nicole and Wells, arm in arm, laughing as they tipped two mugs of beer toward the lens. She tapped the last picture and smiled as the rough but relaxed, proud face of Peter R.B. Peary popped up. He was sitting on the steps of a wooden sidewalk in what any normal person would have guessed as the impending dusk of the Alaskan spring. Over him was a sign reading "PRB Explorations" as an anxious husky with a dark stripe down his back looked up in mid-lick. Joy's smile broadened even more as she secreted away her phone and thought about the taste of that beer Rocky had waiting for her across the river at the University Pub, just four metro stops away.

***

Special Agent Miles Getko waited a few minutes to let the silence fold around him in his office in the modern building at 700 Army Navy Drive in Arlington before he pulled out his computer keyboard. He pressed "enter," triggering a whir from his desktop. The monitor flashed blue as a bright white snowflake grew across the screen before morphing into the letters NP2000. All he could do was smile.

About the Author

SR Staley (www.srstaley.com) is an award-winning novelist and full-time faculty member of Florida State University in Tallahassee, Florida. He has never traveled to the North Pole, but he has always believed in it. This faith is what led him to put down the first words for what would eventually become *St. Nic, Inc.* after his own children asked if he believed in Santa Claus.

In addition to exploring the faith and economics of the Santa Claus myth, Sam has lectured and given speeches in more than 100 cities in the U.S. and traveled to forty-three states. While he has traveled to China nearly thirty times—while working for the Los Angeles-based Reason Foundation—he has yet to make it to Alaska. He hopes *St. Nic, Inc.* might just provide his ticket to The Last Frontier.

His previous novels include *A Warrior's Soul* and *Renegade*, stories also inspired by his children's training in the self-defense oriented martial art of To-Shin Do (a version of Ninjutsu created by Stephen K. Hayes). His fifth novel, *Tortuga Bay*, continues the swashbuckling high-seas adventures of Isabella, an escaped slave who captains a pirate ship in *The Pirate of Panther Bay; Tortuga Bay* will be published by Southern Yellow Pine Publishing in 2015.

He has spent most of his career in the nonprofit sector, starting several nonprofit organizations and serving on the boards of others, including Bicycle House Tallahassee and the Miami Valley School in Dayton, Ohio. He is currently director of the DeVoe L. Moore Center at

FSU and teaches urban economics for the Department of Economics and urban planning in the Department of Urban and Regional Planning. He promises not to quiz his students on the urban economics and design of the North Pole, although its economy and planning are grounded in principles he discusses in class.

Sam earned his B.A. from Colby College, his M.S. from Wright State University, and Ph.D. from The Ohio State University.

You can follow Sam's adventurous journey as a novelist, writer, and self-defense coach by visiting his website or following him on social media.

www.srstaley.com
(blog.srstaley.com)
Twitter (@SamRStaley)
Facebook (SR Staley & Path of the Warrior)